The Body Beneath The Bridge

(Sequel to *The Body Under The Ice)*
An Up North Mystery
By

Douglas Ewan Cameron

W & B Publishers
USA

W & B Publishers

For information:
W & B Publishers
Post Office Box 193
Colfax, NC 27235
www.a-argusbooks.com

ISBN: 978-0-6922600-0-5
ISBN: 0-6922600-0-5

Book Cover designed by Dubya

Printed in the United States of America

Dedication

In memory of:

My father, Angus Ewan Cameron (1906-1981)

My brother, Allan Williams Cameron (1938-2011)

My father-in-law, David Ross Calhoun (1912-1999)

My wife's brother, William David Calhoun (1943-1968)

And for Edna Zonka (1914-2014), who celebrated her 100th birthday February 14, 2014, and upon whom my character of Edna Fitzgerald is based.

Thanks to:

Hibbard Pond and its environs don't exist – if they did Hubbard Lake where we summer and its environs wouldn't. The people in this book are all from my imagination. However, for those Hubbard Lake friends who read this book and see themselves as one of the characters – if you like the person, it's you and if you don't, it's not. In this book, there is a covered bridge across the West Branch River at the south end of Hibbard Pond. In reality, at the south end of Hubbard Lake there is a road under which is a metal tube high enough and wide enough for some boats to go through.

The graphic for the start of the chapters, I downloaded as free clipart from: http://allthings clipart.com and edited for this purpose.

Thanks to

❖ Chris Wright, a diver with the Hammond Bay Biological Center for help with the recovery of the skull from under the bridge and advice about the plane crash. He was previously an Alcona County Deputy Sheriff and founding member of the Alcona County Dive Rescue team.

❖ Bill McClellan for help with description of the plane crash, which is based on one I saw on YouTube (http://www.youtube.com/watch?v=gQ5D0Qa0PBk).

❖ Douglas Atchison, Sheriff of Alcona County MI, for making certain that Nathanial Jefferson and his officers performed their duties correctly.

❖ My wife Nancy Calhoun Cameron and my neighbor Mary von Zittwitz for their proofreading.

❖ David Buchthal, former colleague at The University of Akron and long time friend, for the semi-final editing of the manuscript.

❖ My son Christopher Cameron, who gave up some valuable personal time during his lunch hour and with his family to help with the semi-final editing.

And as I will do in all my books (you can skip this if you've read it before) I must acknowledge two writers who have influenced my work. First (and only chronologically) is Mary Higgins Clark whom I heard speak at a Book and Author Luncheon (or Dinner) sponsored by *The Plain Dealer* of Cleveland OH. She said that many of her works got their genesis with the words "What if?"

The other writer is the late Philip R. Craig, author of the Martha's Vineyard based J.W. Jackson mysteries. My wife and I met he and his wife Shirley on a riverboat trip from Constanta, Romania, to Amsterdam, Netherlands, in 2005 and shared many a happy meal together including my wife's birthday dinner. He told me that in his writing, while he knew the story line, he often didn't know how it was going to come out and let the characters lead him. Frequently that is what I do, and I did in this book.

UP NORTH

In Michigan, Up North is not only a geographical region, but is also a way of life. Also known as Northern Michigan it is basically the upper half of the Lower Peninsula. The Upper Peninsula (The UP) is not part of Up North, but is its own separate entity with its own way of life. The dividing line between Up North and the rest of the lower peninsula is usually thought of as a straight line running just north of Flint and Grand Rapids. How far north is debatable as some people say that the line runs through Mt. Pleasant, home of Central Michigan University. Michiganders enjoy explaining their state's lower peninsula to people using the palm side of their right hand. The Up North line described above basically runs across the palm at the base of the fingers. The famous Mackinaw Bridge joining the lower peninsula to The UP extends north from the tip of the middle finger. Hibbard Pond, where this story takes place, is about a third of the way from the outside edge of the index finger's first knuckle to its tip.

Life Up North is slow, easy, and out-of-doors. Michigan is dotted with rivers and lakes and, supposedly, you are never more than five (or is it three?) miles from a lake, pond, stream or river. To say that everyone who lives Up North is an outdoors person is not totally accurate for there are people who have houses on water but are never in or on the water or the surrounding woods. But these stories are not about them. These stories are about the people who are truly enjoying what nature has to offer them Up North.

PROLOGUE

From where the Eavesdropper stood in the dark hallway, just the left side of Sheriff Nathanial Jefferson could be seen. What was he doing in the kitchen? He had walked out of the Lake Room without a word. Upon noticing this, the Eavesdropper had followed, more curious than anything else.

"My boys are in jail. Two of them for a long time cause of me. The other only because he was the big brother and trying to help them and me. It's all my fault."

Ah, it was Butch, Briel, whomever, he was talking to, thought the Eavesdropper. *Perhaps the sheriff was curious as to why people called him Butch rather than Briel. That was easy. Everybody thinks Dame Edna is having problems with lucidity whether it's senile dementia or early onset Alzheimer's and wants her to feel more comfortable.*

"She's right, Dame Edna. She may be senile, but she was right. That rat Frenchman did come on that plane like she said, and my boys weren't here. It was the first day of deer season, and they was in the woods. Each got a deer that day. Best day ever. Anyways, I helps him to the guesthouse. Mr. Edmund wouldn't let him stay in the house for some reason."

No, it wasn't Mr. Edmund. It is Dame Edna who calls the shots in this house.

"We were there, and that French guy says to me that he needs to see Mr. Rolli. I asked him why, and he says there is a debt to settle. He was mad. He says that Mr. Rolli ratted him out to the cops in Montreal. A bank job or something; I don't remember it all. He was going to even things up. He had this pistol in his bag. He showed it to me. Checks it, and then puts it on the bed. Says we'll go after he uses the loo. Funny that. A Frenchie calling it a loo likes them English do."

What's Butch doing?

"I like Mr. Rolli. He always been good to me. He was a good friend of Dame Edna. They grew up together. I knows that if that Frenchie would kill Mr. Rolli, that it would break Dame Edna's heart, and she just lost her husband. Her son's not around much, so she's pretty lonely – she counts on Mr. Rolli to be company. I can tell they like each other. Not like lovers but like brother and sister. So, I know that I can't let that Frenchie do anything to Mr. Rolli. I takes the gun and stand over by the bathroom door. When he comes out I steps behind him, but he hears me and turns around. He sees the gun and reaches for it, so I shoot him, and he falls back against the bed. Then he starts up, so I puts a bullet in his head."

What? He's confessing to killing LeBeuf. Needed killing, that's a fact. But why confess? He didn't do it. But it did happen somewhat that way.

"Nobody heard the shots I guess cause I go back to the house, and tell Mr. Edmund that the French guy was taking a nap. Says he real tired and would eat in his room that night. I took him a tray like he was going to eat and flushed it all down the toilet. I wrapped him up in the bedclothes that already be spoilt and called my boys. I told them to deep-six him and the gun. But Burke didn't – kept the gun for some fool reason. Biggest mistake that boy of mine made was with that crate. He wasn't thinking. Tired after being in the woods all day, I reckon. He sees the depth as 50 feet like I told him and puts the motor in idle, but that old boat just kept moving and by the time they were ready to dump it, they'd passed up the slope. That's how it got found."

Can't save his boys from the crime of dumping the body, but he's throwing in another decoy as to who called him.

"Then that deputy comes and starts asking questions about that Frenchie, and I know there was going to be trouble. Dame Edna was real upset, and she calls Rolli and tells him about the deputy, so I knows I had to do something. So I calls and tells the boys to sideline that deputy who was causing trouble."

Now he's confessing to another crime he didn't commit. He didn't call the boys.

"Burt and Burl are good boys but not too swift. I should have waited and talked to Burke, but it might have been too late. They took the gun – the Frenchie's gun – and shot that deputy. Nows they's in trouble, and it's my fault. I ruined their lives just like I ruined mine. 'Sides that, me and Dame Edna got the same problem. Getting too old."

Suddenly the sheriff's form disappeared, and there was a gunshot.

"Shit," the sheriff said, followed by silence.

Mon Dieu, Butch shot himself. Why? The Eavesdropper started forward, but stopped when he heard the sheriff talking again.

"Barbara Ann, send some backup including Walker and Roberts to the Fitzgerald house. Also a squad, although that's a formality. Call Wallace Hibbs, and tell him that there'll be a removal."

Having heard all that needed to be heard, the Eavesdropper silently stole back down the dark hallway. *I cannot let Butch take the blame for those crimes. It wouldn't be fair to the boys no matter what they've done. It would kill Edna, too. She thinks the world of Butch. I need to do something to sideline this. Maybe another confession. Or two. I just don't understand why he killed himself.*

Chapter 1

The lobby of the Alcona County Sheriff's office was small, about twelve feet by thirty feet. As one entered after walking about twenty feet down a sidewalk from the parking lot, the jail was on the left. The door was open if there were no prisoners and closed if there were. Straight ahead was the office of the support staff separated from the lobby by a four-foot high concrete block wall with a window covering the rest of the distance to the ceiling. The glass in the window was bulletproof. On the right was a locked door leading to a small hallway in which there were several offices. The sheriff's was the last one on the right.

Early this Monday morning the lobby was empty except for a young man and woman, both of whom looked like they were high school students except for the fact that they were dressed in Alcona County Deputy uniforms. The young woman was Rachel Whitaker, who had just completed her junior year at Western Michigan University with a major in Law Enforcement. The young man was Jeremy Bridges who just completed his freshman year at Grand Valley State also majoring in Law Enforcement. At five feet ten, Rachel was at least four inches taller than Jeremy. He was heavier having a build more like a carrot then her string bean appearance. She wondered if she would ever become a woman, and he wished he needed to shave more than once every two weeks. They were working for the Alcona County Sheriff's Department as Lake Deputies for the summer. Their duties were to be on the lakes throughout the county on a regular but unscheduled basis enforcing such laws as speed limits (fifty-five miles an hour) and to be certain that boats had the proper safety equipment (life jackets for each person on board, throwable floatation device, fire extinguisher, etc.). The part of Lake Huron that abutted the shore of Alcona County was also in their purview. They had been through two weeks of training. This was Jeremy's first year, and Rachel's second. That Monday was the first day they were on their own.

As they stood in the lobby talking, Rich Walker, one of the department's two forensic specialists, entered the lobby through the office complex door.

"We have two choices," said Rachel. "Pine Lake or Hibbard Pond. Which one first?"

Their daily assignment was determined randomly but systematically with their choice of the order to cover the lakes each day. They reported directly to the undersheriff. At the present time there was no undersheriff, a situation that the sheriff had been working on. At least temporarily, the sheriff had assumed the supervisory role.

"Dunno," said Jeremy.

"Easy choice," Rich Walker said as he stopped beside them. "Which of you was hired first?"

"I was," Rachel said.

"Okay, you have a coin," and Rachel reached into a pocket.

"No, no. In the palm of your hand, you have a coin." Rachel looked at her empty palm wonderingly.

"Tails is Pine Lake, heads is Hibbard Pond. Think of heads or tails."

Rachel looked at him.

"Got it?"

Rachel nodded.

"Jeremy, when Rachel tosses the coin, you call heads or tails. Okay, Rachel, toss the coin."

Rachel complied and Jeremy shouted, "Tails." Understanding, Rachel "caught" the coin and opened her hand. "Tails," she said.

"Then it's Pine Lake," Walker said.

"What if they hadn't matched?" Jeremy asked.

"Then you do the opposite of what the non-tossing person called."

Walker started to walk away and then turned back. "One other thing. Loser tosses the next coin. Since Jeremy called the match correctly, that means Rachel loses. Enjoy!" and he was gone.

"Weird," Jeremy said.

"No, not really," Rachel said. "He and Bob Roberts do it all the time. Like when there is something that they have to do and, it is either a plum assignment or something egregious. They used to toss a real coin, but one day they didn't have one and came up with this idea. I heard some of the deputies talking about it the other day. There were two events they talked about. One was a burned-up car that had to be searched. Of course, that meant getting dirty. Not a nice assignment. The other was searching the waste in an outhouse for a gun. They both wanted that one."

"Yuck," Jeremy said. "I'd pass on that. Why did they both want it?"

"Because one of their own, Deputy Arthur Misdorf, had been shot and almost killed, and the gun used was the one they were after."

At that opportune moment, the door to the outside opened and a deputy walked in. Tall, good-looking but a little gaunt was Rachel's opinion.

"Hello, Deputy Misdorf," Rachel said. "Glad to see you back."

Arthur Misdorf smiled at Rachel. "Hello, beautiful. Nice to see you back again."

"I'm Arthur Misdorf," he said extending his hand to Jeremy.

The door to the office complex opened, and Sheriff Nathanial Jefferson emerged. He was a big man, standing six feet eight inches tall and weighing in the neighborhood of three hundred pounds, Jeremy guessed, and he knew from seeing him often for the past two weeks that not very much of it was flab. The other thing about him that was a bit unusual for this part of Michigan was the fact that he was black.

"Deputy Misdorf," Nathanial said, his white teeth gleaming. "Welcome back."

"Thanks, Sheriff," Arthur said, shaking the proffered hand. "It's good to be back. I was going stir crazy sitting at home."

"I know that Shelly was glad to have you around and will miss you. Of course, you know you are on light duty for the next four weeks or until the doctor gives you an okay to return to regular duty. Talk to Ruth Biggers. She's your boss."

Nathanial indicated the tall, comely redheaded woman standing behind the bulletproof glass partition, a broad smile on her face as she waved at Arthur who returned the wave.

"And you two," Nathanial said turning to the two Lake Deputies. "Shouldn't you be on the water someplace?"

"Yes, sir," Rachel and Jeremy said simultaneously.

"We were just leaving," continued Rachel. "Heading for Pine Lake this morning, and Hibbard Pond this afternoon."

With that the two Lake Deputies exited the lobby heading for the parking lot, neither of them knowing how that coin toss would lead to an event which would, for the third time in a year, shake up the Hibbard Pond community.

Chapter 2

It was the time of day that Sheriff Nathanial Jefferson referred to as his "downtime." For about an hour
after lunch—at least when he had brown bagged it and
eaten at his desk—he liked to relax undisturbed, blinds
closed. Today was such a day and he welcomed the
chance to put his feet up on his desk, cross his arms on
his chest, close his eyes and sleep. However, as often
happened, today sleep didn't come. Instead his mind re-
visited the murder of Pierre LeBeuf, a case closed but
with the door left slightly ajar.

The body of Pierre LeBeuf had been removed from
the bottom of Hibbard Pond in early March after
Zebulah Pyke had discovered it while ice fishing. A
team of divers had gone down through a hole they had
cut in the ice and brought the body to the surface along
with the crate in which it had been entombed. The crate
was actually a fish shelter belonging to the Hibbard
Pond Sportsman. Arthur Misdorf, one of his young deputies, had taken the lead on the investigation and had
developed two prime suspects: Rolland (Rolli) Polli and
Edna Fitzgerald. They had become worthy of notice
when both of them used the term, "Not today, not yesterday and not tomorrow." That phrase led back to a retired nun in Quebec who had worked at the orphanage
where they and Pierre LeBeuf had been placed. As the

investigation deepened, someone thought that Misdorf was getting too close. He was shot three times when he stopped a black pickup truck that was being driven suspiciously. His life had been saved by the opportune arrival of Earleen and Dugal McBruce. Her training as a first responder (EMTA or Emergency Medical Technician Ambulance) had kept him alive until the EMTs had arrived. Nathanial and Deputy Mitchell Webster had taken over the investigation. They had managed to track down and arrest three brothers, two of whom were inexorably linked to the shooting of Misdorf using the same pistol with which Pierre LeBeuf had been shot. This also linked all three to having deep-sixed the body in the fish shelter. During a visit to the Fitzgerald home, the sheriff had found the Polli's present as well as the Fitzgerald son who ran an import business in Montreal. Also present was Briel Boswick (Edna thought his name was "Butch Bothwell") whom it turned out had also been at the orphanage. He had confessed to killing LeBeuf and having his sons dispose of the body. Then he had taken his own life. Following that, both Edna Fitzgerald and Rolli Polli had confessed to killing LeBeuf, and that had left Nathanial in a legal quandary. Briel Boswick couldn't be taken to trial because he was dead. Thus, Nathanial had to determine which of the other two had been the killer. That is, if either of them was; but he was now firmly convinced neither was. Mitchell Webster had linked Rolli Polli to arson in a fire in Montreal that had killed his adoptive parents and adopted sister. The Montreal police issued a warrant for Polli's arrest but Polli had suspected his time was up and committed suicide by chaining himself to his Harley and riding it off a borrowed pontoon barge sitting close to the spot where the body of LeBeuf had been discovered. In Nathanial's mind that left Edna Fitzgerald as the primary suspect, but he was convinced that she was suffering from dementia or Alzheimer's and therefore couldn't be taken to trial. Still in Nathanial's mind he didn't think she did it. The question was, "Who had?"

He was wakened from his thoughts by a loud boom. He realized that the room had become dark and suddenly he heard heavy rain on the window. Taking his feet off the desk, he checked the weather on Weather.com and found that a large rainstorm had hit. Using the *Weather in Motion* application of the webpage, he saw that the slow moving storm had crossed Hibbard Pond about half an hour before. He wondered how the Lake Deputies were faring.

There was a knock on the door and Barbara Ann, the daytime dispatcher, stuck her head in the door. "Sheriff, Lake Deputy Whitaker just called in. She and Bridges took refuge under the covered bridge at the south end of the lake. When they were tying off the boat, Bridges discovered a human skeleton buried in the bank."

Chapter 3

The morning on Pine Lake had gone well for the young Lake Deputies. There hadn't been many boats around, but they had proceeded as they were supposed to. They actually left the lake early, heading for Hibbard Pond which, Rachel had explained to Jeremy, was by far the biggest lake in the county other than Lake Huron, of which they were responsible for only a small portion. They stopped at the Hibbard Corner's General Store and picked up some sandwiches, pop and water and were given a bag of blueberry muffins. Rachel had learned the summer before that stopping in to buy homemade sandwiches from Gert Pickard, who ran the store with her husband Peter, would also get them a free bag of that day's special cookies. "And don't youse try to pay for 'em," Gert always said. "Youse just keep things safe on Hibbard Pond. They's a thank-youse from Peter and me."

Rachel had the daily specials firmly set in her mind: blueberry muffins on Monday, fudge brownies on Tuesday, oatmeal cookies on Wednesday, Lemon Crisps on Thursday, corn muffins on Friday ("Cause most folks eats fish on Fridays," Gert always explained.) Saturday was up for grabs but had been Double Fudge Walnut Brownie Delights last summer.

"Thursdays you have to get there before the sheriff and George Haversack, who runs the library across the street, take them all," Rachel had explained to Jeremy.

They arrived at the East Bay DNR ramp shortly before noon and took advantage of one of several picnic tables to eat their lunches. There were several boats in the parking lot. "After walleye or bass most likely," Rachel had explained, as they were the most prevalent fish on the lake and, at that time of year, in close to shore while the water was still cold. They had the Boston Whaler in the water by 12:30 p.m. and, following Rachel's suggestion, headed south along the east shore. They encountered several boats fishing above a rock shelf that extended about halfway down the east shore of the lake. "It's not really a shelf," Rachel explained, "but rather a long pile of rocks fashioned by the winter's ice. But the bass like it for breeding."

The fishermen they encountered were friendly and well-prepared so there were no infractions. They didn't check fish sizes because they had no authority to do that and the fishermen knew it. That was the responsibility of the DNR officers who, because of state budget problems, were thinly spread. "Don't know what your duties require," said the last of the fishermen they encountered along the shelf, "but if I was you, I'd get some shelter. That's a big storm coming." He waved to the northwest where ominous black clouds were moving swiftly toward the southeast. "My wife called and told me that the weather radio was issuing a warning." He waved at them as he started his engine and headed toward the East Bay Launch where he had left his boat trailer.

Jeremy and Rachel noticed that the other fishermen were doing the same, although one of them was headed across the lake for home and another for the south end. The two Lake Deputies quickly donned their raingear and then Rachel headed the Boston Whaler for the south end.

"Why not go back to East Bay?" Jeremy shouted above the roar of the engines.

"There's a covered bridge across the West Branch River about an eighth of a mile above the mouth of the river. We can get shelter under it. We're closer than we are to East Bay and that launch will be crowded with boats getting off the lake."

As they sped across the lake, the winds began to pick up, increasing the size of the waves, and by the time they reached the river's mouth, Rachel had been forced to slow the boat in order to avoid being swamped. At one point she raised her right hand and waved although Jeremy couldn't see anything. "Eyre Spy," Rachel yelled. "Lady lives over there who watches everything that happens on the lake. Has a telescope. Her name is Jane Eyre Polli and everyone calls her 'Eyre Spy', a play on 'Hair Spray' someone told me."

The shallow water of the river necessitated Rachel slowing down as they entered its mouth, but also because they were passing the Negwegon Township DNR ramp with its "No Wake" zone. It was then that the skies opened and dumped what seemed to be gallons of water on them. By the time Rachel eased the Boston Whaler under the bridge, there was at least an inch of water in the boat. Even in the shelter provided by the bridge, the wind buffeted them.

"Get out and tie the bow and stern lines to one of the bridge supports," Rachel said trying to hold the Boston Whaler steady with the engines. Jeremy quickly complied, grabbing the stern painter and leaping to the bank. He slipped a little on landing but quickly righted himself and climbed the bank until he could get the rope around a support beam. He tied it off and started down the bank toward the boat when he slipped and then slid down the bank. Knocking dirt and debris in front of him, he stopped just short of the boat as some of the debris hit it with a resounding thud. As soon as he was on his feet, Rachel tossed him the forward line. Quickly climbing the bank, Jeremy tied the rope to a beam holding the Boston Whaler tight against the shore. Rachel cut the engine and, out of curiosity she would later recount, looked to see what had hit the boat. She saw an almost spherically shaped rock lying above the water, held in place by the bank and the end of the Boston Whaler. Again curiosity got the best of her and she picked it up, discovering that it was amazingly light. She wiped at the dirt trying to identify the rock or whatever it was. As she rubbed, a portion of the rock moved and seemed to open. She shrieked and stepped backward, simultaneously and reflexively tossing the object into the air. It hit one of the supporting beams and ricocheted back toward the Boston Whaler, hit the top of the gunnel and careened unceremoniously into the water.

Chapter 4

"*I am sorry, Sheriff Jefferson,*" Rachel said over the phone. "*It was an awful feminine reflex, I guess.*"

Nathanial was sitting at his desk, listening to Rachel's explanation of the skull getting into the river.

"Natural, I imagine," Nathanial said. "I don't know what I would do."

However, he knew what Dugal McBruce did when he found the skull in the mud beside the earthen work dam. He had put the skull down, stepped away, and called 911.

"Are you certain that it was a human skull?"

"*Yes, sir,*" was Rachel's response. "*After that happened, Jeremy and I climbed up the bank to where his slide had dislodged it. We carefully removed some more dirt, putting it above the hole and discovered some ribs. We stopped there not wanting to contaminate the evidence any more than we had.*"

"You did right," Nathanial said. "Where are you now?"

"*In the Whaler.*"

"Jeremy too?"

"*Yes, sir.*"

"Stay there. I'll be there in about fifteen to twenty minutes. No lights, no siren. Don't want to draw unneeded attention. Word will get out quick enough.

There'll be a squad car there in five to ten minutes. Officer Webster is on the way. Following him will be Walker and Roberts. You do what they say."

"*Of course, sir.*"

"Keep your phone handy. Make no other calls."

"*Of course not, sir.*"

Yeah, Nathanial thought, *but with all this social networking, it will be out there soon enough.*

"No texting, nothing. Make certain that Jeremy does the same."

"*Yes, sir. He doesn't even have his phone out. I told him to cool it.*"

"Good. See you shortly."

Nathanial hung up and saw Roberts and Walker standing in the doorway.

"Rachel and Jeremy say they have found human skeletal remains on the north side of the West Branch covered bridge. The skull is in the water. Webster is on his way. Get there and secure the site under the bridge. No lights. No siren. The cruisers will be enough notification that something is going on. I'll be there in twenty. There'll be a couple of other cruisers there quickly. Don't let any cars stop. Once you have the site marked, tell Rachel to take the Whaler up on the riverside of the Negwegon launch and not to let anyone up the river. If they force their way past, she is to let them go but get registration numbers. She should have a camera, at least on her phone. Get pictures for identification. She'll do the job properly. Now get!"

But Walker and Roberts had already disappeared. They were his forensics team and the best he could have possibly asked for. Their modus operandi might be a somewhat unique, but he wouldn't trade them for any-one. He picked up the phone and punched in a number.

"Chet, Nathanial."

"Sheriff," Chet Willis responded.

"Need a diver or two."

"Where and for what?"

Chet was the head of the Alcona dive team and had led the recovery of Pierre LeBeuf's body from beneath the ice of Hibbard Pond.

"At least a skull in the river under the West Branch covered bridge."

"Be there within an hour. Have to scrape up some people."

The line went dead. The next call was to Wallace Hibbs.

"Wallace, got another live one for you."

"Nathanial, you know I don't deal with live ones."

"It was a joke. Looks like we have a body buried under the West Branch covered bridge. I'll call when I am certain."

"I'll be right over."

"I wish you wouldn't. I'm trying not to attract too much attention. Be best if we just bag it and bring it to you this time."

Nathanial heard Wallace sigh on the other end of the line.

"I never get the good part."

"Yes, you do. You were right there for LeBeuf. Be-sides, this is under the bridge. Be a tight spot for you."

Wallace Hibbs was a big man. Shorter than Natha-nial by about four inches but weighing twenty to forty pounds more. In high school he had been referred to as The Whale.

"Right. I understand."

"And don't say anything to Gert."

Gert Pickard's general store was the focal point of all rumors in Alcona County. Say something spicy in Harrisville and it would be all over the county in thirty minutes – or so they said.

Nathanial sat for a minute pondering what was going on. The bodies of two young girls discovered last year led to a serial kidnapper. Then the body of Pierre LeBeuf had been discovered this past March and now this body, because he had to believe that Rachel was correct. She was too levelheaded to be wrong despite her faux pas at losing the skull. *This place was getting to be as bad as Paradise, Massachusetts, and there isn't even a Jesse Stone*, Nathanial thought thinking about a series by Robert Parker, one of his favorite mystery-writing authors. Although perhaps one might consider Dugal McBruce in Jesse Stone's place because he had been the one to discover the skull in the mud of that dam. He didn't really have a hand in the others although the second body was part of the same case. That one had been discovered by a teenage boy tracking a deer he had shot. Both girls had been kidnapped by Williston, who thought they were reincarnations of his daughter. When they finally had discovered Williston's involvement and gone to arrest him, they had discovered a third young girl. She had been kidnapped from Sylvania, a suburb of Toledo, Ohio. She was unharmed and quickly and safely returned to her family.

Well, Nathanial thought, *I'll have to deal with whatever comes up.*

He got up, grabbed his coat and hat and headed down the hall.

"I'll be at Hibbard Pond," he told his dispatcher as he passed by.

As he passed the office complex he stopped when he heard, "Sheriff?"

"Yes, Misdorf?"

"Need an extra hand?"

"What, and get in trouble with the doctor? No thank you. You're in charge while I'm gone. No change of status. No change of desk. Think you can handle it?"

"Yes, sir," came the response in a tone that Nathanial knew was disappointment.

As much as Nathanial wished Misdorf could be there, he knew it would be irresponsible to bring him along.

Chapter 5

Nathanial stopped his cruiser next to Mitchell Webster's and rolled his passenger side window down.

"Any problems?"

"No, Sheriff. Officer Steiner is on the north side of the bridge about a hundred feet. People stop and ask what's going on. I tell them that I don't know. There is a problem under the bridge and they have to move on. One car stopped in the middle of the bridge and the driver's door opened. Steiner and I hit the lights and sirens at the same time. The door closed and the car drove on."

As he was saying this, a southbound car came across the bridge and pulled over to the side off the road. A man wearing fishing paraphernalia got out and went to the back and opened the trunk.

"I'll get it," Nathanial said putting the cruiser in gear and moving forward until he was aligned with the other car.

As his window was sliding down, he said, "Excuse me, sir. But there is no fishing here today."

"But I always fish here. The walleye are great this time of year."

"I agree, sir, but not today."

"It's a free country, and I'll fish wherever I want." As he was talking he had pulled what looked to be a fishing creel out of the trunk, slipped the strap over his head, took out a rod and slammed the lid of the trunk.

"Sir, there is no fishing here today," Nathanial said, as the man turned and walked onto the bridge. Turning his lights on, Nathanial got out, shut the door and followed the man. By the time he reached him, the fisherman had gotten a bait box out of the creel and selected a worm. He was getting ready to put the worm on the hook when Nathanial put a hand on his shoulder. It can be quite intimidating for a normal-sized man to look up into the face of a six-foot eight-inch three-hundred-pound black man, and he dropped the worm.

"Sir, I said there is no fishing here today."

"I have a right…"

"Sir, may I see your fishing license?"

The man stared at him.

"You have no right to see my fishing license. That's only within the purview of the DNR."

"Sir, if you don't show me your fishing license, I will arrest you for obstructing justice."

The fisherman stared at him, started to say something, and thought the better of it. He grabbed his pole and walked back to his car. Opening the trunk, he tossed the rod and creel into it, slammed it, and walked to the driver's side door. Opening it, he turned back to Nathanial who was five feet behind him and said, "The DNR is going to hear about this."

He got into the car and slammed the door shut. A plume of gray smoke came out of the tailpipe as he started the car and drove away. Shaking his head at the unexpected insolence, Nathanial returned to his vehicle and drove across the bridge and parked just ahead of Robert's cruiser, or maybe it was Walker's. It was slippery going down the slope until he reached the bank of the river, and then he turned to see a well-lit area about halfway up the bank and about a third of the way under the bridge. Two spotlights illuminated an area where Roberts and Walker were on their hands and knees. The generator was sitting on the bank about three feet in front of Nathanial, just a little out from under the bridge. As he looked over the area, he noticed a float about ten feet out from the bank and roughly at the same distance from the edge of the bridge and the dig site.

"What's with the float?" he asked.

"Marks the approximate spot where the skull went down," Walker said without looking up.

"We put it there with just a one pound weight that we let down slowly. Based on what Rachel said, the skull went into the water about two feet from the boat. This was put down right next to the boat."

Nathanial turned and looked toward the mouth of the river. He could see the Boston Whaler sitting broadside in the middle of the West Branch. On the lakeside was another boat; Nathanial thought it was a Lund. As he watched, the prow of the Lund turned toward the lake and the boat motored away.

"Been any problem with the water-based spectators?" he asked.

"Don't think so. We told Rachel and Jeremy to call us if there was a problem," Roberts said.

"Of course there isn't much we could do," Walker chimed in, "what with us not having a boat."

"Pistol is not very accurate at this range and we might hit Rachel," Roberts added raising his head slightly to look at Walker who winked.

"What about Jeremy?" Nathanial asked.

"He's a rookie," Walker said.

"Unproven item," Roberts added.

"Okay, enough. What have you found?" Nathanial said turning back to them.

"Appears to be a kid," Walker said. "Probably stood about three and a half to four feet tall, so young. At that age difficult to tell about the sex."

"Any idea how old?"

"Like I said, young. Four feet means six to eight years at a guess."

"No," Nathanial countered, "I mean how long has it been in there."

Both men stopped their work and sat back on their heels.

"Knew you'd ask that," Roberts said.

"Wanted to see how long we could string you along. You're thinking Williston, right?" asked Walker.

Nathanial didn't say anything.

"Don't think so," Roberts finally said. "Rough guess, it's been here for a long time, maybe thirty or forty years. Take more of an expert than us to be certain."

"How much longer?" Nathanial asked.

"Couple of hours. We've just finished uncovering the top. Getting the bones out, labeling, etc., will be a while."

At this point, Nathanial felt his cell begin to vibrate and pulled it out. Caller ID said it was Rachel, and he turned to look toward the lake. He could see a boat being backed down to the launch site.

"What's the problem?" Nathanial said as he pushed the talk button.

"This boat is loaded with diving gear. Looks like four people."

"That's Chris Willis and some of his divers. Describe the skull to him."

"Right."

"And Rachel?"

"Yes?"

 "Ask him for the password."

Rachel was obviously flummoxed. "What password?"

"Ask him. He'll think of something."

Chapter 6

Nathanial watched the four divers get into the dive boat, back away from the dock, and motor up to the Boston Whaler. They sat broadside to each other for a minute and Nathanial could see Rachel throwing her arms in the air, simulating what had happened when she had recognized the skull. The team waved at her and Jeremy, then motored around the Boston Whaler, and up the river to the bridge. As the boat reached Nathanial's position, Chet Willis put the motor in neutral. Nathanial recognized Yonnie Jones, Skip Andrews, and Fred Fithe.

"Where'd you get the cute deputy?" Chet asked and the other three gave thumbs up.

"She's just temporary. Lake Deputy. Goes to school at Western Michigan."

"A Bronco, huh," Skip Andrews said. "I like to ride..." and stopped when Chet gave him a stern look.

"What's the password?" Nathanial asked.

"Scuba Divers Do It Deeper," Chet said with a smile. "She actually blushed a little. I was going to use 'Scuba Divers Do It Underwater' but was outvoted."

The other three divers grinned at Nathanial.

"So that float marks the approximate location?" Chet said changing the subject.

"So I'm told," Nathanial responded.

"Surface current is pretty good. Probably moved downstream a bit before it hit the bottom. Don't know this bottom well, but it probably has a little murk. We'll tie up here…" Fred Fithe tossed a line to Nathanial who dutifully grabbed it and started pulling the boat toward shore as Chet cut power, "... to get ready and work our way upstream. I'll go down with Skip. Yonnie will tend me and Fred will do the same for Skip.

"We'll use lights. Have to go slowly. Give him the ball, Yonnie."

Nathanial had noticed that Yonnie had a clear plastic spheroid, resembling a football that he started to toss to Nathanial.

"Hold it," Nathanial said. "I was an offensive lineman, not a tight end. I need to get this line attached to something."

By the time he had the boat at the bank, Fred Fithe leapt out with a grapple anchor attached to another line. Moving about ten feet in front of the boat, he anchored the points into the ground, and Chet Willis pulled the line taut and tied it off. The boat rested alongside the shore, held in place by the river's current.

"Catch," Yonnie said tossing the plastic ball to Nathanial. Catching it without a hitch, he noticed that the outer surface was more like a colander and something heavy was inside suspended in the middle by wires.

"What's this?" Nathanial said.

"Drift indicator," Yonnie said. "Or so I hope. Throw this in the water about four feet upstream from the float. When it fills with water it will sink and a light will go on. Hopefully give us an idea of how the skull might have moved."

"Back in a minute," Nathanial said heading up the bank toward the bridge. When he reached the spot on the bank opposite the float, he made a soft underhand toss. The ball tumbled through the air hitting the water with a medium loud plop. As it started to move downstream, it filled with water, a bright yellow light went on, and the ball went under just about the time it reached the float. Almost instantaneously the light disappeared in the murky water. *Lots of luck spotting that,* Nathanial thought.

"What was that?" Roberts asked and Nathanial explained it.

"Lots of luck spotting that," Walker said.

What is he? Nathanial thought. *A mind reader?*

When he got back to the boat, the four divers were already in their wet suits. Chet Willis and Skip Andrews were checking their Buoyancy Compensation Devices (BCD) or vests. The vests contained weights to help keep them on the bottom and their air tanks were attached to the back.

"The light came on, and I couldn't see it more than three feet under the water."

"No problem," Yonnie said. "It puts out a GPS signal. I've been tracking it. Not moving real fast. I'm willing to bet that the skull is about at the midpoint between us and the float."

"Want us to search the bottom all the way up?" Chet Willis asked as he put on his fins.

"Gotta get the most bang for my buck," Nathanial said. "This is straining the budget as it is, what with us losing all that money this year."

Nathanial was referring to the fact that the Alcona County Treasurer Karen Nelson had embezzled three-quarters of a million dollars. This was discovered only after she had fled the country to her native Canada. She and her husband had been apprehended in the Vancouver airport as he and their two children were linking up with her and getting ready to leave the country for Hong Kong, at least that was their first destination. They were in custody in Vancouver, awaiting deportation back to the states. The children were in the care of their maternal grandparents.

"Tell you what," Chet said. "I talked it over with my team and we're doing this as a training exercise. For now at least. Maybe when the budget gets an injection, you can cover expenses."

"Thanks. Be happy to."

"Great! For now, if you could pull the anchor and give it to Fred, we're ready to go."

As Nathanial walked to the anchor, Yonnie started the engine and moved the boat slightly upstream, releasing the tension on the line. When the anchor was securely stowed, Yonnie guided the boat to midstream and shut off the engine. Chet and Skip sat on the right bank gunnel of the boat and were helped into BCDs by their handlers. The two divers put on their masks and inserted their mouthpieces, testing them to be certain they were working correctly. Yonnie and Fred Fithe attached the safety line to their diver's chest harness using locking carabineers. Chet gave a thumb down to Skip and the two tumbled backward into the water. Fairly quickly Nathanial could see the bright lights they used, and using their bubbles, he followed their slow progression along the riverbank as they moved side to side. Yonnie started the trolling motor and the boat followed the upstream progress of the divers staying about twenty feet behind. Fred stood in the bow holding both safety lines.

As they neared the bridge, Nathanial began to despair. Then Fred said, "Diver coming up," as the two streams of bubbles separated and one moved to the bank. Skip Andrews broke the surface holding a net bag in his hand. In it was a brown and white mass that Nathanial could clearly see was a human skull.

"You looking for this?" Skip asked.

Chapter 7

The two divers continued moving slowly upstream swimming side-to-side just feet apart so that their light beams overlapped and they could see about six to seven feet of the river bed. The light held in his left hand, Chet held a GPS receiver in his right. The blip on the screen was the drift ball. Chet wanted to swat the receiver because it didn't appear that the ball was moving. They were swimming a little more slowly than before, if that was possible, because the skull's jaw was missing. Having gotten the story from Rachel, he was certain that the jaw had been what had flapped open, frightened her, and caused her to toss the skull onto the air. Chet hoped that the jaw had not jarred loose then and fallen separately because that would make the search even more difficult.

They had moved under the bridge just a minute before and were getting very close to the drift ball's location. He could sense Skip pointing and looked ahead to see a dim glow – the ball. He wanted to hurry but knew that it was best to keep the slow pace. About ten feet before they had reached the bridge, the bottom had become smooth and he knew that it was mostly rock. Before that had been a deep pool about ten by twenty feet, and it had been fairly clean also. The fish had been rather numerous but naturally skittish, and they could identify them, but only had quick glimpses. There had been one big pike though, probably four feet long, that had paused just a moment before disappearing into the water's murk.

Slowly the drift ball's shape sharpened, and when they were about two feet from it they could see that it was being held against something. With Skip having the free hand, he had been the one to pick up the skull and the few other things of interest they had found. One, Chet felt certain, was a pistol. Reaching the drift ball, Skip reached out and picked it up. Whatever had been holding it came loose also and was raised up about a foot before it fell lazily back to the bottom. *Horseshoe* was Chet's original thought but quickly realized that it was the second object of their search. He gesticulated with the GPS receiver that Skip should pick it up, but he was already reaching for it having stowed the ball in his second net bag. With what they thought was the jaw-bone, Skip gave Chet a questioning thumb up or "Should we surface?" Chet shook his head and motioned with the receiver that they should move on.

In a few more feet, they reached the weight and line of the float and bypassed it. The current had been faster under the bridge because the close banks confined the water, and, being wider upstream, the river was forced to narrow and that caused more speed and pressure. It was a wonder that the jawbone, if that's what it was, had lodged into the bottom. As he swam, Chet pondered this and decided it most likely was just pure dumb luck. He figured that wherever and however the jaw had separat-ed from the skull, it had reached the bottom almost sim-ultaneously with the skull, which had hit on top of it just hard enough to wedge one of the two pointed ends (the Condyle or Coronoid process) into the silt. The drift ball was heavy enough that it was moving slowly and simply became wedged against the jawbone, possibly held in place by a tooth through one of the holes.

He was pulled out of his reverie by a tug on his line and acceded to Skip's surfacing thumb up. They broke surface just a few feet past the upriver side of the bridge. Turning, they saw the dive boat just on the left bank side and swam that way as Yonnie and Fred pulled in the safety lines. Reaching the dive boat, Chet handed his light and GPS receiver to Yonnie with Skip handing Fred his light and the bag. Then each unsnapped the BCD and slipped out of it as their tenders lifted it off their shoulders and into the boat. Once free of that weight, Chet pulled himself into the boat and was quickly followed by Skip.

While they started removing their dive suits, Yonnie maneuvered the boat to shore where Nathanial was waiting. Fred handed him the net bag after removing the drift ball that, once out of the water, had quit emitting light.

"The jaw bone was wedged in the silt and the drift ball lodged against it," Skip reported.

"Good thing too," Chet commented. "That is so small it would have been easy to miss it. I figure that it hit first and the skull pushed it into the silt enough to hold it. If it had landed flat and the skull on top of it pushing it down, we might have missed it."

"Anything else of interest?" Nathanial said holding up the bag.

"Maybe a gun," Skip and Chet answered almost simultaneously.

"You didn't say anything about a gun," Chet said.

"Didn't know anything about a gun," Nathanial said as he thought *Dear Lord, don't let there be another crime. One a day is enough.*

"Thanks for your help, guys," he said, waving as Yonnie started the dive boat's big engine and began turning the boat around to head downriver.

"Tell Rachel and Jeremy to hang tight for another half hour or so. The boys think they'll be done by then," Nathanial shouted after them, and the four divers waved in acknowledgement.

Chapter 8

It took longer than Walker and Roberts had predicted. Nathanial had left them alone and gone to the road to give his deputies a break, one at a time. He relieved Jim Steiner, the northern deputy, first and then walked across the bridge to relieve Webster.

"I'm fine, Sheriff," Webster said. "No problems."

"That may be, Webster," Nathanial replied, "but just for the sake of safety, you need to take a break. There is a facility over at the launch."

Mitchell Webster shrugged knowing better than to argue and started to get into his squad just as a van with a microwave dish on top appeared coming around a bend about a hundred yards south of the bridge.

"I'll stay to help with this, if that's okay."

Nathanial nodded and stepped to the middle of the road holding up his hand indicating that the vehicle should stop. Close behind it was a small red car. Rather than proceeding directly to Nathanial, both vehicles pulled off the road about ten yards behind Webster's cruiser. A woman got out of the driver's door of the van, and a man carrying a television camera got out of the other door. Both were wearing press badges although there wasn't a need. A young woman that Nathanial recognized as a reporter for The Alpena News hurried forward from the second vehicle. Nathanial spoke before any of them had a chance to ask any questions.

"Don't bother turning on the camera. There is nothing here for you to see. I, and my deputies, have nothing to say at this point. I will hold a press conference at my office tomorrow morning at 9:00 a.m. and you are welcome there, cameras and all."

"Come on, Sheriff," said the girl from Channel 11 in Alpena, the local CBS affiliate. "We came all the way down here…"

"I know that you did. But it's a nice day and you might be able to get some shots of weekenders or locals launching their boats over at the DNR site," he said motioning toward it. "But nothing here. I would appreciate it if you wouldn't say anything until after the press conference tomorrow. Idle speculation just draws the curious and makes our job more difficult."

The three reporters turned around without another word and walked back to their vehicles, which they then turned around and drove back the way they had come followed by Webster's cruiser. Webster returned about fifteen minutes later and gave Nathanial a full report.

"The TV crew set up there and started doing as you said, but the locals started asking them questions. They got into one of the boats and started up the river until they reached the Whaler. You've got a good couple there, Sheriff. They stopped the boat and told them they couldn't go up the river. The boat started around and the kids moved the Whaler to block them. Rachel was at the wheel and Jeremy had a digital camera and started taking pictures while she was telling them that failure to comply would be obstructing an official police investigation and they would be arrested and the boat confiscated. That last convinced the boater to turn around. He dropped the TV crew at the dock and took off up the lake."

"How do you know what happened?"

"The TV crew told me. She was pissed – moaning and bitching about freedom of the press. The cameraman was standing behind her taking it all in and smiling. Guess he is used to her bullshit."

"Rachel knows how to handle herself alright. That's why she's back this year. She'll be a good teacher for Jeremy."

Nathanial walked back across the bridge, stopping in the middle to look north toward the lake. He stood there for a few minutes watching several boats being launched. None of them started up the river. The television truck was nowhere to be seen. Continuing across the bridge, he walked and slid down the bank and went to check on his forensics team.

"How's it going?" he asked hopefully.

Roberts and Walker sat back on their heels.

"Slowly," Roberts said. "The top five inches is still fairly soft from the spring's high water. After that it's hard-packed. Years of wet and settling. Dry during the summer so it hardens. If it wasn't for spring flooding, this might never have been uncovered."

"We're doing our best, Sheriff," Walker added. "We're leaving no bone unturned."

There was an audible groan from Nathanial, Walker and Roberts high-fived, and he knew he'd been set up. However, that statement was going to become the forensics team's mantra from then on. With that, Nathanial went back up the road and called in an order of four large pizzas from the Old Mill Inn. By the time he arrived at the restaurant at the north end of the lake, the pizzas were ready.

"These for the crew at the bridge?" Beth Mahoney, the proprietor, asked as she rang up the sale.

"How'd you know about that?" Nathanial answered without thinking.

"Word gets around," she replied.

"Gert?" asked Nathanial and she shrugged.

***

Nathanial pulled his cruiser in behind Steiner's and scooped about a third of a pizza from two different boxes onto two paper plates, which he then gave to Steiner. Munching on a slice of pepperoni and mushroom, he slid down the bank, pizza box in the other hand and walked to the bridge.

"Room service," he said.

"But we didn't order anything," Roberts countered.

"Come back here," Walker intoned as Nathanial turned on his heels to go back up the hill.

He smiled as he handed the pizza box to Roberts. Both had removed their latex gloves before he got to them. Walker opened the box and removed a slice of Italian sausage and green peppers, the gooey cheese tearing away from the adjacent pieces. Roberts grabbed a pepperoni and mushroom and was about to close the box, but Nathanial's big hand was in there first withdrawing a slice of the sausage pizza.

"You've got five minutes," he said as he left, his mouth full of the lukewarm pasta.

"For what?" the two shouted after him, but he just waved.

After delivering pizza to Webster, he drove to the Negwegon launch site and walked out on the dock, pizza box in hand motioning to the Whaler. Rachel guided the Whaler smoothly alongside the dock and Jeremy slipped a rope around a piling.

"Dinner," Nathanial said handing the box to Rachel. "You two are done. Take off. You have a long ride to East Bay and an early day tomorrow."

"What about…?" Jeremy asked motioning up the river.

"I'm here until they're done up there. I think I can handle it … with one more slice of that Italian sausage pizza."

Chapter 9

At precisely 9:00 a.m., Nathanial strode into the small room in which he routinely gave press conferences and knew that he should have chosen the garage except for the fact that one of his cruisers was up on the rack and couldn't be taken down. All of the twenty seats were taken and there were, by his quick count, twelve additional bodies along the walls. Standing next to the door, hands empty, was Deputy Arthur Misdorf being given a break from his office routine. All heads, except Arthur's, turned expectantly upon hearing Nathanial's heels clicking on the tile floor.

All eyes followed his progress to the podium, several noting enviously the sheet of paper he held in his hand. Placing the paper on the podium, he pulled from his pocket a case that he opened and from which he removed a pair of glasses. Putting down the case, he put on the glasses and then looked out at his audience.

"If I had known…"

"Is this another Williston case?" interrupted him in mid-sentence.

"If I had known…" Nathanial started again.

"Is this another Williston case?"

Nathanial looked in the direction of the sound of the voice.

"Who asked that question?"

A short man, standing in the corner of the room, raised his hand and was stared at by the rest of the assemblage who were as curious as Nathanial as to the source of the rudeness.

"And who are you?" Nathanial asked, as he removed his glasses so he could better see the miscreant.

"Harry Livingston."

"And whom do you represent, Harry Livingston?"

"I am an independent."

"Well, Harry Livingston," Nathanial said, putting his glasses back on as he picked up the sheet of paper, "in this room, one does not speak until spoken to."

"Is this another Williston case?" Harry Livingston repeated.

Exasperated, Nathanial once again removed his glasses, shaking his head. The eyes of the assemblage were like eyes at a tennis match following the ball.

"I will repeat," Nathanial said, "In this room, one does not speak…"

"But you spoke to me," Harry Livingston said adamantly.

"Did you get a copy of the statement?" Nathanial asked.

"No, I didn't," replied Harry Livingston.

Nathanial looked at Misdorf. "Deputy Misdorf, will you please escort Harry Livingston from the building and see that he leaves the grounds without a copy of the statement."

Misdorf had already started moving toward Harry Livingston.

"And, Deputy Misdorf," as Arthur Misdorf stopped and looked at the sheriff, "if he offers the least bit of resistance or verbalizes an objection of any kind, arrest him for obstruction of justice, disturbing the peace or something. Just get him out of my sight."

Arthur Misdorf stood aside as Harry Livingston hustled by him, glaring at the sheriff.

"And, Deputy Misdorf, get a picture of this idiot and be certain that he doesn't try to attend another of my press conferences."

Arthur Misdorf followed Harry Livingston out of the room and closed the door behind him. All eyes then returned to the man behind the podium who had re-placed the glasses on his nose.

"Now where was I?" Nathanial mused.

"If I had known..." came a voice from the front row.

"Thank you," Nathanial said without looking up. Then he did.

"If I had known that this press conference would have been so popular, I might have moved it, but the garage is busy at this time."

There were several chuckles from the audience.

"I note that several of you do not have copies of the press release," Nathanial continued. "More are being made and will be available from Deputy Misdorf as you leave.

"Monday afternoon ... that's yesterday, of course..." Again there were good-natured chuckles. "The department's two summer interns were patrolling Hibbard Pond and took shelter under the West Branch covered bridge at the southwest end of the lake. In the process of tying up their Boston Whaler (officially the Department's Boston Whaler), they discovered a skull."

There was a chorus of murmurings from the assem-blage.

"Yes, this is not unlike the discovery of the body in the Perch Pond a little more than a year ago. However, it is not a Williston case. I repeat, it is NOT a Williston case. My forensic team is certain that the body has been in the ground from the early 1950s. I am sorry to say that beyond this, we don't know much. I am being truthful. When we learn more you will be advised. As you came in this morning you were asked to sign in and leave an email contact. You will be mailed further statements and notices of press conferences.

"Some of you know that Deputy Misdorf was shot several months ago. He just returned to duty yesterday. He has requested that he not be asked for a statement. Therefore I implore you to please leave him and his family alone.

"Everything that I feel you need to know about the current discovery is in the press release. Please note that it says that the two summer interns are NOT to be asked about this or any other of their duties. I hope that I have made myself clear on that."

As he was making this last statement, he had removed the glasses from his nose, put them in the glasses case, and then the case in his shirt pocket. He picked up his copy of the press release and left the room, handing that statement to the reporter standing next to the door. Only when he was out of the room did the assemblage make ready to depart. As the reporters exited the room, Arthur Misdorf was standing outside with a fresh supply of copies of the press release, short by the four that Nathanial had taken.

Chapter 10

The crossroads known as Hibbard Corners lies on a direct path from the middle of Hibbard Pond in the direction of magnetic north. It is one of those villages that if you blink your eyes you can miss it. From the middle of the crossroads, East Hibbard Pond Path extends southward until it reaches the bottom of Hibbard Pond, and then it turns westward becoming South Hibbard Pond Path. Reaching the other side of the lake, it turns north becoming West Hibbard Pond Path, which on reaching the north end of the lake turns eastward and becomes North Hibbard Pond Path.

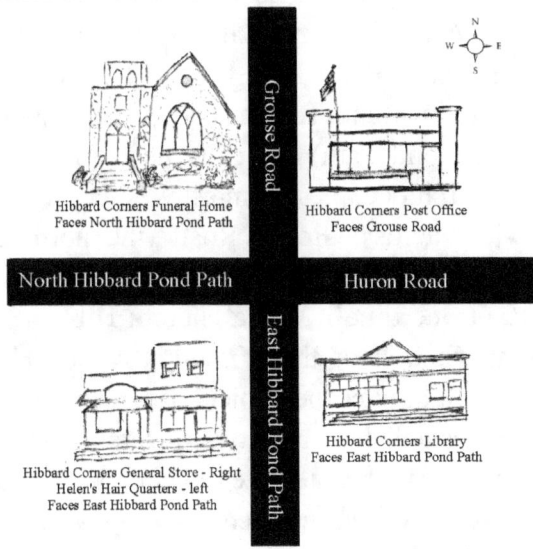

The village, although too small to be a village according to the State of Michigan, consists of four buildings and has a full time population of two: Gert and Peter Pickard who live above the Hibbard Corners General Store that they run. The building, located on the southwest corner of the intersection, also houses Helen's Hair Quarters, run by Helen Trumball-Grant, who lives with her mother several miles away. Before housing the general store, the space was occupied by the post office that now occupies a brick edifice on the northeast corner of the intersection. In this era of economic downturn and cost cutting, Postmaster Owen Whitehawk wages a constant battle to keep the post office in business. Recently he assimilated the Black River Post Office, which had to close because of asbestos in the walls. The move was supposed to be temporary, but Owen Whitehawk (a full-blooded Chippewa) was smart enough to keep hold of this additional business. The general store had previously been housed in what is now the Hibbard Corners Branch of the Alcona County Library, located directly across East Hibbard Pond Path from the general store and across Huron Road (the eastbound extension of North Hibbard Pond Path) from the post office. What looks like a church occupies the northwest corner of the crossroads, just across Grouse Road (the northbound extension of East Hibbard Pond Path) from the post office. In fact, at one time it was a church: Hibbard Corners Lutheran Church of the Missouri Synod. Then a congregational fight over the choice of the next minister resulted in the establishment of two different congregations, neither of which wanted the old church. As a sidelight on this, each of the new congregations hired the man they didn't want when they were part of the old congregation. As Gert Pickard says, "Strange are the workings of the Lord." The building was vacant for a number of years until Steven Hibbs paid the back taxes and assumed control, turning it into the Hibbard Corners Funeral Home. It was currently run by his son Wallace, who also served as the county coroner mainly because nobody else wanted the job. Truth be told, no other funeral director or embalmer in the county was as qualified as Wallace.

Nathanial had come to 'The Corners', as most of the locals referred to it, for that reason. The skeletal remains of the child unearthed by his forensics team had been brought here the previous evening. Wallace would prepare the remains for shipment to the Blodgett Medical Facility in Grand Rapids for an official autopsy. Not being a certified forensic pathologist, Wallace did not feel qualified to issue findings in possible murder cases, although he had no qualms about doing so for garden-variety deaths such as heart attacks or automobile accidents. However, before seeing Wallace, Nathanial had a stop to make at the nerve center of the Alcona County Rumor Mill.

Mounting the steps of the General Store, he knew that someone had either entered or left the store only moments before because he could smell the fattening and tempting aroma of Gert's Tuesday creation. It was chocolate, it was baked, and he could tell it was ready. As he pushed open the door to the store, two heads turned and two faces looked up at him expectantly. The one behind the counter belonged to Gert Pickard, who ran the store with her husband Peter's help, but she was the one who did the baking that brought in most of the customers. She stood no more than five feet and her husband wasn't any taller. Her white hair was pulled back in a bun and her cheeks were red from the heat of the oven. Helen Trumball-Grant was dressed in blue jeans, yellow tee shirt emblazoned with "Blonde, Brunette or Redhead – Only your hairdresser knows for sure" and wearing orange athletic shoes of some type. She straightened from where she had been leaning on the counter, grabbed the small bag from it, and turned to leave. Attempting to sidestep the sheriff, Mrs. T-G, as she was known, almost ran into him. Looking up at him, she felt like a dwarf, as did most people. Even at five foot ten in her stocking feet, she had to bend her head back to look Nathanial in the face.

"Please don't leave, Mrs. T-G," Nathanial said, his white teeth gleaming in a broad smile. "I know what goes on in that shop of yours and, if I have been told correctly, it is second only to what happens in this store. Therefore, I want to set the record straight before things get out of hand."

"Now, Nathanial, youse knows…," Gert started to sputter.

"Yes, I do," Nathanial said. "And I want to know what your rumor mill has started, so you just hush and I'll get the information from Mrs. T-G."

"But Nathanial…," was all she got out before, "Gert, be quiet or I'll call in the kitchen police." He wouldn't have done anything of the sort, knowing in fact that the cleanliness of her kitchen was beyond reproach, but it got her to zip her lips.

"Now, Mrs. T-G, tell me what Gert has been telling you."

Helen Trumball-Grant looked at Gert who shrugged and so Helen started, "Harry Pickens was fishing off the bank near the bridge when it started raining so he moved up onto the bridge. He didn't even have a line in the water when that Boston Whaler come roaring up the river and stopped under the bridge. Those two young deputies …"

"They're summer interns," Nathanial injected.

"Do you want me to tell the story or are you going to keep correcting me?"

"Sorry," Nathanial said, "please continue."

Chapter 11

"Where was I?" Mrs. T-G mused.

"Them … ummm … summer interns coming roaring up the river," Gert offered.

"Yes, so they anchored their boat under the bridge. It was quiet for a bit and then the guy said, 'We might be more comfortable up on the bank.' Guess he got out because then he slipped and said, 'What was that?' The girl shrieked, 'It's a skull!' And there was a splash. They called you and you brought those deputies. Then you told those two young deputies… excuse me … summer interns to guard the river down by the Negwegon DNR launch. You gave them AK-47s to use…."

"That's not what I told youse," Gert interrupted. "I said AR-15s."

"Okay, ladies. I've heard enough," Nathanial said. "Gert, you know the party game of telephone?"

"Which party youse mean? If it's them Democrats, they never tells the truth, and if it's the Republicans, they's knowed to be liars."

"Now, Gert, not that kind of party. I mean…," Nathanial was stopped by the smile on her face and he knew he been had. "This was a setup, wasn't it?"

"Yup," Gert said. "Gottcha." And she smiled at Mrs. T-G who was almost bent over double laughing.

"Gert … ha ha …Gert saw you coming and gave me a … ha ha … story real quick. She said she would step in at the right moment."

"Well, you did well, Gert. Where did you get your information?" Nathanial wanted to know.

"Harry Pickens. He tried to fish there and you made him move off. He was rip-roaring mad and headed for the Old Mill Inn to cool off. He heard a couple of those divers talking about their dive. Picked up enough to know about the skull those two young ones found but not much more than that. He was in first thing this morning. I knew youse be coming to set me straight after that body under the ice last March, so I waited. Only person I talked to was Mrs. T-G and that was to get youse back."

"Well, you did a good job," Nathanial said, handing a copy of the press release to both of the ladies. "Now take a minute to read this and when you talk to anyone, please refer to it."

Both ladies nodded in agreement as they perused the page, Gert's lips moving silently as she read the paper.

"And I don't want to hear anything about AK-47s or AR-15s," Nathanial tacked on.

"Well, then, what do youse use?" Gert wanted to know.

"It doesn't matter and the young deputies…"

"Summer interns," Mrs. T-G injected.

"Yes, the summer interns were not, and are not, armed. Thank you, ladies, for an enjoyable encounter. Gert, could I…"

Before he could finish Gert offered up a paper bag and a cardboard cup of coffee with a plastic lid. "Black, jest like youse."

Nathanial smiled at one of his favorite people. "Thanks, Gert."

She gave him another bag, "This one's for Owen cause I knows youse be going that way and it will save him or Rachel a trip."

Nathanial tipped his hat and held the door for Mrs. T-G, who hurried down the steps and the short distance to her door where a customer was waiting. Setting the two bags on the seat and the coffee in his holder, he started his cruiser and drove the short distance to the parking lot behind the funeral home. Other than Wallace's black SUV and the funeral home's hearse, there was no other vehicle there, so he knew he had time. He pulled out his cellphone and called Chet Willis.

"Good morning, Nathanial," Chet said as he answered the phone. "Got another body?"

"No, have a problem with security. Fellow overheard a couple of your guys at the Old Mill last night talking about the dive. Appreciate a little more closed-mouthness until things become public."

"Aww, dang. Shouldn't have happened. Won't again."

Taking Owen's bag, Nathanial hurried across the street and into the post office's foyer. He looked for some kind of scathing notice to people who used the wrong mail slots (one for local and one for out-of-town) but found none, so he opened the door to the business lobby and entered, a bell tinkling as he did so.

"Be with you in a minute," came the shout from the back.

Nathanial put the bag of brownies on the counter and looked at it. In his mind's eye (or in this case, mind's mouth), he could taste the two different chocolates of the cookie and the icing. He opened the bag and peered in. Five brownies were nestled on the bottom on a paper towel, four on the bottom and one on top. His appetite whetted by his mind's mouth, he took the one from the top and popped it into his mouth in two quick bites as he refolded the bag's top. He was startled as the door's bell tinkled behind him, and he heard a sultry voice, "Hello, tall, dark and handsome."

He spun around and the chocolate deliciousness in his mouth turned into putty. Standing in front of him was the most beautiful woman he had ever seen. Glossy-black straight hair disappeared over her shoulders. Two lustrous black eyes, looking both inviting and accusing, gleamed at him from a brownish-red face highlighted by softly sculpted high cheekbones and a nose of the kind one associates with an American Indian, and she was a full-blood Chippewa. A long neck led to a light blue denim long-sleeved shirt topped with a black vest emblazoned with beadwork hiding soft feminine curves. A wide brown belt at the waist of blue jeans, so tight they had to be painted on, was secured with a big silver belt buckle in the middle of which was a lustrous Petoskey stone. The blue jeans were tucked into the top of red cowboy boots. Nathanial had never met Rachel Whitehawk before and her beauty, as well as his full mouth, left him speechless.

"What are you hiding?" Rachel asked stepping up to the counter. "Ah, just what I came for." She unfolded the bag and peered inside. "Good, I see that Owen has his. Tell him I was here and had to run. Appointment at the beauty shop in Tawas." The bell tinkled as she exited. Nathanial stared out the front window and watched her wave to him as she passed by heading for the parking lot.

"Oh, hello, Sheriff," Owen Whitehawk said from behind him. "You just come in or been waiting?"

Nathanial managed to clear his mouth in a couple of chews and swallows.

"I've been waiting. Your wife…"

He was interrupted by Owen waving and turned to see Rachel drive by in a black Mercedes sedan, waving out the window with a brownie in her hand.

"I see you've met Rachel," Owen said. "Did she leave one for me?"

Nathanial stared at him and then sadly shook his head. "She would have, I mean … she thought you already had taken yours."

Owen looked at Nathanial, peering more closely.

"Better wipe your lips, brownie thief," Owen said with a broad smile revealing gleaming white teeth.

Oh, great, Nathanial thought. *First, Gert gets my goat and then I get nabbed filching a brownie from the postmaster.*

"I'll make restitution," Nathanial said. "I have a bag over in my cruiser." He waved in the direction of the funeral home. "I'll bring you one."

"One what?" Owen asked sarcastically.

"One brownie, to replace the one I ate."

"In the case of Gert's brownies, restitution calls for one bag per brownie," Owen said.

Chapter 12

As Nathanial left the post office to get the brownies from his cruiser, he saw George Haversack, the Hibbard Corners librarian, heading diagonally across the intersection toward the funeral home. He was wearing blue jeans, sneakers and a windbreaker, his head topped with a baseball cap of some sort. Very out of character for George, a former college history teacher, who was usually in dress slacks, coat, and tie, and dress shoes in the library. True, the ensemble was ill matching but that was his way. His pace was extremely determined and in his hand was a paper sack bearing brownies, of that Nathanial was certain. George was so intent on his path that he didn't notice Nathanial at all.

Retrieving the bag of brownies from the front seat, Nathanial returned to the post office. Owen Whitehawk was waiting, hands on the counter, a copy of the press release in front of him.

"You say it's not Williston. Positive?"

Nathanial placed the bag of brownies on the counter and watched as Owen started to open it.

"If my forensic guys are correct and they usually are, it is much too early for Williston. He might not have even been born."

"So, what time frame?" Owen said as he removed a brownie from the bag tantalizingly slowly, holding it in plain view as he awaited Nathanial's response.

"Early to mid-fifties is their guess."

"Oh, so now it's a guessing game," Owen said before taking a bite of the brownie.

"It's an educated guess, which is the best they can do. But they're 98% certain. Even willing to make a bet."

"Yeah," Owen retorted, "use one of the coins they flip when they make a decision, no doubt." And the rest of the brownie disappeared.

"If you see them, ask," Nathanial said, waving as he headed out the door. There was still no hearse in the parking lot other than Wallace's. Entering the building, Nathanial found himself in the small empty lobby. He crossed it quickly to the wall where an always illuminated sign said "Embalming in process" to prevent the curious from going downstairs. There was an intercom under the sign with a notice saying that a visitor should announce himself to the embalmer, but before he could press the button, a voice came out of the speaker. "Come on down, brownie thief." Shaking his head, Nathanial vowed to get even with Owen Whitehawk. As he walked down the ramp, which led to the prep room and was also used to wheel caskets up and down, Nathanial wondered if his entire day was going to be like this.

The door to the prep room was open, which it wouldn't have been if Wallace had actually been embalming and there was no sound of the ventilating fan he would have had on. Nathanial just heard the sound of voices. Entering the room he saw Wallace and George Haversack looking at a small rosewood coffin. Each man had a half-eaten brownie in one hand and full mouths, bites taken just before he entered the room. Another tantalizing punishment no doubt orchestrated by Owen Whitehawk. Ordinarily Wallace or George Haversack would have offered him a brownie, but Nathanial knew that was not going to happen today.

"Morning," Nathanial said. "What's the plan?"

"Morning, Nathanial," Wallace said, mouth full, waving him over with the brownie-held hand. "Take a look."

Inside the casket, the skeleton lay on a bed of purple velvet. It was small but it filled the coffin that was intended for a child.

"Any idea about the sex?" Nathanial asked

"Definitely male," Wallace intoned. "I'd say age six to eight because of his size, about four feet. The average eight-year-old male is four feet four. Blodgett will be more precise," stuffing the remainder of the brownie into his mouth.

"If your forensics team is correct," George Haversack said, completely understandably, through his brownie-filled mouth, "he is most likely not from around here. I spent two hours looking at microfilm of the Alcona County Review from that time period and there is nothing about a missing boy. Could have missed it of course, but if he was from around here, they would have had a notice." And the rest of his brownie vanished.

"Who's taking it to Grand Rapids?" Nathanial asked, unable to manage his salivating. He knew that both Wallace and George Haversack were enjoying this.

Wallace, having retrieved a second brownie from the bag and passed it to George, replied, "George is.

Nobody from the area is free today and I have a family coming to make arrangements."

"But isn't the library supposed to be open today?" Nathanial queried.

George Haversack, mouth full of half the second brownie, nodded in agreement. "But the librarian is ill. At least that's what the sign on the door says." And the second brownie disappeared.

"Who is the chaperone?" Wallace asked. "You?"

Remains involved in a criminal case were always accompanied by a deputy, keeping the chain of evidence intact.

"Nope, Deputy Misdorf will meet us at M-72," Nathanial replied. For the first time it hit him that two of the brownies that he had given to Owen Whitehawk had been destined for Arthur Misdorf.

"Oh, he's back," Wallace said, finishing his second brownie and wiping his hands on a paper towel, which he then gave to George Haversack, who first wiped his lips after licking them slowly.

"Just on temporary duty," Nathanial explained. "He still has a month of light duty, but I don't expect that there'll be any problem with this transport."

Wallace closed the lid of the small coffin, fastening it securely. Then he and George Haversack, preceded by Nathanial, wheeled the litter up the ramp and down a short hallway to the back door where there was a loading dock. The funeral home's hearse was waiting and Nathanial opened the door and stepped out of the way as the coffin was slid into the hearse and secured.

"I'll be ready as soon as I check in, George," Nathanial said and walked to his cruiser. Opening the door he slid into his seat and picked up the microphone.

"Barbara Ann," he said to his dispatcher, "ready to leave the Corners." He vowed that she would pay for it, as would Owen Whitehawk, if the term "brownie thief" was mentioned.

"Roger, Sheriff," was her reply. "Arthur is out the door as we speak. He has been chomping at the bit."

"I'll bet. It is going to be a long month for him. I'll be there in about forty-five."

Hanging up the microphone, he closed the door and started the cruiser. He pulled the shoulder strap of the seatbelt in front of him and, as he turned to latch it, he noticed a paper bag, top folded down, sitting on the passenger seat. He opened it and saw two brownies nestled on a paper towel. He refolded the bag and backed out facing south. As George Haversack pulled in behind him, he started south and looked toward the post office. Owen Whitehawk was standing in the window with a sign that read, "Paid in full." And Nathanial breathed a sigh of relief.

Chapter 13

The weather in May had been mercurial with wind and rain during the week subsiding slightly on the weekends. Temperatures had been equally unstable with snow and sleet mixed in with the rain. In fact, one day in the middle of the month seemed to show at least three of the seasons: the day started with snow and temperatures in the 30s which had warmed the snow until it turned to sleet, and then rain in the late morning. By early afternoon the sun had been out. By mid-afternoon it had been warm enough to be out in shirtsleeves and start or continue the process of winter cleanup.

So when the week before Memorial Day finally promised good weather, the Hibbard Pond Sportsman seized the opportunity to get their shelters built and sunk in the water. So it was Wednesday, two days after the body beneath the bridge had been discovered, that the membership assembled at the south-end launch. Obvious to all was the notice by the docks that access up the river toward the bridge had been closed because of the sheriff's investigation. And of course, rumors were rampant.

"They say that it's another Williston body," Jerry Hatchett said as he expertly drove a nail into one of the slats of the shelter that he and Dugal McBruce were building.

"Don't think so," Dugal said as he started a new nail.

"Why?" Jerry stopped and pulled a handkerchief out of his back pocket to wipe his brow. "Nathanial tell you something?"

"No. It's just that I did a thorough search of the National Center for Missing & Exploited Children and there were no other missing girls within the time frame that match the description."

"Well, maybe it was earlier," Jerry said as he stuffed the handkerchief back into his pocket.

"Could have been earlier," Dugal said. "But it wouldn't have been Williston. Nathanial is certain that Williston's kidnappings came as a result of the death of his daughter to whom the girls were virtually identical." The previous spring, Dugal and Jerry had met when the Hibbard Pond Sportsman were helping to turn a farmer's pond into a perch-raising pond to help bring perch fishing back to the lake. Once a hotbed for perch and pike fishing, shelter-providing weeds had disappeared from the lake. Invasive species had been blamed for this, most notably rusty crawfish. The loss of the weeds had coincided with the sudden downturn in the perch population and had led to the virtual disappearance of the northern pike. The Sportsman had turned to two activities to supplement that of the DNR (Department of Natural Resources) who had been sponsoring pike plants for several years. This was the purchase of pike fingerlings from hatcheries and releasing them in the sheltered waters of both the West Branch River the south end of Hibbard Pond and the north end at Loon Creek.

First, the Sportsman had started building shelters to replace the weed beds. Shelters were wooden crates made of cedar with slats on all six sides permitting the ingress and egress of small fish that hid among the branches of fir trees. The trees were gathered after Christmas from sellers of Christmas trees who were more than happy to get rid of them and write the cost off on taxes since the Sportsman was a 501(c)(3) organization. The shelters also had about six hundred pounds of concrete blocks to hold them on the lake's bottom. The second project was to be the perch pond where perch fry could be raised over the summer to fingerling size before being released into the lake. The first step in the process, as far as the Sportsman's group was concerned, was burying a drainpipe at the bottom of the dam through which the pond could be drained in the fall and the perch harvested as they were carried through the pipe into a waiting wire mesh trap. They would be scooped out of the trap and transported to the lake, which was just a few miles distant.

It was while a backhoe was digging the channel for the pipe that Dugal had discovered a skull in the mud the backhoe had dropped. The local sheriff had been called and when he arrived, Dugal was surprised to see that he was Nathanial Jefferson, Dugal's high school football teammate. Dugal had been the quarterback for the team and Nathanial one of the offensive linemen. Nathanial had gone on to State with a football scholarship only to have a career-ending knee injury early in his freshman season. With hopes for a career in the National Football League literally torn asunder, he had joined the Michigan State Police and upon reaching retirement age, he and his wife Dawn had relocated Up North where he had taken a position as a deputy sheriff. When the sheriff had suffered a massive heart attack necessitating his retirement, Nathanial had been appointed acting sheriff and was elected to the position the following fall.

Dugal, on the other hand, had married his high school sweetheart Earleen just out of high school and turned to truck driving to support his young family. When he had retired, they had relocated to Hibbard Pond where Dugal had joined the Sportsman. Helping to build the perch pond had been his first activity. The discovery of the skeleton of a young girl had brought Dugal instant notoriety and the discovery of the body of a second young girl by a youthful bow hunter on the opening day of deer season the following fall had thrown the small community around the lake into turmoil. However, the second young girl had been identified by DNA and a Tickle Me Elmo doll that had been carelessly discarded at the scene. Good police work had led to the rescue of a third girl who had been kidnapped from Ohio. The kidnapper was Nick Williston who had been killed when his truck hit a tree as he fled from the sheriff. Dugal's role in the mystery, other than the discovery of the first body, had been identifying the first girl by using the database of the National Center for Missing & Exploited Children (http://www.missingkids.com). He had looked for missing girls who matched the description of the second girl and the kidnapped girl.

The discovery of a body in a fish shelter during the previous winter had brought back speculation that Williston's apparent spree had spread, but the body was that of a French Canadian. Who had killed him was speculative as three people had confessed but only one of them remained alive and, with dementia, a trial for her was out of the question.

"You guys going to gab or build shelters?" This derisive comment brought both Dugal and Jerry out of their momentary halt as both of them remembered the past year. They looked up to see Zebulah Pike, the man who had found the body while ice fishing last winter. His hook had snagged on something, and he had brought up a piece of a human finger. He had been in a rush at the time as a blizzard was descending on the lake, and he was in a hurry to get off the ice. It was several days later while he was putting his equipment away when he discovered his "catch" and had taken it to the sheriff's office in Harrisville, the county seat of Alcona County.

"Hey, Zeb," Jerry said. "Not to worry, this one's done. Our third."

"Could be your last. I been designated captain of the barge and need two hands to sign on to sail to the treasure site and drop the bounty."

"Arrgh, matey," Dugal said, picking up on Zeb's pirate innuendos. "For a few doubloons, I might be willing."

"Ah, don't know about the doubloons, but adventures aplenty I've been promised."

"Be there grog aboard if no doubloons?" Jerry asked.

"Bring your own if you feel the need," Zeb said.

Jerry patted a pocket where he had his flask, "Never leave home without it."

"Well, get what you need and get a move on, the loading has started." Zeb motioned to the dock toward which Jerry and Dugal could see several men carrying shelters. "Bring your hammers, we might need to nail the lids on as we voyage. Step lively, you landlubbers."

Chapter 14

As Zeb headed toward the dock, Dugal went to his SUV (a red Ford Explorer he had named Columbus.) He took off his tool belt from which he removed his hammer and put the belt on the back seat. He was about to shut the door when he heard a woman's voice behind him, "And where are you going without saying goodbye?"

"Honestly, Earleen, I was on my way over," he said as he was turning around. Earleen and Liz Hatchett had accompanied their husbands to the shelter building. They had teamed up with Jayne Eyre Polli and were building shelters, at a rate only a little slower than Dugal and Jerry had. The three of them were really a picture. Liz and Earleen were within an inch or two of Jayne Eyre's five feet six and were svelte (at least for people their age) while Jayne Eyre weighed 260, down some twenty pounds on a dieting binge. Liz and Earleen were dressed in faded blue jeans; Liz had a short-sleeved sweatshirt over a long-sleeved tee shirt, while Earleen was wearing a sweater that had seen better days. Jayne Eyre was dressed in spanking new denim bib overalls over an equally new short-sleeved powder blue denim shirt. She was a walking advertisement for adult OshKosh B'Gosh.

"And where are you going?" Earleen was standing in front of him arms crossed, her hammer in her right hand. She truly presented an intimidating appearance, at least to Dugal.

"Jerry and I were going with Zeb to sink shelters."

In the distance he could see Jerry give Liz a smack on the lips and head for the barge, which already had two shelters on it.

"Out on the lake?"

Dugal was stymied. He knew how to swim. "What...?" and then it hit him. Turning around he opened Columbus's door and pulled out his type III PFD (Personal Flotation Device.) This compact device, which looks like a beach towel rolled up lengthwise, is put around the neck so the ends, which lie on the chest, are held on with a web belt. Dugal had purchased two of them when they had moved to the lake because he thought he would be fishing alone. His had a CO_2 cartridge, and if he fell in the water the vest would instantly inflate – at least in theory. He had never tried it. He put the vest on and Earleen uncrossed her arms, putting her hammer in the holder on her belt. She stepped up to him, put her arms around his neck, and gave him a big kiss.

"That's better," she said, settling back and turning toward her waiting shelter builders. "Have fun!"

Dugal took a playful swing at her rear as she started off but missed. He smiled and headed for the barge.

As he got to the dock, a farm tractor with a scoop on the front was sitting at the front of the barge, front wheels in water, the scoop extended out over the deck. Rob and Roy MacIntosh were taking fieldstone out of the scoop and putting them into the shelters. The four foot-cubical crates already were two-thirds full of fir trees cut in half or thirds in order to fit. In prior years, the shelters had been four-by-four-by-eight but, so the argument went, the Sportsman membership had an average age of seventy-two and pushing over five hundred pounds overboard wasn't that easy. So this year the size had been cut in half and also the shelters were built on the spot – in prior years they were built in the fall and stored in an area near the Loon Tavern Inn. Each shelter, when filled with trees and several hundred pounds of fieldstone, still weighed over four hundred pounds. For that reason they were set as far to the rear of the barge as possible so that the front end wouldn't sink into the waves. The barge was a fourteen-foot pontoon boat that had the steering console at the rear. Borrowed from Hibbard Pond Marine, it was standardly used to transport docks and hoists from the business's launch to the owners' properties.

"Ten large stones in each one," George Jamison (known to the other Sportsman as Mr. Warmth) admonished. "If they're not weighted properly, they float and we don't want floaters."

As soon as the fieldstone was in, Rob and Roy started nailing slats on the top. The tractor backed up, two more shelters were loaded on, sitting with three inches protruding over the side to make the dumping easier. Fieldstone added, the tops were nailed on and all but Zeb, Jerry and Dugal went ashore. The bow and stern lines holding the pontoon barge against the shore were untied and tossed aboard. The barge was skillfully and carefully backed away from the dock, stern upstream and then headed out onto the lake where there were waves of about six inches. The ride to the dumpsite took twenty minutes and the joking was rampant between the three new friends. As they neared the site, marked by a floating Tide bottle held in place with nylon rope and a piece of angle iron as a weight, Zeb gave instructions.

"Dump the starboard front first, then turn around and dump the port. Then move sternward and get the port and then the starboard. I'll cut the engine so we'll drift. I'm going to be this side of the bottle for this first bunch."

As he was talking, Jerry and Dugal were putting on gloves to protect their hands. Then they took their positions between the two forward shelters. Zeb shifted the motor out of gear and shouted, "Now." With a shove the starboard shelter went over the side and started sinking. Turning to the port like clockwork, Jerry and Dugal pushed the port shelter and started it moving.

Nobody ever knew exactly what happened. Whether it was a big splinter in a rough-sawn slat or an errant nail head not fully driven in, something grabbed the right cuff of Dugal's shirt and he followed the shelter into the water. As he hit the water, there was a loud POP and his life vest filled with air.

"DUGAL!" Jerry yelled and was starting to jump after him when his arm was grabbed and he was pulled back. Turning, he glimpsed Zeb shedding his life jacket. Then he pulled a hunting knife out of its sheath on his side, put it into his mouth like a pirate and dove into the water.

Dugal had started to yell in horror as he felt himself being pulled over the side but had enough sense to take a breath of air before he was pulled under. The buoyancy of the vest lifted him above the sinking shelter, but he was unable to get his left arm down to try to free the shirt. He was starting to reach for the buckle of the vest when he felt something grab his left foot and then his right. He realized that either Jerry or Zeb had dove in after him and once that person had his feet, he had started working his way down his body. By the time the shelter's first edge hit bottom, Zeb had reached Dugal's right arm and pulled his knife from his mouth. With one quick slash, the shirt cuff was severed and Dugal shot to the surface followed quickly by Zeb.

Chapter 15

Onboard the barge, Jerry had grabbed the life ring and one of the life jackets put there by Chuck Shulmann, owner of Hibbard Marine. He saw Dugal's head break the surface of the water about twelve feet behind the barge. Seconds later, Zeb appeared.

"Heads up," Jerry shouted as he threw first the ring and then the jacket at them. The ring landed three feet in front of Zeb and the jacket six. "Grab them and hang on. I'll bring the barge back."

Jerry moved between the two remaining shelters and, with adrenalin coursing through his body, got them over with two mighty heaves. After throwing the bowline in the water, he raced to the rear of the barge, put it in gear and started making a turn, throttle at full tilt. As soon as he had completed the turn he cut the speed back and set course for the two in the water. "I'm putting you on the port," he shouted. "Grab the bowline."

As he neared them he put the barge in reverse to slow it and then took it out of gear. Dugal was closest and he grabbed the bowline, but Zeb opted for the front of the barge. Jerry hurried to the front of the boat, pulled the bowline in until Dugal was alongside. Dropping to the deck, Jerry grabbed Dugal's right arm and started pulling him up, Dugal helping when he could with his left arm. With Dugal safely aboard and lying on the deck, Jerry moved forward and helped Zeb up. With both safely on board, Jerry helped them to the stern where the bulwarks provided some protection from the wind, put the barge in gear, and headed for the Negwegon DNR ramp as fast as the barge could move, which was a lot faster than it went out with its approximately one ton cargo deep-sixed, or maybe deep-twentied.

He pulled out his cellphone and called Liz. "Hey, just listen. We have an accident. Everyone's okay, but Zeb and Dugal are soaked, and the water isn't very warm. They're going to need blankets and a fire to get warm, so get hopping." He paused. "No time to explain – just do it please."

Putting the phone away, he reached into his back pocket and pulled out his ever-present flask. "Bet you guys are going to be happy I filled this with brandy today," he said as he handed it to Zeb who was closest. Unscrewing the lid, Zeb took a deep draft and handed it to Dugal who drank equally deeply. Then he looked at Zeb and said, "Thanks. I owe you my life."

Zeb smiled and said, "I don't want your life. You keep it and hold on to it tightly."

Always cool in the face of adversity, George Jameson had organized things. By the time the barge docked twelve minutes later, there was a roaring fire fueled by shelter slats and Sportsman members were waiting on the dock with blankets pulled from vehicles, where they were part of the winter emergency kits that hadn't been put away yet. Earleen, who was trained as an EMTA, had organized the preparations. Hearing that warmth was needed, Jayne Eyre Polli, who lived closest, had hurried home and returned with two thermoses full of soup. By the time she had come back, the two drowned rats had shed their clothes, were wrapped in blankets and standing in front of a roaring fire. "Hope you like tomato or chicken noodle," Jayne Eyre said. "The tomato is from a can, but the chicken noodle is homemade. Rolli loved my homemade chicken...," the end of the sentence died off as she realized what she was saying. Her husband Rolli Polli had committed suicide just barely a month ago rather than face an investigation into his part in a fire, which had killed his adoptive parents many years before. Dugal took the chicken noodle and Zeb the tomato. Earleen had not left Dugal's side since he staggered off the dock. She had helped him to the fire and in getting his clothes off. Liz had been equally helpful with Zeb, this being no time for modesty.

With adversity over and things beginning to return to normal, the Sportsman returned to shelter building, each man silently thanking his lucky stars that he hadn't been the one in the lake. Only Zeb, Dugal and Earleen were left around the fire

"When George started the fire using the slats, a couple of the guys were upset, 'Hey, those are needed for shelters.' George said, 'Don't you idiots think that one or two fewer shelters are worth a couple of lives?' That quieted them," Earleen told Dugal and Zeb, who both laughed.

"Hey, Dugal," Jerry called from nearby where he was busy building a shelter with Liz and Jane Eyre, who surprisingly could drive one of the nails in with two strokes of her twenty-ounce framing hammer.

"What?" Dugal said, looking at his friend.

"Hell of a way to find out that the vest works!"

Dugal waved at him and watched as Jane Eyre sunk another nail.

"What's she doing here?" he asked Earleen.

"She told us that after Rolli took his life, she went into a drunk for a week or so. Then something worked its way through the fog – she didn't say what – and she straightened up. She quit drinking, started dieting, and using her treadmill – that was a surprise hearing they had a treadmill. She found a copy of the *Sportsman's News* somewhere and read about the shelter build. She called Ed Stockwell and here she is."

"Wonder what turned her around?"

***

The shelter project took all day although Dugal, Earleen, and Zeb left as soon as the men's clothes were dry. Exhausted by the experience, both men got home and fell into bed and slept many hours. Jane Eyre was also exhausted when she finally got home. She got a long hot shower, dried and dressed in a pair of purple silk pajamas. Getting a glass of ice water, she settled herself into her lounger and found herself looking across the room at Rolli's. Draped on the chair was the Greek flag that he had held when he took his hog and drove off the Hibbard Marine barge. Raising her glass in a toast she said, "Stin ijiasas. We will make this right."

Chapter 16

Jane Eyre Polli slept the sleep of the proverbial dead that night and didn't wake up until midmorning. It was the first good night's sleep she had had since Rolli died. Her sleep had been dreamless, or at least there were none that she remembered. She showered, dressed in her trademark purple silk pajamas (these with little red crowns on them), and then had her breakfast of tea and dry toast sitting in her rocker looking out the window at Hibbard Pond. The day was bright and there were several fishing boats dotting the lake, probably manned by local fishermen getting their fishing done before the onslaught of weekenders opening their cabins for the first time in preparation for a summer of weekends enjoying the peace and water sports that Hibbard Pond offered. Previously on days like today, sitting in her rocker, she would have her eye glued to her telescope watching the lake for some interesting occurrence. Before Rolli's death, she had mainly hoped to find some guy's Johnson exposed when he urinated from the end of his boat, unaware of Eyre Spy's penchant for spying and seeking an entry in her Johnson diary (kept only in her head.) However, at least for now, she had lost interest in that undertaking.

As she sat there, teacup (a mug actually) in hand, her thoughts drifted to her promise to Rolli of the night before. What had to be put to rights was two-fold: first, it must be made clear to anyone who cared to listen that his suicide had nothing to do with the body found under the ice earlier in the year. This despite the fact that he had confessed to murdering that idiot Frenchman – Pierre LeBeuf, that was his name – to Sheriff Nathanial Jefferson. And, in fact, that was item number two: convincing everyone that his confession had simply been to save his dear friend Edna Fitzgerald. They had been friends – extremely close friends – since childhood in the orphanage in Montreal. What was its name? Sisters of the Poor or some equally silly title. No, it was Sisters of Care. That was it! The rat-faced fink (Rolli's description) Pierre LeBeuf had been a member of a trio, but after Edna had been adopted, he and Rolli had really started drifting apart as though Edna was the glue that held them together. Then Rolli had been adopted and Pierre had turned to crime and almost had gotten Rolli involved when they reconnected in their late-teen years. Pierre had never been adopted. Who would adopt a rat-faced kid? A rat-faced ratfink kid. She giggled at the thought of "rat-faced ratfink."

But the first confessor – he was the real mystery. Edna (Dame Edna as he called her) had always called him "Butch," but in that last hour of his life, he apparently had his fill and told her his name was Briel Boswick. They had later learned (Rolli had remembered) that Boswick had been in the orphanage also. He had a crush on Edna but she had no interest and would rather pal around with Rolli and Pierre, who were several years younger. On second thought, she was that much younger than Butch or Briel or whomever. The question that both she and Rolli had was, "Why had he confessed?" The only possible reason could be that he did it to save his sons who were in jail for disposing of the rat-faced ratfink's body and for the attempted murder of Arthur Misdorf, a sheriff's deputy. How appropriate! How effing appropriate! But his death really did nothing to change the boys' outlook. If anything, it had darkened it, because they were without their father, their mother having died years before. It was rumored that he had Alzheimer's, or at least dementia. That could have been enough, but they (she and Rolli) had believed that he was protecting Edna. And she had confessed, but only after Butch had confessed and killed himself. But why? With his confession, the case was closed, wasn't it? The sheriff had the gun used to kill Pierre; the boys had kept it when they deep-sixed the body. And that had been the crux of the matter. Rather than sinking the body-containing shelter in fifty feet of water, they had dropped it in thirty. And then that Zebulah Pyke had hooked it and brought up a part of a finger. Game on for the sheriff.

But who had killed Pierre LeBeuf? Rolli hadn't! He couldn't hurt a fly – except for the bestial adoptive parents of his. It had been his father really – adoptive father, asshole adoptive father – who had molested his sister. He had been unable to do anything because his mother – asshole adoptive mother – had refused to confront her husband. At least that is what she told Rolli. So when Rolli had gone to college, he had majored in chemistry. And what a brilliant chemist he would have been. He figured out how to make a chemical time bomb – a firebomb. The residue from the chemical timer was harmless non-descript compounds. How ingenious! Until that Deputy Webster had started digging, the Montreal police had written the fire off as an accident. Rolli had ridden his motorcycle from Ann Arbor to Montreal, set the device unbeknownst to his adoptive parents, and returned to Ann Arbor with nobody the wiser. Then the plan had gone awry as will most best laid plans. His sister had come home from her college for the weekend and had died in the fire along with his adoptive parents. Good riddance to them, but he had loved his sister – no biological relation. He was so torn up by her death that he had left chemistry and changed to business. But on the other hand, Jane Eyre had to admit, if Rolli's sister hadn't died, the two of them might have gotten married. If his sister hadn't died, he wouldn't have changed his major, and she and Rolli wouldn't have met. They wouldn't have shared those wonderful years. Those years whose memory was now tarnished by his confession. The confession brought about because for whatever reason that rat-faced ratfink Pierre LeBeuf had come to Hibbard Pond and gotten himself killed.

And that death, in the long scheme of things, had contributed to events that lead to the discovery of Rolli's arson and thus to his suicide when the thoughts of his sister's erroneous death had once again surfaced after lying dormant all those years. And now Jane Eyre had to clear his name – at least for the death of that rat-faced ratfink Pierre. Old rf-squared. That thought – clearing Rolli's name – was what had brought her out of her drunken malaise. And now, one concern out of the way: the Sportsman group knew nothing about the death that wasn't common knowledge. Thus, moving on to concern two: confronting the only remaining confessor – Dame Edna Fitzgerald.

Chapter 17

It was well over an hour later when Jane Eyre pulled her purple van up in front of the front door of the Fitzgerald estate. "There just was no other way to describe it," she had always told Rolli. She got out of the van, stepping down cautiously because of her size – she couldn't see the ground despite her new weight loss. Well, she could see the ground, but she couldn't see her feet. She was wearing a purple muumuu and purple tennis shoes although her small purse was red. At the front door she rang the doorbell and listened to the first notes of "O' Canada." She didn't have long to wait for the front door to be opened. She was greeted by a woman several inches taller than herself, wearing a light blue dress with a white collar and dark blue buttons down the front. It almost looked like a uniform. She had dark hair, almost an unnatural color, cut in a bob. Her makeup was well done. So well done that Jane Eyre wasn't certain how much she was wearing. Her lip gloss (because her lips were shiny) was basically peach. She had a decent figure – a little top heavy, Jane Eyre thought. On her feet were white deck shoes, no socks.

"Yes?" the woman said.

"I would like to talk to Edna," Jane Eyre said.

"Mrs. Fitzgerald is not accepting callers," the woman said in an almost haughty tone.

Mrs. Fitzgerald is not accepting callers? Might have well said "Dame Fitzgerald" from her tone, Jane Eyre thought. *Does everyone think the lady is royalty?*

"I am not a caller," Jane Eyre said as she started to push past the woman. "I am a good friend."

Her attempted intrusion was met with a brick wall as the woman refused to budge.

"Friend or not," the woman retorted in a definitely haughty tone, "Mrs. Fitzgerald is not accepting visitors." She emphasized this by placing her right hand in the center of Jane Eyre's chest and giving a gentle but decidedly firm push while her other hand was kept firmly on the door.

"And who are you to make this decision?" Jane Eyre said trying to sound as indignant as possible.

"I am the housekeeper and...." At this point there came a rumbling from inside the house as though a cart with wooden wheels was being pulled or pushed down a cobblestone street. Both adversaries stopped being adversaries and the woman turned around, releasing her hold on the door as she did so. The door swung open as though pulled by a spring and Jane Eyre could see a decidedly aged Edna Fitzgerald wearing a green Chinese style kimono with an orange border with red embroidery around the neck. Down the front, three wooden pegs serving as buttons were visible. Her hands were propped on the sides of a wheeled walker, and it was the hard rubber or plastic wheels that had been making the sound on the granite floor of the entry.

"Who's there, Alix?" Edna's voice definitely quavered as she said this.

"Just someone...," Alix started before Jane Eyre said, "It's Jane Eyre, Edna. I've come to call."

"Oh, yes, dear," Edna said as she made a surprisingly adroit about face with the wheels of the walker lifted off the floor. "We'll be in the Lake Room, Alix. Bring some tea, please," this was barely audible over the rumble of the wheels, which died when she reached the hallway and turned to the left. "I know where the Lake Room is," Jane Eyre said as she brushed past Alix.

Edna was moving spryly and had disappeared through the doorway to the living room as Jane Eyre hurried down the hallway. As she turned into the living room, she could see Edna entering the Lake Room, where the rumble began once again. It had ceased by the time Jane Eyre got there and Edna was sitting in a large high-backed white cane chair that faced Hibbard Pond, clearly visible beyond an expanse of sodded lawn. Jane Eyre took another of the high-backed white cane chairs and turned it to face her friend and sat down. Edna was staring at the lake.

"What happened, Edna?" Jane Eyre asked.

There was no response as Edna continued to stare at the lake.

"Edna?"

"Edna, what happened?" Jane Eyre said again, starting to rise from the chair to approach Edna.

"She had a stroke," Alix said over the rumble of wheels of a teacart she pushed out into the Lake Room. The teacart bore a silver tray with a teapot, sugar bowl, creamer, two white china teacups, some silverware, and a silver plate of cookies. *Lorna Doones or another shortbread*, Jane Eyre thought.

"When?"

"When she heard that one of her friends had committed suicide," Alix said. "She was in the hospital for a week. That's when Mr. Fitzgerald hired me. To take care of her." Alix started pouring tea.

"I had heard that he wanted to take her home to Montreal."

"He did, but she wouldn't hear of it." She handed a teacup and saucer to Jane Eyre. "Cream or sugar?"

"No, thank you," Jane Eyre said. "Where did he find you? I mean, you don't sound like you're from around here. You have an accent."

"Yes," Alix responded as she put a spoonful of sugar in the second cup. "I am from Montreal." She stirred the tea and then placed the teacup and saucer on the glass-topped white wicker table next to Edna's chair. "Will there be anything else?" she said looking at Jane Eyre.

How did you make this tea so quickly, she wanted to say. "No, thank you. This is fine."

"Well, if you do, ring the bell there," Alix pointed to a crystal bell on the table. Then she turned and left.

Strange, Jane Eyre said. *Everything was directed at me. Nothing to Edna and it's her house.* She looked at her friend who continued to stare fixedly at the lake.

It didn't take long for Jane Eyre to determine that she wasn't going to get anything from Edna on that day. She stood, walked over to her friend and leaned over, looking at her. "We'll get them for what they did," she whispered to Edna. "We'll make them pay." She patted her friend on her knees, straightened up and walked out of the Lake Room into the living room where Alix sat reading a magazine.

"Is she always like this?" Jane Eyre asked as Alix stood up.

"She has her good days and her bad days," Alix said. "Edmund says she was pretty much like this before the stroke."

Edmund, Jane Eyre thought. "I can see myself out."

She continued on out of the living room, turning left, down the short hallway and into the foyer. Behind her Alix appeared and stood watching and listening. She heard the door close behind Jane Eyre and then from the Lake Room, the faint tinkle of the crystal bell.

Chapter 18

After a good night's rest, Dugal was ready to tackle that day's big project for the homestead – roto-tilling Earleen's garden plot. But not before he had another offer.

"Ready to do some walleye fishing?" Jerry asked when Dugal answered the phone.

"Not today, I don't think. Let's go tomorrow."

"But the place could be lousy with Downstaters," Jerry said and Dugal could sense the smirk on his face.

"Well, we'll just go armed."

"You're certain?"

"Yep."

"So then what exciting thing are you up to today?"

"Roto-tilling."

"Wow, can I help?"

"Sure, come on up."

"No, thanks, got my own to do. Liz has the beast primed and ready to go."

"So you weren't really going fishing?"

"Nope. Just needed to jerk your chain."

"Well, when I jerk your chain, it will be to the trap door under your feet with a noose around your neck."

"Ouch," Jerry grimaced. "That'll hurt."

"Yep, see you in the morning."

And so the die was cast and a fortuitous roll it had been.

Dugal was about halfway done with the first go-round of the garden when he heard someone calling. Looking up, he saw Herbert "Norm" Smythe, neighbor to the north from Kitchener, Canada. The nickname "Norm" was self-imposed because he thought his laugh sounded like that of Norm on *Cheers* although no one else was of the same opinion. Dugal shut down the roto-tiller and walked to the garden gate, shucking his gloves as he went and eagerly accepted a mug of coffee that Norm offered.

"Looks like a lot of work to me," Norm said. "Thought you could use a break."

"You can pitch right in, you know."

Norm laughed. "I have my own bucket list to get at."

"You mean a 'Honey-Do' list," Dugal countered.

"Most people would call it that, but Pauline says that this will be untouched when I kick the bucket."

"Ah, always the weasel, eh?"

"Speaking of weasels, whatever became of that rat-faced French Canuck they pulled out from the ice this winter?"

Norm knew about Pierre LeBeuf because all Canadians who lived near Hibbard Pond were contacted by the sheriff's department in an effort to find out how he had gotten to the lake, much less in it. In fact, the Kitchener police had come out to his home to see if he knew the man.

"Oh, he died," Dugal said trying to keep a straight face.

"I know that, you idiot ... Oh, ha ha," Norm said.

So Dugal brought him up to speed on what he knew of the case, which was as much as anybody other than the sheriff knew. He ended with Rolli Polli's suicide jump.

"What a way to go, eh?" Norm said. "So the case is tied up in knots?"

"Legalese – three confessions, two of the confessors dead and third is non compos mentis."

"Guess we'll never know."

"Never is a long time," Dugal said, finishing his coffee and handing Norm the mug.

"Time to get back to my list. Glad you're up," and Dugal started into the garden, pulling his gloves on. Then he turned.

"If you're not doing anything Monday, I'm having some friends over to celebrate the start of summer. You and Pauline are welcome to come."

"Thanks, but we have a prior commitment with some friend from Kitchener down near Hale."

"Well, enjoy and stay safe."

When he finished the garden, he cleaned the roto-tiller and stored it in the back of the garage until needed again. Then he went into the cabin and told Earleen about Norm and his "bucket list."

"That list is of his own making," Earleen said. "Pauline says it's as though he sits around trying to think up projects. He just can't seem to get used to the fact that in retirement you don't have to do a damn thing."

"Then what's this list of stuff you've given me to do?" and Dugal ducked to avoid a playful swing from Earleen.

Chapter 19

Nathanial looked up from his paperwork at the sound of a rapping on his doorjamb to see Arthur Misdorf standing there, hat in hand.

"Arthur," Nathanial said extending his hand toward his visitors' chairs, "just the man I wanted to see. You must be psychic."

Arthur moved and took a seat while Nathanial was talking. He put his hat on the other chair. Then he leaned forward, arms on his upper legs, hands clasped together.

"Sheriff, I'm in a quandary."

Nathanial wanted to say, *"No you're not, you're in my office,"* but he sensed that Misdorf had a serious problem.

"What's up, Arthur?" Nathanial inquired, hoping it wasn't about quitting because of the shooting.

"The first time I went to interview Edna Fitzgerald, something strange happened."

"Strange? How so?"

"Well, I was standing in the foyer while Butch went to see if she was available."

"Not that it's important, but his name was Briel Boswick. Mrs. Fitzgerald had trouble remembering his name."

"Right, he was the father of those...," *men who shot me,* Nathanial knew he was going to say.

"Yes. So, you were standing in the foyer...," Nathanial said trying to get him to move past that point.

"I thought it was extraordinarily long just to ask if I could talk to her. It must have been about five minutes."

"She might have had to fix her makeup. You know how women are."

"She doesn't wear much makeup or at least she didn't that day. A little blush on her cheeks and some lip gloss – could have been a chap stick of some sort. But that wait is only part of it. As I walked down that hall I noticed the artwork."

Nathanial nodded.

"But there was artwork missing. I could see the outlines on the walls. Things had been there a while and were now gone."

"Change of decoration?"

"No, don't think so. In the living room, there was a glass coffee table with books lying on it, stacked, but there were outlines on the glass of what could have been bookends. The space between was about the same as the height of the stack of books."

Nathanial nodded understandingly.

"Then in the Lake Room, there was more artwork missing."

"Again..."

"But when I had the second visit, there were pieces of art where the missing ones had been both in the hallway and in the Lake Room."

"As I said...," the sheriff put in.

"But," Misdorf continued, "there were bookends on the coffee table. They looked like stone but were resin of some type."

"Yes, but..."

"But they fitted the outline of the missing ones exactly. I lifted one to look at it and could still see the outline. Some sloppy housekeeping."

"Well, Briel didn't seem like much of a housekeeper. He was hired to cook and look after Mrs. Fitzgerald."

Misdorf nodded in agreement. "Granted, that's my thought too. But there was a door just opposite the entry to the living room. The room there doesn't have a window. I know because I noted the layout of the windows on the front of the house."

Nathanial started to say something, but Misdorf held up his hand indicating he wasn't done.

"The lake side is ordinarily called the front, but this place is majestic and the side of the house with the driveway is the front of the house. I just have this feeling that artwork I wasn't supposed to see was removed and put in that room and not replaced. There was time. As I said, that wait in the foyer was about five minutes."

"And that's been bothering you?"

"Yes. I don't like where this case seems to have ended. I really don't. I know that Butch ... Briel ... confessed to killing Pierre LeBeuf, but maybe he didn't. I don't ... didn't ... have much of a feel for him. However, I would bet my pension that Edna didn't do it. She would really have to be pushed, and the relationship between her and Pierre wasn't that push. Same with Rolli Polli. He was milquetoast. Couldn't hurt a fly. Yes, we think ...," and he put air quotes around "we", "... he set a fire that killed his adoptive parents and, unfortunately, his sister. That was never proven and there may be something there that could have caused it."

"Yes, I agree. I am also not happy with where this has gone."

"You mean, you don't think it's over?"

"Well, unless we can come up with some concrete evidence to the contrary. Clemson Mathers won't prosecute Edna Fitzgerald because of her dementia or Alzheimer's, whichever it is, and she has had a stroke. A little one, but her faculties seem diminished."

"Well, what about the artwork?"

"You don't have enough grounds for a search warrant. Clemson would laugh me out of his office."

"Well, I could go back to see her and ask about the artwork, or take a look in that room."

"And if there is anything in there of an incriminating nature, it is long gone."

"Still worth a shot. And I'd like to talk to Jane Eyre Polli again and find out about Rolli if she'll tell me."

Nathanial was quiet for a moment.

"Have to take you off light duty for that. What's your doctor say?"

"I'm ready the first of the month."

"Good, glad to hear. But in the meantime, I have a job for you and Webster."

Misdorf straightened up at the thought of some action with his friend Mitchell Webster.

"Is this about the body beneath the bridge?"

"No, but there is a bridge involved. Saturday, you and Mitchell are to drive to Sault St. Marie and pick up the Nelsons at 1:00 p.m. They have agreed to return without contesting extradition. They will fly to the Soo Saturday morning accompanied by some Mounties who will turn them over to the Canadian Border Patrol. They will meet you on the Canadian side of the U.S. gate. Get them and return them here."

"Handcuffs?"

"Not necessary. Stay with them. If she needs to use the bathroom on the way down, one of the two of you go in with her. The other stays with her husband."

Misdorf picked up his hat and stood up.

"Mitchell know?"

"I'll let you tell him. Take an SUV."

His face wreathing in smiles at the thought of action, Misdorf turned smartly and left the office.

"Misdorf," Nathanial called and Arthur appeared in the doorway.

"Just because they said they are coming back peacefully, doesn't mean you don't carry a weapon."

Instinctively, Arthur reached for his weapon, which wasn't there.

"I'll clear it. Good luck," Nathanial said.

Chapter 20

The Friday of Memorial Day weekend was the last day that Jerry and Dugal expected to get anything close to quiet fishing done until the Weekenders had gone back Down State, either late on Monday or early Tuesday. They were out early and had five nice walleye in the live well by 10:00 a.m. Jerry had just finished putting out his line from the most recent catch (a 14.8 inch walleye, just 0.2 inches shy of keeper size) when they heard the sounds of a plane. Locating it, they could see it was a pontoon plane arriving at the lake from the south and starting to make a low pass up the west side of the lake.

"Looks like the Fitzgeralds are here for the weekend," Jerry commented as he took his seat. The family had been become the talk of Hibbard Pond since the suicide of Rolli Polli and the implications of the connection with the body under the ice.

"It's not even a Canadian holiday," Dugal commented from the captain's chair as he watched the plane lift into the sky and begin to circle back to the south. "Should be okay to land, waves are only six inches."

"That's on this side of the lake. Never know about the other side," Jerry chided him. This was true because a wind from the west would make higher waves on the east side than the west, but the light breeze was out of the southwest this morning and so waves on the west side would be minimal. The two continued their southbound path watching the plane turning northbound and preparing to land on the lake. As it touched down, the left pontoon seemed to touch the water and then bounce up. The pilot appeared to try to correct it and sent the left wing down into contact with the water and then seemed to bounce up as the pilot tried to counteract his original action. But he over corrected as the left wing rose and the right wing tip came into full contact with the water. The airplane's nose was pulled to the right and the right wing dug into the water. Another correction by the pilot brought the right wing and pontoon high out of the water causing the left wing to dig deeply into the lake. The airplane flipped forward burying its nose and the tips of both pontoons in the lake. The tail continued in its travels flipping the plane onto its back and it started to sink. Unseen by the pilot was a barely submerged piece of flotsam that the left pontoon had hit: a four-foot-by-four-foot piece of decking the storms of the previous week had wrested loose from its dock.

By the time this sequence had ended Dugal had started turning Jerry's pontoon boat toward the crash site and Jerry had rushed forward, grabbing each of his poles and jerking each line to break it loose from the clip. That completed, he started pulling his planar board in. Once the boat was aimed toward the crash, Dugal cut back the speed and moved forward, duplicating Jerry's movements with his own lines. With his planar board stowed on the deck, Jerry moved to the captain's chair and started inching the throttle up. As soon as Dugal had his planar board out of the water, Jerry slammed the throttle fully open while simultaneously yelling, "Hold on!" and

Dugal grabbed the planar board mast and sank into one of the fishing chairs. By the time they reached the crash site, another boat was sitting in the water beside the plane and they could see movement inside the cockpit through half-submerged windows. Dugal removed his inflatable life vest and was taking his shoes off when a head burst into view in front of the plane's wing. Whoever it was sputtered and thrashed at the water trying to swim. Dugal grabbed the boat's life ring and yelled, "Grab this," and threw it toward the person. The ring splashed just in front of the person who grabbed it and stopped thrashing.

"Where's Tom?" the person yelled.

"Who's Tom?" Jerry asked.

"The pilot...." More splashing interrupted the man's answer and two heads broke the surface behind him.

"I need help," one of them said. "He's unconscious."

"It's Zeb," Jerry yelled grabbing an orange disk and yanking at a Velcro tape, revealing yellow twine wrapped around it. Holding one end of the twine, he threw the disk at Zeb. It landed within reach of an arm, Zeb grabbed it and Jerry began hauling in the line. Jerry had Zeb and his unconscious partner to the boat about the same time as the first man reached it. Jerry and Dugal managed to pull the unconscious man onto the pontoon with Zeb's help pushing. Then they got the other man aboard.

"God, it's cold," the man said through chattering teeth.

"I'm good," Zeb said as Dugal reached to help him aboard.

"You'll freeze," Dugal said remembering the water's cold from two days before.

"I've got my wet suit on," Zeb said as he treaded water. "I always wear it in the spring when I'm fishing alone in case I fall in."

"Well, we need to get these guys ashore and get them warmed up."

"Go ahead, I'm going to check the plane and put up markers in case it sinks. Then I'll wait for the cavalry."

Jerry got the boat in gear and backed away from the plane and then headed for the nearest dock, where he could see people standing and watching. It was a ride of just a few minutes and eager hands grabbed the bowline and side of the pontoon as they came alongside the dock on the side where there was no boat hoist.

"Get this guy in the house and get him out of his clothes and into something warm. Have you called 911?"

"Yes," the woman said as her husband helped the conscious man toward the house. "As soon as we saw the crash."

In the distance, Dugal could hear the sound of sirens and two men appeared running from the direction of the house, one of them carrying a bag.

"Down here," Dugal yelled, waving at them. "We've got an unconscious man."

The two men reached the pontoon and came aboard, Dugal and Jerry moving out of the way, as the First Responders (qualified volunteer EMTAs) started work on the pilot. Dugal recognized them as First and Second, two men he knew by no other names, who helped Tater Miller with docks each spring and fall. As they worked, Second looked up, saw Dugal, smiled, and returned to his work, saying something to First. In a moment, First looked up at Dugal, "Seems like you're always in the thick of it, doesn't it, Mr. McBruce?" Without waiting for an answer, he returned to his job.

With nothing else to do, Dugal and Jerry each grabbed a pole and started reeling in their lines. Each man had the legal limit of three lines out and each had lost about half of his equipment. Jerry lost two lures and one weight while Dugal fared slightly better, losing only one weight.

"Could have been worse," Jerry said, "We could have had a fish on."

"Maybe we did," Dugal said.

Within minutes, two paramedics arrived with a litter, and five minutes later the pilot was on his way to Alpena General Hospital.

"Anyone else in the plane?" First asked, his question punctuated by Jerry's cellphone ringing.

"It's Zeb," Jerry announced looking at the caller ID.

"Hey, merman," Jerry said and then listened.

"Nobody else aboard," Jerry reported. "The plane is basically stabilized and doesn't appear to be sinking – could be a low fuel load and not much cargo. Zeb called a friend who is bringing some airbags to stabilize the plane temporarily. He also called the Alcona dive team and they will come and help right the plane. He'll wait there for them."

Chapter 21

After First and Second left to see if help was needed in the house with the passenger, Dugal cast off and Jerry backed away from the dock, and headed to the crash scene. By the time they got there, a second boat had arrived to help and several others were gathered around with their passengers gawking. Zeb was in the water holding a hose leading from a compressor on the other boat where a man, also in a wet suit, stood. Zeb waved to them and soon the edges of a large yellow air bag appeared on either side of the left wing lifting it and starting to lower the right wing. Zeb disconnected the hose and swam around the plane's nose while his friend, whom they learned was Howard Hawes, pulled in the hose. Then he fed what looked like a huge blue air mattress over the side and Zeb dragged it to the plane's right wing. He next dove under the wing dragging one end of the air mattress, and reappeared on the other side. Returning to the side of Howard Hawe's boat, he took the air hose and swam back to the right wing where he plugged the end into a valve on the air mattress. Howard closed a valve on the compressor and air began to fill the air mattress until the right wing tip was level with the left. The hose was disconnected, retrieved by Howard, who then moved his boat around the right wing and near the tail, and then fed a red air mattress over the side. Zeb repeated the process as he had with the right wing and soon the tail section rose out of the water. Zeb disconnected the hose and Howard pulled it back after shutting off the compressor. Zeb swam to Howard's boat and was helped aboard.

Jerry maneuvered his pontoon near Howard's boat. "What the hell are those things?"

Zeb laughed. "They're air mattresses that kids bounce on. Also can be used as a raft in a lake. Howard sells or rents them as a sideline."

"Good thinking," Dugal chimed in. "What's next?"

"We're waiting for the dive team. They're bringing the barge from Hibbard Marine and we'll try to right this thing. Then we'll tow it to the South End and see if the FAA wants to investigate. From what I saw, it is an obvious pilot error."

The discussion was interrupted by the arrival of another boat, the sheriff department's Boston Whaler bearing four people: Bob Roberts, Rich Walker, and the two summer interns, Rachel Whitaker and Jeremy Bridges.

"What's the situation, Zeb?" Rich Walker called.

"Two people aboard, pilot and passenger. Think the pilot's name is Tom, and the passenger is Edmund Fitzgerald. Pilot was unconscious and evacuated to Alpena General. Fitzgerald was taken to the ... that house over there." He pointed and then asked Dugal, "What's their name?"

"In all the excitement, forgot to ask."

"Well, who saw the crash?" Rich Walker asked.

Zeb, Dugal and Jerry raised their hands.

"We'll need statements. The FAA might be minimally interested. Private plane, no one apparently hurt. Come over to the sheriff's office in the next day or so."

"So we're not needed?" Jerry asked.

"Nope."

"Then we're out of here." He and Dugal waved and Jerry motored slowly away, reporting events to other boats as they passed and asking if they had seen the crash to make a statement at the sheriff's office, although they knew that the Boston Whaler would make the rounds. As soon as they were clear of other boats, Jerry hit the throttle and the pontoon boat roared across Hibbard Pond as fast as its forty HP Mercury would take it.

"Howard and I will wait around," Zeb told Rich Walker. "Those are his air mattresses."

It was an hour before the dive team arrived on the barge. There were five members plus Chet Willis, dive team head: Fred Fithe, Skip Andrews, Yonni Jones, Bill Smythe, and Susan Swartz who usually functioned, as she did today, as the dive team's official photographer. Skip Andrews and Yonni Jones went in the water and replaced Howard Hawes's air mattress with air bags that were used to raise cars and other things from the bottom of lakes, and had been used just a few short months before to raise the shelter that had contained the body of Pierre LeBeuf. Bill Smythe and Chet Willis erected a twelve-foot tall metal tripod, which usually is used on the ice to pull up a truck (or car) that had the misfortune to hit a weak spot in the ice. The tripod was bolted into the barge's flooring near the bow and two cables affixed from the top of the tripod to each stern corner. Zeb had jumped into the water to help with the removal of Howard's air mattresses and volunteered to help with the righting of the plane. When the team's floats were in place, a heavy rope was fastened to the tail section of the plane and led down the belly, past the front to the pontoon where it was fastened to the top of the tripod. With the help of Fred Fithe, a rope was attached near the tip of each wing and then run back behind the tail to the front of Zeb's boat. With all divers out of the water and communicating with cellphones, Zeb backed his fishing boat with its powerful 250-horse power motor until the lines to the plane were taut. Then the barge began to back up until its line to the tail was taut. Once set, the two boats began to back up in unison. At first nothing happened other than the props churning water. Then slowly, punctuated by a sucking sound as the cockpit broke free of the lake's grasp, the tail section began to rise, and the nose dipped under the water's surface. Once the motion was started, it went smoothly, and the tail reached the apex of its arc and quickly began to descend. With a loud kerplop, the tail section hit the water and the pontoons popped up and settled on the surface. There were cheers from the dive team, Howard Hawes, Zeb and the small flotilla of onlookers.

Zeb and the dive team made short work of retrieving the flotation bags and rope to the tail. The ropes to each wing tip were transferred from Zeb's boat to the sheriff's boat and fastened to the tow bar at the stern of the Whaler. With things clear, the Whaler started its slow process pulling the plane toward the Negwegon Launch at the South End, with Zeb following close behind keeping an eye on the plane. He noticed Edmund Fitzgerald standing on the dock with his hosts and, as the plane passed, he shook hands with them and then hurried across the lawn and disappeared around the house. The dive team took down the tripod as the barge motored back to the East Bay landing where it would be retrieved by Chuck Shulmann, owner of Hibbard Pond Marine.

It was close to half an hour until the plane was at the south end. The Whaler pulled into the dock, and Rich Walker and Bob Roberts got out with the ropes that had tethered the plane. Bob Roberts went and got their SUV, which they had left there, and the Whaler went back out on the lake to continue its unplanned second visit to Hibbard Pond that week. The ropes were attached to the SUV and carefully Bob Roberts pulled the plane, riding on the wheels under the pontoon, up the ramp. Edmund Fitzgerald was waiting for them.

After introducing himself, Edmund asked, "Can I retrieve some personal belongings?" He was ready to add, "It is my plane after all." But that was not needed.

"Be our guest," Bob Roberts said. "But you will need to sign for whatever you take and we'll need to photograph it. That FAA can be picky."

"There's going to be an investigation?"

"Who's to say?" Rich Walker said.

"It's up to the FAA," Roberts added, "but we like to cover our asses."

Edmund got into the plane and, after a few minutes, exited carrying an aluminum briefcase.

"That's it?" Roberts asked.

"It's all I brought with me. I have clothes at the house."

He signed a sheet Walker had prepared, let the briefcase be photographed both open and closed, and walked to his gray Cadillac Escalade and drove away, leaving Walker and Roberts to get the plane to a storage area at the Alpena Airport where the FAA could look at it. Out on the West Branch River, Zeb was watching interestedly from his boat. He noted all that had taken place, then started his engine and headed for home. He thought he would have a busy weekend ahead of him.

Chapter 22

The distance from Harrisville to Sault Ste. Marie, Michigan, is approximately 180 miles and three-and-a-half hours driving time on a good day. But this was Saturday of Memorial Day weekend – a beautiful Memorial weekend and the roads were liable to be crowded with tourists, both in-state and out-of-state, visiting Mackinaw City and taking one of the many ferries to historic Mackinac Island. The easiest route is following US-23 north to Mackinaw City, across the Straits of Mackinac via the five-mile long Mackinac Bridge on I-75, and continuing north to the Michigan-Canadian border. I-75 ends there, but to get to Canada one crosses over the St. Mary's River on the International Bridge, providing a good view of The Soo, as the Sault Ste. Marie locks have come to be known. Another option is to cut across from Harrisville to Indian River using back roads where you would pick up I-75 about 28 miles south of the Big Mac, as the Mackinac Bridge is known to Michiganders. The time difference is about half an hour.

Had it been a joy ride, Arthur and Mitchell Webster would have opted for the latter, but this was business and it wouldn't do to have a vehicle break down in the middle of the Michigan wilds – especially while transporting two "criminals" or on the way to pick them up. This being said and considered, Arthur and Mitchell met at the Alcona County Sheriff's garage at 8:00 a.m. on Memorial Day weekend Saturday. Both were dressed in clean and freshly pressed uniforms, their boots polished to a high gleam, their holstered weapons clean, polished and loaded. Rich Ross, the duty deputy had the required paperwork, which Arthur signed before being given the keys.

They had flipped a coin (actual) and Mitchell drove north and Arthur was to drive south. They pulled out of the parking lot between the sheriff's office and the courthouse turning left onto M-72 at 8:07 a.m. They made the light and turned left onto US-23 and headed north toward Sault Ste. Marie. Initial conversation centered around the plane crash on Hibbard Pond the day before. That didn't take them much further than Alpena, about thirty miles to the north.

"You took over my investigation," Misdorf began after the plane crash conversation lagged.

"Which one?" Mitchell responded.

"You know which one."

"Oh, ze body in ze lake, eh?"

"Yes, what's your feel about it?"

"He ez dead," Mitchell said smiling.

"Cut the crap, Webster. Who killed him?"

"Nobody who confessed."

"Why not?"

"That butler guy, Butch, or Briel I guess in reality, confessed to try to ease the burden on his sons. Didn't help any. I guess he had Alzheimer's or dementia and didn't want to face its reality. Had a good way out."

"What about Polli?"

"Ole Polli. Now there was a guy for you. Had it made. Nice house, loving wife – not my type but then....

Anyway, he confessed third, after Mrs. Fitzgerald. They went way back. I think he did it to protect her. I mean, you can't try two people for a crime only one could commit."

"Actually there were three."

"But you can't try a dead man. Whatever, Polli had his own problems for which I think it will turn out, if the Montreal police pursue it, he was guilty of arson and the resulting deaths."

"But...," Misdorf tried to get in another word but Mitchell held up his hand and continued.

"Rolli was smart – a good chemist according to his professor. If the Montreal Police have the residue from the chemical timer, my guess is they won't be able to figure out what the chemicals were. Maybe, but my guess is not. Therefore that turns up a dead end and he is a free man."

"Except for the confession."

"Yep, but that is going nowhere. Mrs. Fitzgerald could recant hers but maybe in her condition that wouldn't be accepted. Even if it is and Rolli recanted his, you've got Butch's and that can't be broken without some hard evidence."

"Like what? The real killer stepping forward?"

Mitchell laughed. "Like that's going to happen. The only thing I can figure is that someone who knows who the real killer is will step forward and speak up."

"Who? Burt, Burl or Burke?"

Mitchell shrugged. "If they knew, but I think their contact was their dad. They don't know anything else."

"Good point."

The rest of the drive to the Soo was filled with talk of Misdorf's family soon to expand, Misdorf's hope of being able to take part in a reenactment of a Civil War battle, and Mitchell's new desire to own a motorcycle.

They got to the Soo about forty-five minutes early and stopped at a McDonald's to use the facilities and get some lunch: two Big Macs, a large order of fries, a chocolate shake and a strawberry shake.

Between bites of a Big Mac, Mitchell said, "Man, I wish they had McRibs all the time."

"Oh, yes," Misdorf said, finishing a mouthful of fries. "When those things come out, I get a couple and just wolf 'em down. That's lunch every day while they have them."

"But if they had them all the time, I'd get fat," Mitchell said, finishing his strawberry shake and wiping his mouth with a paper napkin. Misdorf looked at his watch.

"Fifteen minutes. Better get hiking." They policed their table and headed out.

They were expected on the bridge and let through to a parking area on the other side of the tollbooths. A Canadian Border Guard SUV pulled up at precisely 1:00 p.m. and two men got out. Through the darkened windows, Misdorf could make out two figures in the SUV. One of the border guards had a clipboard with requisite paperwork, releases stating that Karen Nelson and Norm Nelson were being released into the custody of the Alcona County Sheriff's Department. While Misdorf read the releases and signed them, Mitchell and the other border guard went to the rear of the Canadian SUV and retrieved four pieces of luggage (two suitcases and two carry-ons) that were put in the American SUV. Then one of the Canadians opened the rear door of their SUV and stood back, hand on his pistol's hilt, while the Nelsons got out. Misdorf compared their faces with photographs they had brought with them and asked each of them their names.

Then, "Are you accepting extradition from Canada to the State of Michigan in The United States of America willingly?"

Norm Nelson replied, "I am."

Karen Nelson nodded.

"Mrs. Nelson, I need a verbal answer."

Karen Nelson mumbled something.

"Mrs. Nelson, I need a clear and intelligible answer."

She looked up at him and for a moment anger flashed on her face. She seemed to grit her teeth and then said, "Yes, damn it, I am."

Misdorf looked at Mitchell and shrugged. Then he led the Nelsons to their vehicle with Mitchell trailing, opened the door and let the Nelsons get in, Norm letting Karen go first. She paused, looking back across the bridge at her native Canada for what may be the last time in a long time, sighed and entered the SUV.

Misdorf got in the driver's side and Mitchell the passenger seat. They waited until the Border Guard SUV had made a U-turn and was proceeding back across the bridge before Misdorf started the SUV and proceeded through the tollgates heading south on I-75 toward Mackinaw City. On US-23 about thirty minutes south of Mackinaw City, Karen Nelson said, "I'd like to make a rest stop."

"Okay," Misdorf said and shortly signaled a turn and pulled into a small rest area with two picnic tables and restrooms in a small building, with men's entrance on one end, women's on the other, and metal ventilators on top spinning slowly in a light breeze. There was only one other car in the lot. At one of the picnic tables a middle-aged black couple sat facing each other, eating an obviously homemade lunch. Before he could stop, Karen Nelson said, "I meant, a proper restroom, like a McDonald's or Burger King."

Misdorf pulled into a parking space in front of the restrooms, shut the engine off and turned around so he could see Karen Nelson. "Let me give you the McDonald's scenario. We get there and I go into the restaurant and get the manager to clear the ladies restroom. Then after I check it, you and I will go in and you use the facilities. After that we will do the same with the men's restroom for your husband."

"You mean you'll be in there with me?" Karen said indignantly.

"Yes but the stalls have doors. You will have your privacy."

"You're treating us like criminals," Karen said.

"No, ma'am," Misdorf said. "I am treating you like prisoners. It's just either here," he said, indicating the middle-aged couple, "or more in public. Your choice."

She chose "here." The rest of the trip to Harrisville was uneventful and eerily quiet.

Chapter 23

"I haven't done anything," Norm Nelson had said repeatedly since his return. "I didn't know what Karen was doing. When she left, it was a shock to me. I hadn't heard from her until her message the day before we left. She said go to the Toronto airport on the Friday with the kids, use my credit card to take flights, and she would meet us."

"That's partially true," Nathanial said. "You looked and acted innocent on the surface. You know the saying, 'Beauty is only skin deep'? Well, when you've got a beauty sometimes you have to use cold cream to see what's under the makeup. Is it real or is it Memorex?

"In your case, it started with the three phone calls from Karen the night she vanished. Call number one, you said was informing you that shopping was done and they were going to dinner. No woman with children at home would do that. She would ask about how they were, maybe want to talk to them and then she would tell you about shopping. What she saw, what she didn't buy, and what she did buy." Nathanial had to thank his wife Dawn and Earleen McBruce for that little scenario.

"You can't do that in fifteen seconds and that is how long the call was."

"But the bill says one minute."

"True, but cellphone companies charge you for whole minutes. A five second call is one minute. That's how they make their money on calling cards, pay-as-you-go plans."

"Well, that's what she said. Brief and to the point. I was fixing dinner and the kids were playing computer games."

"No way I can check that of course."

"Right. What about the others?" Norm Nelson said indignantly.

"The second one – we're done with dinner and I'm on the way home. Well, that could have been that short, but the kids were ready for bed. She's going to tuck them in."

"Kelly was in bed and Josh was in the bath. She wanted to get going."

"Possible but not plausible because, like any good husband, you knew she'd call and want to talk to the kids."

"I've already explained that."

Nathanial nodded. "And the third. She's had car trouble, called a wrecker, has to spend the night in a motel in Hale. Nobody, man or woman is going to get that off in less than a minute."

"The tow truck had just arrived and she had to deal with that."

"And she wouldn't call back later saying she was in the motel and all was well?"

"I'm not a big talker. Check the bills since then."

"Oh, they back that part of the story up alright, but you know how in books and TV shows they can isolate the cellphone towers that calls are made from? Well, you know what? That's true. So here's what we think.

First call, from the Windsor Casino or in that area, 'I'm in Canada. No passport record.' That's enough. Kids don't need to know it's Mom, she's gone on a business trip just like the one she supposedly had just gotten back from according to Sandra Deevers. Same with the second call, 'I'm at the Windsor airport.' The Canadian cellphone people were very helpful, eh?" Nathanial had to grin.

"And the third, from the Toronto airport, 'I'm aboard.' Guess that was the flight to Vancouver. We're still running down where she stayed, etc., looking for the paper trail. But it's there. We'll find it."

"Look at her all you want. She's the one who took the money. Chase her down. I'm innocent except for meeting her. And what's that, not informing the police? I'll get minimum time and not serve any."

"That was probably the plan, and it was pretty good. But last and not least, there's the laptop for your office, the one you were setting up when I came to see you. It's a Dell, just delivered that morning by FedEx, special overnight. You said you had called them the day before to send it."

"So? I needed it for work. You took the others."

"So … you had ordered it ten days before and asked them to hold delivery until you called. Told them it was a special present and you didn't want it until the right time. That time being after we seized your office and home computers. You hadn't thought about home, and the kids had to make do until we were done. But you knew we'd take the office computer because Karen worked there on weekends."

Norm said nothing. Just sat there with hands folded on the table, eyes down, and his confidence shaken. Nathanial smiled.

"This is supposed to be the paperless age. But there is always a paper trail. This time it was e-paper but there is always a trail. If there's more, we'll find it. So if you're so innocent and what you say is true – that's a big IF by the way – tell us how you got that message from Karen. The one telling you to meet her."

Norm was silent.

"I thought so. Should have had her do that, shouldn't you? Of course, maybe you didn't think that this Up North sheriff was up to snuff, eh? Well, surprise!"

Nathanial slapped his hands flat on the table and Norm jumped.

***

"So why, Karen?"

"We needed the money. The business was hurting, we couldn't pay our bills. When things were good, our lifestyle got out of hand. The treasurer's job didn't pay much, but I had time to help with sales and things were good. If I'd thought – God, if we had only thought – we could have saved more money. Nuts, we wanted a nice home, nice cars, good things for the kids. What everybody wants. And we had it. We had it. And I wanted to keep it."

She was quiet for a minute, remembering her Camelot.

"Then the market tanked. Sales didn't just slowly die, they quit. And there were bills. Mortgage, car payments, braces – all the good stuff that now we couldn't afford. Our savings disappeared and we were hurting. A mortgage payment was due. We didn't want to lose the house. So I borrowed. I was going to pay it back, I really was."

She looked up at Nathanial and Clemson Mathers, the County Prosecutor.

"They all say that, though. Don't they?"

Neither Nathanial nor Clemson Mathers said anything.

"I just kept borrowing. Kept thinking that things were going to get better. They had to. Didn't the President say so? We're Republicans, but we voted for him. The Republican ticket was a laugh. That bimbo from Alaska – one step from the presidency. That was scary. But Obama was adamant. Things were going to turn around. 'Yes we can.' Isn't that what he said? Isn't that what he promised?"

Neither man said anything.

"Then I learned about the audit. I was going to get caught. No way to put the money back. So I panicked. Should have just admitted it and taken the medicine. We should have downsized. Now Norm is in trouble because he came to meet me. We don't have the kids. It's all gone."

"So when did you know all this?" Clemson asked.

"I had a week. Getting the identification I used to fly to Vancouver was the hard part – the expensive part. Don't ask me how I got it. I won't tell. There are innocent people here."

"Nobody involved in helping you is innocent, Karen."

"My parents and Norm's parents knew nothing about this. They didn't help."

"We believe that," Clemson said.

"Well, I tell you what I did. I'll tell you where the money is. At least most of it. Some of it's gone."

"We appreciate that."

"But I'm only doing this because of the children. They need their parents."

"Guess you should have thought of that some time ago," Clemson said.

Chapter 24

"To tell you the truth, the scary part was that I couldn't reach my hand to try to free it. The life jacket worked to perfection and inflated almost instantaneously when I hit the water. It was trying to take me to the surface, and the shelter was trying to take me down. I really didn't have time to think much about it because, almost in a flash, Zeb was there. He got my leg first of all."

"I would have thought he would get your other hand or something," Nathanial said. "I mean with the life jacket trying to pull you up."

"Except the barge was moving and he had gone past where I went in and had to swim back."

"Yeah, I forgot about that."

Nathanial and Dugal were standing on Dugal's deck looking out at the lake. It was late afternoon on Monday, Memorial Day. All day watercraft of all sorts had been cruising or zooming around the lake enjoying the benefits of a beautiful Monday, putting an end to a beautiful weekend. Mother Nature had cooperated to the fullest as though in recompense for the past couple of weeks. As the afternoon had lengthened, the number of watercraft had diminished as people with jobs and school to face the next day, pulled every boat, covered it, and tied it down to await the next weekend when they could get away. Until school was out those times would be infrequent, but it was only a couple of weeks. Then for the rest of the summer, the full-time summer residents of the lake would have control during the week and the Down State or Down Below invaders would rule the weekends. But the ordinary weekends wouldn't be that bad because not everyone would be up the same weekend. Of course there was Fourth of July, which was probably the busiest the lake would be, and the week before and after with people coupling vacations with obligatory days off. Then the summer would be drawing to an end celebrated by the last big splash of the summer – Labor Day. For the months of September and October, the lake would again belong to the full-timers until the majority of them underwent metamorphosis by turning into Snow Birds who migrated to warmer climes for the winter – Florida, Texas, and Arizona being popular.

"He really had the knife in his teeth like a pirate?" Nathanial asked shaking his head at the thought.

"Well, that's my impression. I don't think he could have pulled himself along my body with just one hand and having a knife in the other would risk injuring me."

"And when he cut you free?"

"Pop – like being shot out of a gun. My vest got me to the surface. I don't remember getting on the barge or the ride back to the South End. I just remember the bone chilling cold. Zeb and I huddled together, arms around each other like newlyweds, but we were trying to get warm."

"That guy is truly amazing. But what's so weird is that it was the three of you again at that plane crash."

"True," Dugal said after finishing his Lumber Logger Red. "But it really was all Zeb. He was the one in the water. He was wearing his wetsuit, if you can believe it. Saying if he fell in he wanted to be ready. But without that, I don't know if he could have rescued both the pilot and Fitzgerald. Hear anything about the pilot?"

"Yes, he was released Saturday afternoon. Had a slight concussion. Hit on the back of the head. Nobody can figure out how. Fitzgerald had a briefcase. Aluminum thing, watertight. It could be the culprit, but usually things like that are stowed."

"Yes, on an airline. This was a private plane. There were no stewardesses. It could have been sitting on a seat. Been anywhere. What about the plane?"

"It's being worked on. No structural damage. Engine being underwater wasn't good, but getting the water out should make it good as new. Electronics might need to be repaired. Don't know exactly what's going to happen to it."

"I'm going to get another beer and check on the food preparations. Those two women have been at it for a while. Should have something we can nibble on while we cook the ribs."

"You're cooking ribs?" Nathanial said as the two walked toward the door.

"Sure, why not?" Dugal stared at Nathanial curiously while opening the door and letting his friend enter first.

"Cause ribs are what we do best."

"Who's we?" Dugal said letting the door shut itself behind them.

"My people, of course."

"Is he talking about cooking ribs?" Dawn asked from where she and Earleen were preparing potatoes and salad.

"He is," Dugal answered.

"Don't let him get any cooking implement in his hands unless you like your ribs charcoal black and about as tasty."

"Your people, huh?" Dugal said nudging Nathanial with his elbow.

"Did I hear ribs?" Jerry said, holding the door for Liz who was carrying a big bowl of coleslaw.

"You brave the denizens of the lake and come by boat?" Dugal asked.

"Sure, it's going to be quiet by the time we head home. Oh, Zeb is right behind us. He tied up next to me."

"What's he bringing?" Liz asked.

"I told him just to bring himself," Dugal said.

"How about smoked walleye and pike?" Zeb said as he came in the front door holding a plate piled high, held in place by plastic wrap.

Nathanial laughed. "What is this, a meeting of 'Find-a Corpse-a'?"

"Can't be," Jerry said. "I'm not a member and don't want to be."

"Maybe 'Rescuers Be We'," Dawn said laughing.

"None of the above," Dugal said. "It's a simple gathering of old friends and new friends to celebrate the start of a beautiful summer on Hibbard Pond."

"Hear, hear," they all said with Jerry adding his standard, "I'll drink to that," and the celebration began.

Chapter 25

By 8:30 a.m. Tuesday morning, the Alcona County Supervisor's meeting room in the courthouse was packed with media from all walks of life. Reporters from the Detroit Free Press, Detroit News, Lansing State Journal, The Alpena News, Alcona County Review, Alpena Channel 11 (local CBS affiliate), Detroit Channel 7 Action News (ABC affiliate), Fox 66 from Flint (Fox affiliate), and even The Wall Street Journal. Some had gotten up very early for the four- or five-hour trip to Harrisville, and some had gotten in yesterday because there is only one flight a day into Alpena, and its arrival would have been too late to make the press conference. Sheriff's deputies had closed the doors when the room was fire marshal capacity full, and had told those who waited that the press conference would be aired via loudspeakers, and at the conclusion written copies of the statements distributed. They would be able to ask questions, but the supervisors had requested that no questions be asked when they entered the press conference and when they left the press conference. Asked about that, some individuals were told that the sheriff had given orders and anyone who transgressed would be arrested for lawful misconduct.

While they waited for the supervisors to appear, the room was abuzz with rumors about the Nelsons. Everyone knew that they had been apprehended in Vancouver trying to leave the country, but had been shocked to learn that they had not fought extradition. All knew it would have been a losing battle, simply delaying the inevitable, but they had expected Karen Nelson to fight. And how had they gotten back? No one knew anything. She had possession of at least three quarters of a million dollars. Why had she given in so easily?

At nine o'clock, sheriff's deputies, led by the sheriff, formed a wedge to get through the press of bodies outside the room, but it wasn't needed as the press parted willingly, apparently not wanting to test the sheriff's wrath. Inside the room, the three supervisors mounted the six-inch high stage where their usual desks were. Then all but two of the deputies left the room, but were not far away outside. The sheriff remained inside, standing to the right of the podium. The three supervisors huddled behind their desks in deep discussion, as though deciding who would be the person to conduct the proceedings.

Finally, the huddle broke. First to leave was William "Willie" McComb from Glennie. Although he was an avowed outdoorsman, when not campaigning or appearing in his supervisor role, he dressed in dirty bib overalls, a red shirt and a straw hat, all of which had seen better days. He was thought to be gay, but he had a rotten marriage early in his life and that had soured him on women. He was well educated although no one knew where because he had disappeared from the county on his eighteenth birthday for eight and a half years and he wouldn't talk about it. He returned when his mother died, being predeceased by her husband, and Willie inherited the farm.

After he was seated, the other man took his seat. Donald W(acker) Trump had been a dairy farmer. He was a man only his mother could love with yellow buck-teeth surrounded by a scrawny goatee and an even more sparse, rarely trimmed mustache accentuating his mouse-like appearance. He was elected unopposed only because his opponent had his life terminated by two blasts from his lover's husband's shotgun. The only way that Trump was going to be reelected was to perform some act that would grab attention and help him get a second term. He had sold his farm and bought a lakeside condo and, other than being a supervisor, had nothing to do.

Beth Carmody, the third supervisor, unanimously chosen by her colleagues to be the spokesperson, sur-veyed the audience, took a deep breath, crossed her fin-gers and stepped forward around the desks to the micro-phone placed there for the occasion. She had been elect-ed when her opponent made the mistake of saying that a woman's place was in the home, barefoot, pregnant and flat on her back. Her decision to run had been inspired by the fact that she had no one to share her bed. She was married to Alcona County Sheriff's Deputy Andrew Carmody who had the midnight-to-eight shift and then slept from eleven to seven. Truth be told, the fact that she had no one to share her bed was her fault. They had moved Up North to the south end of Hibbard Pond when he had retired from the Huntington Woods (Michigan) Police Department. After two years of him being under-foot she had urged him to get a job and he had – the midnight shift was the only one available.

"Ladies and gentlemen, it is a sad state of affairs when the only thing that can draw the interest of the press to what is undoubtedly the poorest county in the state is tragedy. But that is the way of the press, isn't it?

"As you know, several months ago, it was discovered that Karen Nelson, the county treasurer, had fled the country after embezzling one million three hundred fifty dollars and twenty-three cents. Don't ask me about the odd amount because I don't know."

This brought a round of laughter.

"This is the first time this amount has been announced because the auditors wanted to be certain they had found it all. Not that they know where it is hidden or has gone, but that they had uncovered all her transactions. Soon after, her husband took their children and left the country meeting up with her in Vancouver from which they were to flee to China. However, diligent work by both United States and Canadian law enforcement enabled them to be apprehended shortly after reuniting in the Vancouver International Airport. Most of the credit in this goes to our own Sheriff Nathanial Jefferson, who – according to him – smelled a rat."

This brought a round of applause and Nathanial turned a brown shade of red.

"After lengthy discussion with both Canadian and U.S. attorneys, the Nelsons agreed not to fight extradition. In an agreement with us, their children are in the custody of her parents. The Nelsons were picked up at the United States-Canadian border in Sault Ste. Marie Saturday afternoon where they had been brought by Canadian officials. Two of Alcona County's finest, Deputy Arthur Misdorf and Deputy Mitchell Webster, were the detail the sheriff assigned to that mission."

Several hands shot up.

"Please, hold your questions until I am finished. Upon arrival in Harrisville, Karen Nelson willingly told officials where the money was secreted and how to retrieve it. We are happy to say that all but four hundred thousand, one hundred ninety-three dollars and twenty-three cents has been returned."

The identical number of cents brought forth a low murmur.

"Again, as you can guess, I cannot explain the twenty-three cents. Karen Nelson and her husband are in custody and will be tried. No deals were made except for the care of the children. Thankfully, that was the only stumbling block. Both Nelsons have stated that they will not make any public statements."

Chapter 26

Beth Carmody looked at each of her colleagues questioningly and both shook their heads. Then she turned to the audience.

"We will try to answer any questions."

Hands shot into the air and questions were shouted. Beth picked a reporter from The Alpena News.

"You said that Deputy Arthur Misdorf was one of the officers assigned to transport the Nelsons. Isn't it true that he is on light duty?"

Beth Carmody turned to Nathanial.

"Sheriff, would you like to answer that?"

Nathanial stepped up on the podium.

"I don't need a microphone..."

"Sheriff, remember this is being broadcast in the hallway for the overflow," Beth Carmody reminded him and he stepped to the microphone.

"Yes, Misdorf is on light duty, but the Nelsons were returning willingly and I felt there was no danger of difficulties. I had the approval of his doctor and the county prosecutor. And, for further information, Arthur Misdorf has been cleared to return to more active duties but still not able to patrol. That is about two weeks away pending the doctor's approval."

Nathanial started to leave the podium when another question rang out.

"There was a moratorium on spending during this crisis. However, money from the sheriff's discretionary fund was used to make payments on his deputies' insurance premiums, which they were expected to cover. Isn't that contradictory?"

Nathanial stepped back to the microphone.

"Who asked that question?"

A man stood up.

"I did. Jim Crenshaw, Genesee County Herald."

"Where did you get that information?"

"I have a source."

"The source has a name, doesn't he or she?"

"Yes, but he asked not to be named."

"Well, I know you like to protect your sources but, by agreement with the supervisors, that information was not public, so someone has gone against the rules. I want to know who that was."

"I won't say," Crenshaw said.

Nathanial motioned and two deputies moved to apprehend Crenshaw.

"You can't arrest me," he insisted. "That's privileged information."

"Public disorderliness will do. Get him out of here." The deputies complied with Crenshaw yelling vilifications at the sheriff. When order had been restored Nathanial stepped to the microphone.

"I didn't want to have to do this, but now I have no choice. I know your kind – don't take that the wrong way– and some of you will dig and dig and dig until they get to the bottom of this, so let us cut to the chase. The money used to pay the insurance premiums was my money – where I got it is my business, but it was mine. With the approval of the supervisors, I put it into the discretionary fund so that it could be dispersed appropriately. It was easier to keep the funding chain in place as much as we could. I did it because I had officers – especially Arthur Misdorf – who needed to keep their insurance intact without straining family budgets."

Beth Carmody stepped to the microphone.

"Under the circumstances, we do not feel that more questions are appropriate. I am truly sorry."

"Please remain seated until the supervisors are out of the room," Nathanial said and he led the supervisors out of the room and out of the building with no one wanting to cross him again.

Leaving the supervisors to their own devices once outside the courthouse, Nathanial strode purposefully across the parking lot and into his office complex via a locked back door. He went straight to his office without a word to anyone and sat down to think matters through. Sitting in the middle of his desk blotter was a steaming cup of coffee. He smiled to himself – as usual Barbara Ann was on top of things. Of course she knew that Crenshaw had been brought in and put into a "conference" room where he would be left to stew and consider his misdeed. He would be handcuffed, attached to the table by a heavy eyebolt. He wasn't going anywhere.

Nathanial picked up the mug of coffee and took a sip. Then he sat with his hands around the mug as though warming them. Thinking. Didn't take much thought. Whoever had planted that information with Crenshaw did it for one reason. He wanted to shed some doubt on Nathanial's integrity. Why? To make it easier to defeat him in the next election, still more than three years away, was the obvious answer. But why start now? Throw shadows of doubt a bit at a time, and it would build up. And why choose a reporter from a small paper? Genesee County – Birch Run Outlets. Didn't make any sense. But only one person had to bite. Take the first who would regardless of where they were from. Only thing is, if he was right, he couldn't do much about it. Raising a stink would play right into that person's hands.

Leaving the rest of the coffee, he walked to the room where Crenshaw was. There were two such rooms, but the other wasn't being used. Crenshaw looked up as the door opened, his shoulders sagged perceptively and he looked down at his folded hands. Nathanial took a chair on the other side of him. A cardboard cup of coffee sat near enough for Crenshaw to get and drink. Nathanial didn't say anything for several minutes.

"This isn't fair," Crenshaw finally said, raising his head and looking Nathanial straight in the eyes.

"What isn't fair?"

"Me being arrested. You have no reason."

"Public disorderliness."

"A judge will throw that out."

Nathanial sat back.

"Let me give you the scenario as I see it. I can keep you twenty-four hours. Of course, you can get a lawyer, but you'll still have to go before the judge. Nine tomorrow morning. The county prosecutor will explain to the judge what went on."

"The prosecutor?"

"Yep, see the books are under lock and key because of the audit. Still ongoing. Takes awhile and the state can't stay here all the time. Other audits and stuff. So they come and go. Books under lock and key. For that reason, the prosecutor and the supervisors – oh yes, and the judge who will hear the case tomorrow – all had to approve what happened. So someone either got at the books without permission – broke the law – or got the information from someone else who broke the law. So there is a chain there and the judge, as well as the prosecutor, are going to want to know the links leading back to the person who broke the law. So he is going to ask you who told you and you will..."

"Take the fifth," Crenshaw said smugly.

"Look, you're not Woodard nor Bernstein. This contact of yours is no Deep Throat. Go ahead. Take the fifth. Refuse to answer." Nathanial slammed his fist down on the table causing Crenshaw to jump. " 'Contempt of court. Put him away until he gives me that name.' That's what the judge will say. Then it's up to you. Is it really worth it, Crenshaw? How long do you think the Genesee County Herald will support you? Can they afford a lawyer?"

Nathanial stood.

"But it's your call. I'll have one of my deputies come in and get you some jail clothes and show you to your room."

He opened the door to leave.

"Wait...."

An hour later, Clemson Mathers, armed with a tape recorder, Nathanial and Jim Crenshaw were in the conference room. Crenshaw seemed a lot more relaxed but slightly nervous with the county prosecutor in the room.

"No need to worry, Mr. Crenshaw," Clemson Mathers said. "If what you say is true, so that we can verify it, you will be free. Is that agreeable?"

"No time in jail? I can go home today?"

"Yes. Now please tell me what you told the sheriff."

"I was sitting in the last booth in the Flour Garden. Not necessarily by choice, but I had waited and it was the first table to come free. I had ordered and had just gotten my coffee when this man slid into the booth across from me. He had his own coffee. He said, 'You're a reporter, correct?' I said yes and started to tell him about the paper and he waved me off. 'You're going to the news conference in the courthouse?' I said I was and he said, 'I can help you break a big story if you're interested.' I guess I looked askance or something because he said, 'This isn't about the Nelsons.' We talked about the fact that the county had been running on empty with strict guidelines and that someone had broken the rules. As a reporter, I was naturally interested and said, 'Who?' He said, 'If I give you the information, you cannot reveal your source.' I told him that since I didn't know his name I couldn't reveal the source and he seemed to accept that. So he told me that the sheriff had used money from his frozen discretionary fund to pay for his deputies' insurance. He said that all I had to do was ask a question and I wouldn't have any problem. Boy, was he wrong!"

Nathanial then said, "At this point, I asked if he could identify the man and he said he could. I called the Alcona County Review and said I needed a variety of campaign pictures from last fall from the League of Voters forum and they sent over ten."

He pulled the photos from a manila envelope and gave them to Crenshaw.

"Can you identify the man?"

Crenshaw looked at the first picture.

"This isn't one of the one's you showed me."

"No, none of them are. If you can identify the man again, I'll be more inclined to believe you as will Mr. Mathers."

Crenshaw shuffled through the pictures, then started through again and stopped at the sixth picture.

"That's him. Not as clear as the others, but it's the same man."

Nathanial gave him a grease pencil. "Circle the face."

Crenshaw did and Nathanial picked up the pictures and put them in front of Clemson Mathers. Clemson looked at the pictures and then at Nathanial and mouthed, "Leonard Hilbreth?"

Nathanial nodded.

Later, after Crenshaw had signed a written statement from the tape, he had been released and warned by both Nathanial and Clemson Mathers that if he was contacted by Leonard Hilbreth, or if he contacted Leonard Hilbreth, he was not to mention that he had identified him as the instigator of the questioning.

"We can't go after him because we have no proof. He got the information from someone on the auditing team and we have to find out who," Clemson Mathers said.

"True. So it's out of our hands. You will notify the state?" Nathanial said.

"As soon as I get back to my office. I guess he is a sore loser!"

"I hope he is going to be a lot sorer."

Chapter 27

The opening notes of "Hymn to Liberty" echoed within the house and Arthur Misdorf stood patiently on the porch waiting for Jane Eyre Polli to answer the door. The music of the Greek national anthem died away and there was no sound within. Without, birds were welcoming the warmth of a late spring day and the promise of summer with its official astronomical start just three short weeks away. Misdorf knew she was home because the garage door was open and the purple van sat inside. To its right, at the rear of the garage, sat the hog to which Rolli Polli had been chained when they flew together off the Hibbard Marine barge and ended up in Hibbard Pond on almost the exact spot where the fish shelter containing the corpse of Pierre LeBeuf had been found.

The opening of the door startled him out of his musing. Jane Eyre stood there in a pair of her trademark purple silk pajamas. These were dotted with small red roses. But what he saw was not that same Jane Eyre from before. This was an ever so slightly thinner Jane Eyre and her face seemed to brighten appreciably when she saw him.

"Oh, Deputy Misdorf," she said extending a hand of welcome, "I am so happy to see you. I was going to call and ask about you, but now I don't have to. Please come in, come in," as she stepped back to permit his entry. Doffing his hat, Misdorf entered and stood in the entry way as she closed the door behind him. *What a difference from Rolli Polli*, Misdorf thought. *He usually walked ahead of you, letting you close the door.*

"Can I get you a glass of water, iced tea, or me?" she said, and then giggled as his face showed his shocked reaction. "Just joking. No young stud like you is going to want an old fat battle axe like me."

"Iced tea, unsweetened with just a squirt of lemon juice," Misdorf said, trying to be both businesslike and sociable and also because he was thirsty.

Leading the way into the great room she disappeared to the left into the kitchen. "Make yourself at home, I'll be right back."

Misdorf wandered toward the glass wall facing the lake where Eyre Spy's infamous telescope sat. He heard a cabinet shut, then the tinkle of ice from a machine, probably in the refrigerator door. He bent over and peered into the eyepiece. A fishing boat, or at least its stern, was visible, and he could see the telltale yellow and red planar boards trailing behind and off to the side indicating whoever it was fished for walleye.

"You can adjust it if you want," Jane Eyre said behind him.

Misdorf stood and turned to face her, her right hand holding a glass of iced tea extended toward him. Another was in her left hand. Misdorf accepted the iced tea and moved toward one of the large wooden chairs – all the furniture in this house was large because of the size of the owner.

"To what do I owe this pleasure?" Jane Eyre said as she backed into her lift chair and started it lowering her into a sitting position. "I hope soon to be able to sit in this chair without help, but that soon is a long soooon." She giggled again.

"I have some questions I would like to ask you, should you decide to listen to them."

"Why wouldn't I?" Jane Eyre said and took a long drink of her iced tea. Had Rolli still been alive, it would have been Long Island Iced Tea, which only looks like iced tea and, in truth, contains no tea at all, iced or otherwise.

"Because they concern your late husband," Misdorf said, watching her reaction.

There was a brief trace of her body stiffening as though in shock and then it was gone.

"I have no objection. I will listen but may not answer," followed by another long sip of her drink. "Unless not answering gets me in trouble."

"I don't think the questions will get you in trouble. In fact, I am hoping the answers will get Rolli's memory out of trouble."

Jane Eyre smiled. She had hoped that someone from the sheriff's department would come asking about Rolli. She liked this young man and was glad it was he.

"Did the sheriff send you?" Jane Eyre asked.

"Not directly, although this is official business. I asked if I could try to clear up some concerns I had about ... the Frenchman and your husband's death."

"It was suicide," Jane Eyre said. "I saw it. No need to sugar coat it."

"Yes, ma'am," Misdorf said. "First, Pierre LeBeuf. From what I know of your husband – and I didn't know him that well, but I think I understood him – I don't think he killed Pierre."

"Why?"

"He just didn't seem to be the kind of person who could kill someone unless really driven to it."

"What do you mean by 'driven to it'?"

"I mean, he would have to be threatened with grievous bodily harm to take another person's life."

"Or have someone he loved threatened in that manner?"

"Yes."

Jane Eyre looked at Misdorf in a contemplative manner, "Or horribly abused?"

Misdorf was stunned by this segue. He had never considered abuse. "Yes, ma'am. That would work."

Jane Eyre sat silently for a few minutes. "You haven't tasted your tea."

Misdorf complied with her request and hoped that his face didn't show his dislike of the tea.

"Interesting," was his remark.

Jane Eyre just smiled at him. "Wretched would be a better word. But that's neither here nor there. You realize that whatever I tell you would never stand up in court. I am no lawyer, but what I can tell you is hearsay. If Rolli were here ... to tell you, it wouldn't be."

"Yes, ma'am. I know," Misdorf replied. "But we – really I – have questions that bother me and I cannot rest easy not knowing the answers."

"I understand. What's your first question?"

While Misdorf sorted through his mental question list, he took another sip of tea. She was correct – it was wretched.

"Why are you willing to answer my questions?"

Chapter 28

Jane Eyre sighed. "I, too, rest uneasy. I am hoping that by letting the truth be known – or at least my understanding of the truth – Rolli's legacy will be clearer." She paused and sipped the wretched tea. "It won't be clean, but it will, I hope, be understandable."

Both were quiet as Misdorf picked his next probe.

"Rolli confessed to killing Pierre LeBeuf. Did he?"

Jane Eyre looked straight at him when she answered, "Yes...."

Misdorf was visibly shocked, but he relaxed as she continued.

"... he confessed, but he didn't do it. He didn't even know he – that rat-faced ratfink – was here ... there ... on Hibbard Pond. The first he knew was when everyone else around the lake knew – after the body was pulled from the lake and identified."

"Why the confession?"

Jane Eyre smiled. "To save Edna. She was his oldest and dearest friend. If she did kill Pierre – and Rolli thought it was possible – then he wanted to help. He knew it was risky. Stupid. He said he was an idiot for taking that chance but then ... it didn't matter."

"Why not?" Misdorf was intrigued.

"Because the thing about the fire started flickering. He had a call from his professor – I don't remember the name. He said that some deputy sheriff was investigating and learned about what Rolli had been working on the semester before the fire. He figured it would all come out."

"And so that is why he committed suicide – to escape prosecution?"

"No ... and yes. All the memories of his childhood came back. The happy ones at the orphanage and the bad ones of his adoption."

Jane Eyre started to take a sip of her tea and stopped. She pressed a button and the seat started rising. Misdorf stood, assuming that the interview was over.

"No, Deputy. You don't have to go. I'm just going to pour this wretched brew out and get something better. Can I replace yours with something else?"

"No thanks," he said handing her his glass.

Jane Eyre hurried from the room. He could hear ice cubes tumbling into the sink, water being run, ice clicking into a glass from a dispenser, then water being added. She reappeared, crossed to her chair and lowered herself into it. Taking a sip of the water, she began, "You want to know about the bad things, I guess."

"It would help to understand," Misdorf almost sounded apologetic. "If it is going to cause grief...."

"I need to do it. I want to do it." Jane Eyre seemed to gather herself. "His adoptive parents were beasts. They beat him for the slightest foible – that's not right. Infraction. That's what I wanted to say.

"Beat him?"

"With a belt – a wide leather belt. On his bare bottom. There were scars. I should have taken a picture, but it was ugly. Then they adopted Jeanette. For several years, things were good. The beatings lessened. Became private. He had gotten too big to be handled without a fight, and Rolli threatened to kill his adoptive father if he touched him. When he was a senior in high school, Jeanette matured. She was four or five years younger than he. Their father started molesting her. First touching her, having her touch him...."

"I understand," Misdorf said. "But didn't she ... they ... tell their mother?"

"Oh, she laughed. 'Ridiculous,' she said. 'He has all he can handle in me. Why would he want some young inexperienced girl?' Back then, going to the police wouldn't have done any good. There was no proof. They – the parents – would have claimed she was promiscuous, having sex with one of her friends. Rolli was going to do something violent, but Jeanette convinced him it wasn't smart. He'd end up in prison and he would be a nice target for the perverts there. She told him to wait until he graduated – it was a week after his eighteenth birthday.

"The morning after his graduation, Rolli appeared at breakfast carrying a duffel bag with all his belongings. He told them he was leaving and he would never come back. They laughed at him. 'Good riddance,' his adoptive father said. 'You were a rotten son anyway.' That didn't surprise Rolli, but it hurt him. He told his adoptive parents he would see them burn in hell. They laughed and he left. He worked in Buffalo for a couple of years getting enough money to get into college. He kept in touch with Jeanette during that time and they would meet. He had bought the Harley – he never told me where or how he got the money. He would bike to Montreal, and they would meet. Then she graduated and went away to school. Then it was time for him to make his bomb. She was away and wouldn't be hurt. He never learned why she came back that weekend. Her death shocked him to the core. That's why he quit chemistry and turned to business. Causing her death could never be forgotten. He pushed it away over the years and then...."

Both sat there for a few minutes.

"Thank you, Mrs. Polli," Misdorf said, standing and picking up his hat. "You've answered my questions. If you think of anything else, you know where to reach me."

He started for the door and had reached the foyer when he heard her calling him. He turned back and met her.

"No one ever told us when Pierre was killed. The date I mean. There was an accident late in that fall. Rolli fell and badly twisted his ankle. He was laid up for two weeks in mid-November. If it was then, he couldn't have done it. He couldn't put any weight on it."

"I'll check and see what I can find out. Thanks again."

"Thank you, Deputy," Jane Eyre said stepping forward and trying to wrap her arms around him, but she was too fat and her arms too short. "I'm glad those Boswick boys didn't kill you."

Chapter 29

Tuesday afternoon at 2:00 p.m., the outside door to the lobby in the sheriff's office opened, and Zeb Pyke stepped through and stopped just inside the door letting it swing shut behind him. The lobby was empty. There wasn't a sound to be heard except the ticking of the electric clock on the wall and that was more of a hum with a slight click of the minute hand as it moved after sixty seconds of stillness. In his left hand he held a small burlap bag, hanging low and taut indicating that the contents were heavy. He walked to the glass partition separating the lobby from the small office complex and waited to be noticed. A woman dressed in civilian clothes was bent over a desk apparently sorting some papers. A middle-age deputy sat at another desk intent on the computer screen in front of him. Neither seemed to notice him. He raised the burlap bag and set it on the small metal ledge at the bottom of the glass partition. It made a slight clunk when he set it down. Both people in the office heard it – the man looked up and the woman turned around.

"I'm sorry," Ruth Biggers said. "I didn't hear you come in. Can I help you?"

"I would like to talk to the sheriff," Zeb responded.

"Is he expecting you?"

"No."

"May I ask what this is about?" She smiled at him either trying to relax him or herself, Zeb thought.

"I want to report a possible crime."

That really got the attention of both of them. Rich Ross got up and moved to the window and stood beside the woman.

"Possible crime?" Rich Ross asked.

"Yes, I believe a crime has been committed. A crime that would interest the sheriff."

"Exactly what is this crime?" Ross asked, Ruth Biggers having turned around, her body and the deputy's blocking whatever she was doing.

"I am sorry," Zeb said. "I hate to be secretive, but I would rather talk to the sheriff."

Rich Ross looked at Zeb for a moment. "May I tell the sheriff who you are?"

"Zeb," Nathanial's voice boomed.

Zeb turned to his right and saw Nathanial standing in a doorway.

"Come in and tell me about this crime. Did you catch another finger?" Both men laughed as Zeb walked to where Nathanial stood and shook his outstretched hand.

"No, but there may be a connection."

Nothing more needed to be said as Nathanial led Zeb down a short hallway to his office. Taking his seat behind the desk, Nathanial waved at his visitors' chairs. "Have a seat and tell me about it."

Zeb did as he was bid and set the burlap bag on the seat of the chair next to him. He could tell by Nathanial's eyes following the bag that he was interested.

"What's in the...?" Nathanial started.

Zeb held his hand up. "All in due time.

"I was the first one at the crash site. The plane was starting to sink and the cockpit windows were almost submerged. I could see movement inside so I went in the water. I was wearing my wetsuit after my experience on Wednesday and, fishing alone, I didn't want to fall in without extra protection against the cold. I managed to get one of the cockpit doors open and something fell out, hitting my leg – it was hard."

Nathanial's eyes went to the bag.

"Someone was yelling, thrashing the water. He was sitting in a seat behind the pilot. He was yelling about his seatbelt. I reached him, unfastened his buckle – guess he was too panicked to get it open – and pulled him out the door. The pilot was just hanging in his harness unconscious. I freed the belt and dragged him out. I noticed in my efforts that he had a bump on the back of his head. There was nothing he could have hit the back of his head on.

"When Dugal and Jerry took the two to shore, I dove under the plane. The water was about twenty feet deep, my limit nowadays in a free dive. I didn't know what I was looking for. Luckily the bottom was fairly clean and sandy and right where it should have been was a rock, or what I thought was a rock. Found it on my second dive.

"I brought it up and put it over the side of the boat. Just as I pulled myself in Howard Hawes arrived, and we were busy with the mattresses, then Dugal came back, the sheriff's posse arrived, and all was pretty busy until the plane was being towed. Then I happened to see what I had salvaged. It was a stone carving – about the size of a bookend or big paperweight on some executive's desk. Then when we got to the south end, I sat in the river in case help was needed and watched Edmund Fitzgerald get into the plane and retrieve his briefcase – it was aluminum, big enough to hold the statuary. He didn't seem distraught or anything. He let your guys photograph his briefcase open and closed – I guess in case the FAA is upset about it being removed, although I cannot imagine why in a private plane crash that was clearly pilot error. So I kept it until I knew more about it. Maybe that's withholding evidence – that's your call."

Nathanial waved his hands sort of brushing it off and saying nothing.

"Anyway, I did some surfing this weekend – on the Web – and found a lot of things that look like it. I don't know whether it is Aztec or Mayan, but it is illegal to export and/or possess such artifacts. So if it does belong to Edmund Fitzgerald, he's in trouble. I know that he is in the import business and manufactures and sells a lot of resin statuary that look much like this one. I found that on the web also."

With that, he pulled the statuary head from the burlap bag and set it on Nathanial's desk. It was about two-thirds the size of a football and showed weathering.

"Beautiful," Nathanial said. Then he pushed a button on his intercom. "Walker or Roberts, bring me copies of the pictures you took of Fitzgerald's briefcase."

While they waited, Nathanial picked the head up and studied it.

"Heavy."

"Yep," Zeb agreed. "Heavy enough to knock someone out."

"You don't think it was intentional, do you?"

"I sure as hell wouldn't knock someone out who was landing a plane I was on."

"Who knocked whom out?" Bob Roberts said as he walked into the office closely followed by Rich Walker holding two eight-by-ten photographs.

"Whoa," Walker said handing the photographs to Nathanial and looking at the head, "that looks deadly."

"Definitely," Nathanial agreed. "Zeb salvaged this from the crash site. Thought it might be what knocked the pilot out."

"Could be," Walker agreed. "There was a cloth bag in the briefcase. It was empty. Big enough for the head and the briefcase was big enough also. He could have been looking at it when they landed ... or tried to land."

"This puts a new light on some things that Misdorf said are bothering him about the Fitzgerald house," Nathanial added.

"Then I was not withholding evidence?" Zeb said satisfactorily.

"On the contrary," Nathanial said. "You have brought new evidence to light."

"Then I am glad I found it," Zeb stated, " 'cause the sight was crawling with local divers this weekend."

Chapter 30

After sitting for half an hour in his cruiser a quarter mile from the Fitzgerald "estate" as he thought of it and scaring motorists who thought he was a speed trap, Arthur Misdorf screwed up his courage and drove to the house. It was quite different from the last time he had been here in the late winter. There was no snow, annuals in red and white were in bloom along the walk, and rose bushes were budding at the "front" of the house. Having prepared himself as best he could, he got out of his cruiser, adjusted his hat to just the right cockish angle, and walked to the door. Before he could ring the bell, the door opened and he found himself face-to-face (although a foot shorter) with an attractive dark-haired woman with bedroom eyes. She was attired in a light blue dress with a white collar and dark blue buttons down the front. She was wearing white deck shoes with no visible socks. Misdorf thought that if Hollywood had set this up, she would have a little starched white cap of some sort and be carrying a feather duster which she would rest over one shoulder and say...

"Yes, Officer? I am sorry, I don't know American police uniforms."

Misdorf gulped. Her voice was as seductive as her eyes and that accent gave him goose bumps.

"Misdorf. Alcona County Sheriff's Deputy Arthur Misdorf. I would like to talk to Mrs. Fitzgerald."

"Cèrtainement," (which she pronounced 'cer-tain-mon', adding to the goose bumps.) "Madame is in the Lake Room having tea and I am cèrtaine she would be happy to have you join her." While saying this, she had stepped back, opening the door wide and indicating with a wave of her right hand that he should enter, which he did. Knowing where the Lake Room was and wondering if Edna Fitzgerald was ever anywhere else, he started in that direction.

"Excuse me, Deputy," he heard her say firmly but politely as he heard the door close behind him. "I will be happy to show you the way."

"I've been here before," Misdorf said, removing his hat and trying to appear nonchalant although every muscle (even relaxed ones) was quivering.

"That may be true," she said as she brushed past him, "but it is my duty to be cèrtaine that guests do not get lost."

And stray through closed doors, Misdorf thought.

The artworks that had been there before were still there, discoloration in the wallpaper showing the ones that were new (*replacing what?*) after his first visit. And the door to the storage room possibly holding answers to his questions was still closed. Crossing the living room, Misdorf stopped by the glass-topped table. The books were still there but turned ninety degrees, and the glass-top was pristinely clean.

"You like those books?" the maid's voice (who else could she be in that uniform) asked.

"There were different bookends before," Misdorf said. The current ones were sailboats battling a rough sea and were made of wood, whether hand carved or not he could not discern.

"I wouldn't know," she said. "If we may continue?" She moved on and Misdorf followed like a little puppy, happily following the slight twitch of her rear beneath the skirt. Just enough twitch to keep his muscles twitching and starting other things to stiffen.

"Mrs. Fitzgerald," the maid said as she entered the Lake Room, "a Deputy Misdorf from the sheriff's department would like a word with you."

"Thank you, Alix. Would you please get him some tea."

Arthur moved in front of her.

"Please sit down, Arthur," Edna Fitzgerald said to him smiling and indicated a white high-backed cane chair facing hers. "You would like some tea, wouldn't you? It is tea time after all."

"Yes, ma'am." *It had to be better than Jane Eyre Polli's iced tea,* he thought as he accepted the cup Alix offered.

"Thank you, Alix. That will be all for now. I'll ring if I need you."

Misdorf noticed the crystal bell on the table at Edna's right.

"Were you one of the people who rescued Edmund when his plane crashed?"

"No, ma'am, I ..."

"It was a new plane. Eight-seater. Cessna, I think. Sounds like a trip to the desert. What is that ... oh, yes ... caravan. He bought it for his business. Terribly expensive but he says he can afford it. It was his first flight in it. Don't know what made Tom crash land. He's an awfully good pilot. I know, because he flies me when I need to go somewhere."

"I'm certain that he is," Arthur got in. *She's jabbering like a blue jay.*

"Now, what can I do for you this time? Last time it was about that murder. The body under the ice, wasn't it?"

"Yes, ma'am," Arthur said. "Pierre LeBeuf."

"Yes, I knew him, you know. Way back when we were kids in that orphanage. Me, Pierre and Rolli...."

Her eyes watered and she stared straight ahead.

Yes, Arthur thought, *and shortly after that visit I was shot. Was it by your orders?*

"Dear Rolli. I can't believe that he killed his parents. And his sister too! He lied about it, you know. To save me, I think. Or maybe to save Butch. I don't know. He said he killed Pierre. But he couldn't have. He was an invalid then. I remember. I didn't then, but I do now. He hurt his knee, I think. Couldn't walk for two weeks. No way he could have come here and killed Pierre. I don't even think he knew he was here. I certainly didn't know he was coming. It was a surprise. Edmund thought he would surprise me. What a terrible surprise."

She took a sip of her tea. "Oh, this is cold," she said setting the cup and saucer on the table.

"I'll refresh it," Arthur said starting to rise but she had picked the bell up and rung it. Before she could set it back down, Alix was there. *Must have been just outside*, Misdorf thought. *Eavesdropping.*

"Yes, Madame," Alix said with just a hint of exasperation in her voice.

"My tea is cold," Edna said. Alix picked up the cup, took it to a tea cart that Arthur had failed to notice. It too, like the cane furniture, was white with a glass top and the tea set on the silver tray was white. Alix set the cup and saucer on the tray, picked up another, filled it from a teapot, and brought it back. Then she turned and left without a sidewise, or any other way, glance at Arthur.

"That's better," Edna said taking a sip of tea. "Sorry we don't have any biscuits or crumpets. I just like tea at teatime. Never did like crumpets. Don't like scones either. Too dry."

She paused and stared out at the lake. *Well, it's over now*, Arthur thought recalling his previous visits when she seemed to go off in La-La Land staring at the lake.

"I'm awfully sorry, Arthur, that you were shot after your last visit here. I'm so glad you weren't killed. I didn't think...."

She stared at the lake.

She didn't think what? Arthur wondered.

"Then Butch," Edna said. "Dear Butch. Saying he killed Pierre. Then killing himself. He didn't though. He said he did, but he didn't."

"Who did, Mrs. Fitzgerald?"

"I...." She stared at the lake, her eyes vacant, unseeing.

And after several minutes of Edna Fitzgerald not moving, Arthur picked up his hat from the floor where he had placed it when he sat down, and stood.

"Thank you, Mrs. Fitzgerald," Arthur said walking to the tea cart and putting his cup and saucer on it. *Now for the storage room* and Arthur quickly stepped into the living room.

"Leaving already, Deputy?" Alix said from a chair halfway across the room. She put the book she had been reading back between the sailboat bookends. "I will show you out," and led him out of the living room and down the hallway to the foyer. Arthur gave the storage room door a longing glance as they passed it. Alix opened the door and Arthur stepped out, putting his hat on. "Please feel free to come back whenever you need to," Alix said. "She likes you."

As the door closed behind Misdorf, Alix heard the faint tinkling of a crystal bell.

Chapter 31

"Dugal, let's take a walk!"

Knowing this was more than a friendly request, Dugal got out of his boat where he was doing some mindless cleaning and headed for the cabin where Earleen waited on the deck.

"What's up?" he asked as he drew near.

"What do you mean?" Earleen said somewhat suspiciously.

"You just don't come out in the middle of the afternoon and ask me to go for a walk. Come in for a nap maybe ... Oh, is that what you meant?"

"Oh, you. No, I meant that someone is looking at the 'mansion down the road' and I wanted to check them out. After all, they are potential neighbors."

The "mansion" was a big log cabin two doors down the road. Leaving their cabin, the McBruces walked about a hundred feet where Spruce Drive continued left toward the East (Hibbard Pond) Path. Continuing on Spruce Drive, which makes a left-hand turn and continues an uphill slope starting back at their cabin, they first passed a small bungalow owned by a couple in North Carolina. They had been up only in August last summer, remaining through Labor Day and then heading south again. They had hoped to be able to spend more time this summer, but there had been no word as yet.

Continuing past the bungalow, they came to the "mansion" as Earleen had called it. First, they passed the garage complex on the left side of the road. This building had six two-car garages with one converted into a shop by the second owner. The "mansion" was a huge log cabin with four bedrooms, two of which had private baths and the other two shared one. There was also a game room complete with pool table and a poker table seating eight, and a gigantic cathedral-ceiling great room. For most women (and some of the men) the pièce de résistance was a huge kitchen with a six-burner gas stove with two ovens and a built-in grill with a spit big enough to roast a suckling pig. Propane had been the fuel source for the heating and cooking until natural gas had been introduced in the early 2000s.

Along the front of the house was a porch with glass sliders. The highlight of the porch was a built-in hot tub that had been added by the third, and thus far last, owners who surprisingly were the couple from North Carolina who now owned the bungalow next door. As they had aged, they longed to spend winters in a more hospitable climate and when the bungalow next door had come on the market two years before, they had snapped it up and put the "mansion" on the market. So far, there had been no takers.

This was not really surprising because the asking price was $750,000, which had dropped to $600,000 earlier in the spring. That had brought a steady stream of lookers, including Earleen and Dugal just out of curiosity. The house was too big for their needs, but what had intrigued them (other than the kitchen) was the boathouse. From the house there was a fifty-foot lawn to a lakeside drop of approximately twenty feet to a rocky beach (Hibbard Pond had no sand beaches) about ten feet wide except where the boathouse was.

Located almost at the extreme left hand side of the two-hundred-front-foot shoreline lot, the boathouse was set back about five feet from the lake's standard high water mark, and was big enough to house a modern twenty-five-foot pontoon boat. But that wasn't the best part: above the boathouse portion was an apartment. Except for a walled-off bathroom at the back left (which had a tub, sink and toilet), the room was open. At the back next to the bathroom was a kitchen. There was a counter running the remaining width with a sink and two-burner electric stove with a small oven and a refrigerator under it. Cabinets were above the counter and there was storage below. The rest of the room was given to a living area with two comfortable chairs, a hide-a-bed sofa, a large circular coffee table and a king-sized bed. On the wall opposite the bed was a 52-inch high definition television. The lakeside wall was virtually solid glass with a slider in the middle. To the left was a built-in desk. A four-foot wide deck surrounded three sides of the building. On the left hand side, as one faced the lake, was a stairway with a landing providing access to the deck before the stairway continued to the beach. In the wall of the boathouse facing the landing there was a solid wood door with a dead bolt. What Dugal had really liked about the boathouse apartment was that it was paneled in real barn wood, very expensive unless you could find an old barn and be the first to get at it.

Dugal really wanted to have a boathouse to store his boats in, but the state powers that be (Department of Environmental Quality or DEQ, and the Department of Natural Resources or DNR) had decreed that no further boathouses be built. You could rebuild one on the original footprint but that was all.

The boathouse was built in 1946 and the owner lived in it while the house was being constructed. Stephen Fisher Thompson was independently wealthy, inheriting his money from his mother who had wisely invested in the stock market, and her portfolio had miraculously survived the 1929 crash. Stephen had discovered that the fortune was his when he returned home from the South Pacific where he had served with the Navy, enlisting after Pearl Harbor, just one semester before he was to graduate from Harvard with a major in political science. When he returned, he had thrown himself full tilt into Michigan politics, although remaining in the background.

He had been raised in Charlevoix, the area that many call the "tony" (stylish and expensive) part of the state and somewhat infamous for Leopold and Loeb, the latter's family having a summer home called Castle Farms in the area. However, Thompson eschewed the public life, sold the family home and bought the property on Hibbard Pond. The home he built was intended for his friends and their friends with hunting being the guise for weekend and weeklong getaways during the late forties and early fifties. Suddenly that ended and Thompson became a recluse, although no one knows why. It could have been the onset of an illness that was never properly diagnosed and took his life in 1959.

Put up for sale, the property was snapped up by two families who were supposed to share responsibilities for maintenance, but that fell apart in five years. One couple bought the other out and kept ownership until their children were out of high school and then they sold it to Bob and Betsy Williamson, the current bungalow-owning North Carolina snowbirds.

The McBruces had enjoyed their semi-privacy with their only full-time summer neighbors being Pauline and Norm Smythe. Consequently both were interested in knowing who was going to share their serenity. Dugal sensed that Earleen could swing either way in describing the area depending how she felt about the potential buyers.

There was a white Suburban in the parking area near the mansion's granite-floored foyer resplendent with head mounts, obtained who knows where, because none of the locals could ever remember Thompson, or any of his friends, hunting. In fact, only one person could remember anyone with a gun, and that was questionable.

"There they are," Earleen announced pointing to a couple standing on the edge of the twenty-foot bluff overlooking the lake. The woman of the couple noticed them, and Earleen waved and started moving that way, drawing Dugal with her. The couple met them halfway.

"I'm Earleen McBruce, and this," she said waving in the direction of the trailing Dugal, "is my husband Dugal. We live at the other end of the road."

"Glad to meet you. I'm Kathy Jo Paul and this is my husband Michal."

"Glad to meet you," Dugal said, shaking Michal's hand, then Kathy Jo's. "Don't think I've ever met a woman with three first names."

"I get that all the time," Kathy Jo said. "It's really...," and she looked at her husband.

"It's was 'Pawlak'," he explained, pronouncing it 'PAV-lack', "Polish last name from Pawel, Polish first name for Paul. But my grandfather changed it when he immigrated to help him blend in. Just like my name, which is Polish for 'Michael.' It would be pronounced 'meehaaw', so that's Anglicized also except for my mother, may she rest in peace."

"So what brings you here – other than this place?"

"We've been staying at the Loon Creek Inn for a couple of Memorial Day weekends and have fallen in love with the area. We've seen this place from the water and saw the 'For Sale' sign hanging on the boathouse and thought we'd give it a look."

"So, looking for a summer place when you're not working?"

"Yeah. That's our thought – at least for now."

Dugal started to ask what work was, but was interrupted by a "Yoo hoo," coming from behind the McBruces. It was Irene Stockwell who had the listing on the place. She and her husband Ed, who ran Hibbard Pond Outfitters, lived just across East Path from the end of Spruce Drive. Obviously, she had chosen to walk down.

"Well, there's your guide," Earleen said to them. "When you're done and have any questions that Irene cannot answer, stop down. All the way to the end..." indicating the direction of their house, "... and then head toward the lake."

Chapter 32

"Did they pass muster?" Irene had asked as they passed her. Out of the corner of his eyes, Dugal thought he could see a smile on Earleen's face. Walking home, he said, "Well?"

"They appear nice."

"I sense a 'but' at the end of that sentence."

"Let's wait until they stop down."

"If they stop down, you mean."

"They'll stop down...," Earleen's reply stopped by the barrier of Dugal's arm in front of her. He was looking to the left, near a small group of bushes in back of the bungalow. Next to it stood a doe looking at them but not moving.

"Oh," whispered Earleen, "how neat."

"I think she's the one who has been around recently," Dugal whispered, "but something's different."

"What do you mean?"

"Well, she was great with young but doesn't appear to be so now."

"You think the fawn is close?"

"Unless I'm mistaken, I think it is in that bunch of bushes. Great place to give birth and keep the fawn hidden."

"Can we look?" Dugal sensed Earleen starting to move toward the doe.

"No," he hissed and taking her hand, they continued their homeward walk, each casting discreet glances at the doe whose head followed them, but nothing else moved. Safely out of earshot, Dugal said, "If she hangs around here for a day or so, we'll see the fawn. When it's strong enough, she'll take it into the deep woods."

"I can't wait," Earleen said.

Back at the cabin, Dugal headed for his boat to continue his work while Earleen went into the cabin "to putter." Dugal knew that was making certain the place was clean, although that wouldn't take much, and see what she could throw together for nibbles, hot or cold, when the Pauls showed up. Earleen was uncanny when it came to predictions like that, so he expected it to happen. Sure enough about an hour later, Dugal heard Earleen yell, "Company." He finished what he was doing, put everything away, raised the boat back up under its canopy and headed up.

Michal Paul was standing on the deck looking out at the lake, a bottle of beer in his hand.

"Beautiful place you have."

"Yes, it's great for us. Not too big, not too small..."

"Just right," Michal Paul finished and laughed. "I hardly know you, and here I am finishing your sentences."

"Would not take much sometimes," Dugal said. "I see the hostess has provided you with a libation."

"Yeah," Michal Paul said looking at the label. "Lumber Logger Red."

"Fletcher Street Brewing Company," Dugal said. "They're in one of the old buildings of the Fletcher Paper Company."

"Right," Michal Paul said. "Isn't that shipwreck museum in one of them?"

"That's the Great Lakes Maritime Heritage Center Museum. They offer glass-bottom boat rides of wrecks in the Thunder Bay National Marine Sanctuary. Really a great trip."

"We've been meaning to do that, but find it hard to break away from the lake when we're here."

"Where are the ladies?" Dugal asked.

"Inside fixing some sauerkraut balls. What are those, anyway?"

"A specialty of Akron, Ohio. Had them one summer when we went to see the World Golf Classic at Firestone Country Club."

"Not into golf, prefer fishing."

Dugal laughed. "I'm with you, but Earleen had the hots for Tiger Woods until his infidelity ruined it."

"I understand. Kathy Jo had a thing for Jim Tressel at OSU until his infidelity to the job came up. Now it's Urban Meyer."

"Did she go to OSU?"

"Nope, neither of us did. She just likes the coach."

"Dugal, come and help," Earleen called and then let the screen door slam.

"Probably have to carry some heavy plate," Dugal said. "Be right back."

Inside, Dugal discovered that Earleen had "thrown together" sauerkraut balls (from the freezer, thawed and heated in the toaster oven) and a cheese (Edam, Cheddar and Brie) and cracker plate. Both ladies were was standing there with glasses of red wine, Kathy Jo with a sauerkraut ball on a toothpick, and Earleen with an empty toothpick.

"Those are great," Kathy Jo said, obviously the one she held was not her first.

Earleen indicated the two plates.

"Would you be so kind as to take those to the deck?" she said.

"What about my libation?" Dugal asked.

Earleen pointed at two opened bottles of Lumber Logger Red.

"I can't carry two plates and two bottles," Dugal said.

"You can come back," Earleen said as Dugal dutifully picked up the plates and headed back out to the deck. Behind him, Kathy Jo popped the sauerkraut ball into her mouth and then she and Earleen each picked up a bottle of beer and followed him.

"Try one of these kraut balls," Dugal said, offering the plate to Michal who responded by taking one without a toothpick and popping it into his mouth.

"Waa," he wailed as he bit into it, "that's hot."

"That's why you usually have a toothpick, so you can cool it or just take a bite."

Michal finished his bottle of beer.

"Hot but delicious. What's in them beside sauerkraut?"

"Pork sausage, cream cheese, and bread crumbs," Kathy Jo said handing him a full bottle of beer.

"We make them for New Year's Day. They're the pork you are supposed to eat up here in the north, but in the south its Hoppin' John," Dugal explained.

"Hoppin' John?" Michal said.

"It's black-eyed peas and rice basically, with some bacon, ham or pork for the meat. I learned that on a run to South Carolina. Also learned that on New Year's Eve you should wash your car because the way it is on New Year's Day is the way it will be the rest of the year."

"I'll stick with the sauerkraut balls," Michal said, picking up one by the toothpick and taking a little bite before closing his lips over the entire thing.

"I'm getting the recipe," Kathy Jo said.

"Only if you buy the mansion," Earleen said.

"Oh, you mean the Spruce Street Cottage?" Kathy Jo asked.

"You've already got it named?" Dugal and Earleen looked at each other incredulously.

"No," Kathy Jo answered.

"But we have put in a bid," Michal Paul said. "If we get it, the first thing we are going to do is hold a party on the lawn."

"A wedding party," Kathy Jo said.

"For whom?" Dugal and Earleen asked simultaneously.

"Us," Michal and Kathy Jo answered simultaneously.

"You're not...?"

"No. We've been together for ten years," Michal explained. "Neither married before, and at our age there won't be kids, so we kept the status quo. We're both professionals. Kathy Jo is a high school English teacher and can retire at any time. I'm an investment broker and I can work from anywhere. I've got an office in East Lansing and one in Detroit. I have a small staff in each place. I've done well and recently invested in property in Florida."

"The price has been right down there with the economy in the tank," Dugal agreed.

"Yep, but it's going to need management, so we're thinking Hibbard Pond is summer and Florida the rest of the year. With all this, we felt that getting hitched is the proper thing to do."

"Well, we hope you get the place," Earleen said. "I love weddings."

Kathy Jo and Michal looked at each other and then at Earleen.

"Who said you'd be invited?" Kathy Jo said.

Earleen looked chagrined and then smiled when the Pauls laughed.

"Gotcha," Kathy Jo said.

Chapter 33

Misdorf's report to Nathanial was not as good as they both had hoped.

"So Rolli's confession can be broken by an alibi, provided the murder occurred during a two-week span?" Nathanial said.

"Yes, and there are only two people who can provide an answer to that question: Edna Fitzgerald and her son Edmund, who based upon that piece of Mayan statuary, has something to hide. If Edna has dementia or Alzheimer's, she might not be able to provide an accurate answer, although she did mention it, so that's hopeful."

"If either is the killer, a correct answer will not be forthcoming. But there are three other people you can add to the list of possibilities," Nathanial said looking at Misdorf quizzically.

"Three ... oh, the brothers."

"Yep. You certainly aren't going to let a body lie around for someone to discover. So the burial was done immediately."

"Too bad we can't pinpoint when the shelter went missing."

"The best we can do is to know that it is after mid-October when they were built. No one is around the

Loon Creek Inn after Labor Day or end of September at the latest, so they won't be of much help."

"Any chance Clemson Mathers will give us a search warrant?" Misdorf asked hopefully.

"Everything is circumstantial," and Nathanial started enumerating on his fingers. "One, your suspicion that art work was removed and later replaced is countered by the fact that people remodel all the time, and the bookends that were replaced are no longer there. Two, this piece of statuary may have gotten to the bottom of the lake some other way and there is no way to tie it to Fitzgerald. Again the briefcase is circumstantial."

"So we should work on the brothers?"

"Worth a shot, but they're pretty closed-mouthed about it."

"Understandable, but maybe Clemson Mathers would offer a deal."

"Might work. I can give it a shot, but for now I've got something else for you and Webster to work on."

"The skeleton from the bridge?"

"Yes, heard from Blodgett this morning. Kid was male, six to nine or ten, buried in the mid to late fifties. That's the best they can do."

"DNA?"

"No. We just have the skeleton. There is no retrievable DNA there."

"But in many cases, a missing relative – especially a young one – is not forgotten."

"We would need a picture for that. Blodgett is going to do a facial reconstruction based on the skull. When we have that we can do more. For right now, I want you to concentrate on getting any pictures you can of Michigan children missing in the fifties."

"You're assuming that he was from Michigan."

"Taking an educated guess. In the fifties, traveling very far with a kid who wasn't yours would have been difficult. There weren't as many drive-thrus where you could get food and not be seen, at least not as if you were in a restaurant. There weren't any video cameras. None of the modern stuff, so we'll start there. Give that Missing Kids site a shot first."

"Yes, sir. I'm going to keep going on the Fitzgerald aspects though. I really think that's going to get us the killer."

"In that case, cross your fingers and pray to your patron saint since it is going to take some dumb luck to crack this case because it's already so muddled."

It took Misdorf less than an hour to get what he needed. He first went to the missingkids.com web site of the National Center for Missing and Exploited Children. Using their search engine, he looked for children missing from Michigan from 1/1/1950 to 12/31/1959 and came up with no hits. That was disappointing. He expected something. So he Googled "Michigan Missing Children 1953" just to see what happened. The first link on the page of results was

1969 & Prior - North American *Missing* Persons Network

www.nampn.org/mp1969-prior.html

Joseph Laurence Halpern *Missing* since August 15, 1933 from Estes Park, ... Ronald Henry Tammen, Jr. *Missing* since April 19, *1953* from Oxford, Butler County, Ohio ... since September 18, 1958 from Ann Arbor, Washtenaw County, *Michigan*

The only person in that time frame who went miss-ing in the 1950s was Ida Dean Anderson, who went missing from Ann Arbor on September 18, 1958. Other than being a girl, she was 21, had just received custody of her children and was to fly to Florida with them. However, she disappeared before that.

The second link was

Michigan - National Center for *Missing* & Ex-ploited *Children*

*www.**missingkids**.com/**missingkids**/.../PubCa...*

National Center for Missin...

Records Found: 66 *Michigan* ... Location: DEARBORN, *MI*, US ... Location: DETROIT, *MI*, US ... Location: STURGIS, *MI*, US .... DOB: Jan 10, *1953* Age: 61

That link turned up a page with 66 missing children. Five of those went missing in the 1950s but, again, they were all female.

He sat back, frustrated. It was as though boys never went missing. His mind raced and suddenly he said, "Cracks. Things fall through the cracks." Ida was not one of the people missing on the Missing Kids website because she wasn't a kid, and not one of the five missing girls on the Missing Kids list was on the North Ameri-can Persons Network. The Internet didn't exist in the 1950s and so all this data had to be uploaded later and the cases were cold. Maybe some didn't get listed.

With at least a partial resolution in hand, Misdorf went to see the sheriff. He knocked on the door and caught the sheriff with his feet up, in a contemplative mood.

"Got a minute, Sheriff?"

"Certainly, Arthur. Come in."

Misdorf told the sheriff about his findings.

"Not looking good," Nathanial said. "I'll bet the FBI can't be of any help unless state lines were crossed."

"No, but here's what I think is our best option. I will send an email to all the sheriff and police departments as well as the state police. I'll write a paragraph or two about the discovery and what we know. Then I'll ask if they have any records of any disappearance in the 1950s. I'll wait until we get the facial reconstruction from Blodgett and include that."

"I approve of that plan. We'll send it out under my signature for the greatest clout. Let me know when you're ready to do that and we can both cross our fingers and pray to the Archangel Michael."

"Who's that?" Misdorf questioned.

"You don't pray to the Archangel? I thought every cop did, believer or not. Michael is mentioned in Jewish, Christian and Islamic teachings, appearing in the Bible's Book of Daniel three times. In the late Middle Ages, Michael was considered the patron saint of chivalry, and over the years he became the patron saint of police officers, paramedics, and the military."

"I thought that was Saint George," Misdorf said.

"You are not alone. We'll pray to them both. What can it hurt?"

Three days later they received a picture from Blodgett and the emails were sent and they waited.

Chapter 34

By nature, solving a crime involves a lot of work. Some just searching for clues. Some just putting the pieces (clues) together to see the whole picture, or at least a part of it that enables the rest of the puzzle to be put together. On television, for the most part, what you see is a brilliant piece of deduction time after time – as though every good police officer is a Sherlock Holmes. That's not the case in real life. Grunt work, long hours and, you have to admit it, luck. "Yep, just plain dumb luck," according to Sheriff Nathanial Jefferson. And that's how the important link to the Pierre LeBeuf murder came to light.

Though somewhat expected, there wasn't a lot of curiosity about the plane crash despite what Zeb Pyke thought. There weren't gawkers like a situation with a train wreck with tens and tens of derailed box and tank cars, or a shooting where a house is sealed and marked with yellow police tape identifying it for the curious. In the case of the Hibbard Pond plane crash, there was nothing to see. Water leaves no holes marking the spot, and there weren't that many people who actually saw the wreck. Among those who did, among those who went to the scene initially to help or just out of curiosity, nobody – not one person – marked the location with a GPS. On an open body of water, a big open body of water like Hibbard Pond, distances are deceiving. Even if Jerry or Zeb or Dugal had gone back the next day, their mark would have been off by twenty or thirty feet. So if someone wanted to dive for something that had been in the plane and lost, there was a lot of bottom to cover. It would take a good team of divers hours to cover the area and, face it, there wasn't any wreckage. The plane was intact and had been hauled carefully and slowly away from the Negwegon launch site to a hanger in Alpena, so there was nothing there to see.

Dumb luck brought two teenage boys close to the area. Dumb luck and youthful curiosity. Sam and Jack Pickens were part of a weekend family, one of the many with a small cottage on the lake who had come up for the opening weekend of summer. The boys had spent the winter taking scuba lessons in a local YMCA and then, earlier in the spring, in a local lake near their home in Fenton. They had received their diver certifications just the weekend before, and naturally had brought their gear with them to dive in the crystal clear Hibbard Pond water. Water that was so clear that on a sunny day you can see the bottom in depths of fifteen to twenty feet. And, for the weekend, that was the limit established by their parents. For the most part they were good boys and obeyed their parents. In this case, not abiding and getting caught would possibly mean no diving for the rest of the summer. They were not going to risk that.

The older of the two was Sam, short for Samuel, middle name Clements – no relation to the creator of the Tom Sawyer and Huck Finn characters. At eighteen, he was six foot two, two hundred twenty pounds, a good-looking strawberry blonde basketball player. Not good enough for a big college, but he had a scholarship to

Eastern Michigan where he hoped, with grit and deter-
mination of which he had plenty, to start at point guard
by his junior year. Jack was two years and three months
younger. Jack was short for Jackson, which was his
middle name, Andrew was his first – again no relation to
the American president. Both middle names were family names – Clements was their mother's maiden name
and Jackson their father's mother's maiden name. Jack
was an inch taller than Sam, twenty pounds heavier with
sandy brown hair and no promising athletic skill at all.
His forte was mathematics at which he was a whiz. His
hope was to go to M.I.T. and become a computer engi-
neer.

But this weekend was for diving. "No, Mom, we're
not going to spear any fish. That's illegal." That was
Jack's answer to his mom's second mandate. The first
had been water depth, and they both had vowed to "not
go deeper than twenty feet, and not stay down more than
twenty minutes." Saturday and Sunday had been spent
within eyeshot of the cottage, with their mother keeping
a vigilant eye on them and a stopwatch. Their father had
kept one eye out also, but he had a father's sense of his
two sons and wasn't worried. His wife would do
enough of that for both of them. So it was with their
parents' consent, their mother's reluctantly, that the boys
had taken the family boat down to the area of the crash
"just to look around."

Arriving at the scene, or what had been described to
them, they anchored the boat and put out the divers
buoy. A divers certification present from their parents,
it was a red buoy with a painted banner proclaiming
"Diver Below." The buoy was topped with a red flag
with a diagonal white bar from upper left to lower right,

a bar sinister in heraldic terms. Attached to it was a twenty-five foot nylon line at the other end of which was a two-pound plastic enclosed weight. They threw it into the water about ten feet from the boat from which another diver's flag was flying. Then they changed into their wet suits, fins, goggles, Buoyancy Compensation Devices (BCD) or dive vests with newly filled oxygen tanks, set their watches for twenty minutes, gave each other a thumb up and then fell backward off opposite sides of the boat.

In the water they joined up on the bottom and, with Sam leading the search, started swimming away from the boat toward the middle of the lake until they were about twenty feet away. Then they started a clockwise search staying three feet apart, Jack on the inside. The bottom was fairly clean with rocks every so often and an occasional school of baitfish. They were nearing the end of their first circuit when Jack saw Sam motioning him and starting to swim deeper. When Sam stopped, Jack saw that he was trying to pick up an object that appeared greyish-green unlike the nearly black, dark gray or amber brown stones they had seen. Jack gave him an okay with his forefinger and thumb making the "O", and put the item into a nylon mesh bag. Then they returned to their circular search. The next ten minutes revealed nothing further and they surfaced on the lake side of their boat.

Chapter 35

"Any luck?" a girl's voice said just as Sam was about to lift the bag over the side of the boat. They both turned in the water and saw a red ski boat sitting about twenty feet away with two boys and two girls in it, as well as a chocolate lab. On the stern, a yellow and red towing tube sat at a tilt.

"Nothing," Sam said.

"You need a spear gun to get fish," one of the guys said, nudging his friend indicating a "gotcha."

"Think that's illegal in Michigan," Sam said.

"Yeah, who's going to see?"

"That would be us," a female voice said from the other side of the ski boat. The surprised occupants of the ski boat whirled around in the direction of the voice to see that the sheriff's Boston Whaler had coasted to a stop fifteen feet behind them.

"Oh, hi," the boat's captain said.

"Do you recognize that flag?" Jeremy Briggs asked.

"Yeah, that's a diver's flag," the guy replied.

"What are the Michigan laws about that flag?" Rachel Whitaker asked. While this questioning was on going, Jeremy indicated that Sam and Jack could get out of the water.

The captain (driver) looked at his friends who all shrugged to indicate they were clueless. "I don't know. Just that people are diving."

"There are two diving flags. Red and Blue. Red means stay away two hundred feet. Blue means stay away one hundred feet. You are about twenty."

"But they're not diving!"

"They were when you stopped. You were here a couple of minutes before they surfaced."

"You were watching?"

"Yes, we saw you tubing and wanted to talk to you but before we could reach you, you came over here."

"Yes, we were tubing. So what?" the captain said indignantly.

"How many people were on the tube?" Rachel asked.

Nobody answered.

"I believe that a video would show three on the tube," Rachel said and watched the startled reaction of the four.

"You have a video?" one of the girls asked incredulously.

"No, I just said a video would show three on the tube. You have four in the boat. That means you didn't have spotter."

"I've got a rearview mirror," the captain said.

"Doesn't count. You **must** have a spotter."

Then Rachel went through a checklist to see if the boat was properly equipped including a life vest for each person and a throwable ring for someone in need among other things. Finally she asked to see a boating safety card for each person aboard. The captain was the only one who could produce his.

"Since you are the only one with a card, you are the only one who can pilot the boat so no tubing for you. It's early in the season and we don't want to spoil your weekend, so we are not going to give you a ticket. Let this serve as a warning. DNR officers and we will be on the lake all summer, so be certain that you are always in compliance with the regulations. We are making a note of the boat's registration. Next violation this summer will mean a ticket. Have a nice day."

After the ski boat had departed, Jeremy performed the same boating safety check for Sam and Jack's boat.

"So were you guys spear fishing?" Rachel asked after giving them a pass.

"No."

"Well, if you do, check out what you can fish for. This time of year, there's nothing very good except maybe white fish and they would be real deep now. Have a good day," Rachel said as they prepared to depart. "Enjoy your diving."

As the Boston Whaler pulled away, Jack said, "They didn't ask what we were doing."

"Of course not. We weren't doing anything illegal."

"Let's see it," Jack said, reaching for the net bag.

"It" was a carved head about six inches tall with a flat bottom.

"Do you think it's Indian?" Jack asked.

"If you mean Native American, not unless they made things out of resin," Sam said.

"You think it came out of the plane?"

"Could be. Don't think it's been in the water very long," Sam said as he turned it over in his hands. Then he looked at it closely and frowned.

"What's wrong?"

"It's cracked at the seam," Jack said. "Looks and feels like it was made in halves and then something put in for weight and it was glued together, but the seam either wasn't complete or has cracked."

"Well, maybe someone threw it away."

"Could be," Sam said looking at his watch. "Oops, got to go. Mom and Dad said they wanted to leave at four."

The boys stowed their gear and then headed for the cottage. When they got there, their mother yelled at them to hurry because their father wanted to get going. Jack grabbed their wet suits and took them to the house and hung them in their mud room/laundry room. Sam put their air tanks in the shed and locked it. Then both boys put the cover on the boat, raised it, and headed for the house with Sam stopping to turn off the power to the hoist and locking the switch cover. They quickly changed out of their bathing suits, dressed and hung the suits with their wet suits. Then, hastened by their father blowing the car's horn, they hurried out and got in the car. Quickly they were headed south on the East Path on their way to Fenton.

Their parents were talking about an old friend who had stopped in to visit, and soon they were on M-72 headed west toward M-65 where they would turn south toward Glennie.

"Did you have fun diving?" their mother asked, who had been visibly relieved when they had returned.

"Yes," the boys responded and proceeded to regale their parents with the story of the ski boat kids and the sheriff's summer interns.

"Did you find anything interesting?" their father asked as he stopped before turning left on M-65.

"Just some old resin bookend someone tossed in the lake," Sam responded, realizing they had left it in the boat.

Chapter 36

It was two weeks before the Pickens got back to the cottage. There had been some debate about the weather with rain predicted Friday afternoon and night and ending mid-morning Saturday.

"You know the weather up there is always wrong," Jack offered.

"Yeah, it could rain all weekend," his mother answered.

"Or not at all," Sam impinged pleadingly.

In the end they decided to go and they were amazed that t he weatherman was correct for once. Regardless, Sam had plans for the morning. He and Jack were both up early, breakfasted on bagels and cream cheese, and headed out. Sam went to the boat and got the net bag and Jack went to the garage, pulling the car out so they could get at the workbench. On the workbench was something that Sam needed – a vise. He had brought superglue with him, and his plan was to fix the crack in the head. He put superglue in the crack, wrapped the head in a rag towel so the vise's jaws wouldn't mar it, leaving the spot with the crack visible and stuck it between the jaws of the vise. With Jack holding it in place, Sam started closing the jaws. Once they started making contact with the head, he turned the handle carefully and watched as slowly the crack started closing. When it was closed, Sam gave it one more half turn and quit.

"How long do we wait?" Jack asked.

Sam was answering, "About ten minutes," when, in midsentence, there was a CRACK.

The two boys looked at each other and then Sam unwound the vise handle and Jack caught the towel-wrapped head and handed it to Sam. Setting it on the workbench, Sam started unwrapping the towel. When it was off, he looked at the head and could see a jagged crack running from the mid-top of the head down between the eyes, continuing the length of the nose, across the lips and chin and then disappearing. As he carefully picked up the head, it separated into two pieces – the right side of the face fell off and onto the workbench. Sam found himself looking at a plastic baggie filled with white powder the consistency of powdered sugar. They had been around drugs, although neither had ever used, but instinctively knew what the bag contained. They didn't even think but left the head on the workbench and went to get their father.

***

Midmorning, Nathanial burst through the door into the foyer to see the duty deputy holding two fingers up. Twelve seconds later, Nathanial opened the door to Interview Two. Rich Walker looked up from where he was bent over the head on the table and holding a camera. Standing back against the wall were two teenage boys wearing cargo shorts – one navy, the other camouflage – and tee shirts claiming support for the Detroit Tigers, both white. Both were wearing flip-flops. Standing next to the tallest boy was their father, probably in his mid-forties, sandy brown hair flecked with gray, a day's worth of stubble on his face. He was wearing a Detroit Lions tee shirt that had seen better days, jeans of the same description, and fairly new brown boat shoes, no socks. Of the three, he was the only one using a belt to hold up his pants, the beginning of middle age spread starting to show.

"Hello," Nathanial said stepping to the father. "Sheriff Nathanial Jefferson. You must be Derrick Pickens. Bet they called you 'Slim' as a kid."

Derrick Pickens grinned ear to ear as he shook Nathanial's hand. "Still do – at least sometimes although lately it's been 'Hard Pickens'."

Nathanial turned to the boys. "Which of you is Sam?" and shook his hand when Sam said, "That's me." Then he turned to Jack and said, "That leaves you to be Jack.

"Okay, while my tech guy does his job, let's go next door and talk," and headed for the door.

"All set up in there, Sheriff."

In Interview One, the Pickens men took seats and Nathanial went and got three coffees – one black (his), one with cream (Derrick's) and the other with two sugars "not sweetener" (Jack) – and one non-diet pop (Sam). Back in Interview One, everyone took a sip or two of his drink, and then Nathanial started the tape, provided names and date, and then said, "Tell me about your find, Sam."

Sam did with Jack chiming in, as he felt it was needed. "When we realized that we had a potential package of heroin, we got dad."

"Fortunately, I had just gotten up and was having a cup of coffee on the front porch when they found me. Don't think Nikki was too thrilled when they woke her up looking for me. I went to the garage while they filled me in. Seeing the head and the bag, I just put it in a box from the recycling pile and we came here. I guess I should have called and asked what to do, but that seemed natural."

"No problem. Didn't make a difference because it wasn't at the scene of discovery," Nathanial said. "You think it was at the crash site?" he asked Sam.

"Well, that's where we went, but I don't know. Nobody seemed to know exactly where the crash site was."

"The head wasn't buried?"

"Nope. Sitting there plain as day."

At this point the door opened, and Rich Walker came in. "Heroin," he said. "Uncut." Both boys whistled at this point knowing how much it was probably worth.

After explaining that this was potentially part of an ongoing investigation (without mentioning any particulars) and that he wanted them to keep it to themselves, the Pickens men went back to the lake.

"You think this is related to Pierre LeBeuf?" Walker asked.

"The head is very similar to the one Zeb found. Might be, might not be. Things for you to investigate. I want the answers first thing Monday morning."

Chapter 37

Monday afternoon Clemson Mathers found himself looking at three heads sitting on his desk on top of a towel to protect the desk's finish or possibly the heads themselves.

"So the one in the middle is obviously different," Nathanial was explaining. "That's the authentic one – at least we suppose it is authentic, we have been unable to get anyone to authenticate it from afar. It is the one that Zebulah Pyke pulled from the bottom of Hibbard Pond. It was directly under the plane.

"The one on the left is the one found by the Pickens boy and it contained a kilo of extremely high quality heroin. The one on the right we got from 'Antiquities and Not'. There is no manufacturer ID, but they got it from Fitzgerald Imports which, according to the name, deals in antiquities and remembrances."

He placed a clear plastic file containing a shipping invoice on the desk in front of Clemson Mathers. Clemson Mathers picked up each of the heads in the order that Nathanial had described them, removing the broken piece of the one that Sam Pickens had discovered.

"This one is heavy like the real one," Mathers said hefting the "Antiquities and Not" one in his hand.

"Filled with sand," Nathanial said, "Mexican sand if I trust my techs, and I know I can. It was put in through a hole in the bottom, which was then plugged. Walker and Roberts drilled another hole in it to get at the sand and then plugged it with cork."

Clemson Mathers looked at the bottom to verify this.

"The one that Sam Pickens found has no such plug in the bottom. Either this was an oversight which I doubt, or enabled someone to identify the ones containing the happy dust."

"Happy dust?" queried Clemson Mathers.

"Yeah, we watched *Porgy and Bess* this weekend," Nathanial said. "It's the term used for heroin."

"Really? Ira and George Gershwin wrote a musical about heroin?"

"Yeah. Pretty powerful story too."

Clemson Mathers put the last head down and leaned back in his chair.

"And you want me to do what?"

"Give me a search warrant for the Fitzgerald house and property."

Clemson Mathers looked at Nathanial with disbelief.

"You've got to be kidding?"

Nathanial shook his head to indicate he wasn't.

"Then you did more than watch a movie about happy dust, you've been sniffing some."

Nathanial sat back in his chair and sighed. He'd known it was a long shot. but he had nothing else.

"Face it, Nathanial," Clemson Mathers said. "You are not going to find evidence to tie Fitzgerald to anything. He's too smart."

"He's made a mistake, though," Nathanial said. "Maybe two," indicating the two heads found in the lake.

"Yes, that's possible, but it is all extremely circumstantial. We don't even know how close to the wreck the Pickens boy found the second head. It's a no win situation."

Nathanial sagged back in his seat as though defeated. Then he sat upright, stood and started packing up the heads. "No, it's not," he said.

***

"May I speak with Sergeant Kimbria Shaw?"

"Who is calling?"

"This is Deputy Sheriff Arthur Misdorf of the Alcona County Michigan Sheriff's Department."

"Oui, just a moment and I will transfer you."

There was a brief pause.

" 'Ello."

"Is this Sergeant Shaw?"

"Lieutenant-Detective Shaw speaking."

"Oh, congratulations. This is Deputy Arthur Misdorf."

"Ah, yes. How are you? I 'eard you have been shot."

"Yes, but I am fine."

"That eez good. I was worried."

Misdorf laughed. "You weren't the only one."

"What can I do for you, Deputy?"

"We have come across some information that may be of interest to you or someone in your department."

"What kind of evidence?"

"Well, two different kinds, but related. One is a head, Mayan or Aztec relic, that may have been illegally imported, and the other is a kilo of heroin."

"And these were found where?"

"On the bottom of Hibbard Pond."

" 'ibbard Pond?"

"Yes, a big lake in our county."

"And so, why would we be interested?"

"We believe that they were originally imported into Canada by Fitzgerald Imports."

There was silence for a minute.

"Deputy, we are very interested."

"I thought you might be."

"How did you acquire them?"

Misdorf related the stories.

"Interested, but I am afraid that is as much as we can be. The manner in which they were found is circumstantial. You cannot tie them to Edmund Fitzgerald or Fitzgerald Imports."

"True but..."

"Yes, there is a 'but.' There has been a steady supply of drugs reaching our streets recently, and we have been at a loss as to how to proceed. We have people undercover but nothing has surfaced. Now you have given us a place to look."

"How are you so aware of this? I thought you were sort of public relations."

She laughed.

"I was there on temporary assignment following a pregnancy. I had put in for a transfer and when I got my promotion recently, the transfer came with it. Thanks for the tips. If you get anything further, please let me know."

The next morning Misdorf knocked on Nathanial's door and entered without waiting for an answer. Nathanial looked up from a stack of papers.

"We've got a very possible identification of the bridge boy. I just had a call from Officer Dinsworth of the Lansing Police Department. He's on limited duty like me and was given the task of looking at their past cases. He went looking and recovered an envelope from storage – it was sandwiched between boxes and was easily overlooked. In it was a file containing only basic information about a missing eight-year-old boy named Nathan Biggins. He disappeared April 16, 1958. He was living with his mother, recently divorced, and her boyfriend. The latter was apparently physically abusive to the boy, although that wasn't proven. The boy had recently had a broken left arm and had run away two days after the cast was removed. The file contained x-rays of his arm when it was broken and when the cast was removed. The police got them to be used for possible identification in a case like this. The mother and boyfriend split up after Nathan ran away and couldn't be found. The father went to Alabama, remarried. No kids. Nathan had no siblings. The father had a sister, but nobody knows anything about her. Both parents and the boyfriend are dead. I had Dinsworth send the x-rays to Blodgett. We'll get confirmation in a day or so."

"That's good," Nathanial said. "Congratulations. Fine job. Now to find out how he got here. Prepare a poster and when it is confirmed, get copies out. I think there's a Hibbard Pond Sportsman meeting Wednesday. If we know by then, get some to Ed Stockwell to spread around."

"Will do, Sheriff."

Chapter 38

"I am not an authority on covered bridges. Hell, I'm not an authority on anything." There was a chuckle from the audience. "Least of all women," he said bowing to the few women who sat at the tables in front of him, "having been married four times." This drew a roar from the men at the tables.

The speaker was a small man of about five foot six, solidly built although sagging with his age as shown by the unkempt shock of white hair that crowned his head. He had beady blue eyes set above a medium-sized craggy nose under which was a dour mouth when it wasn't open which was most of the time because he loved to talk, even to himself. He was wearing a brown plaid short-sleeved shirt that seemed hastily tucked into a pair of green corduroy pants showing the wear and stains of years and held up by an equally worn and stained brown belt. His name was Maurice Logan, the self-proclaimed unofficial historian of Hibbard Pond, having lived here all his life except for four years during the Korean War when he was in the Navy serving off the coast of Korea.

"I am not a historian. If youse wants one, go see George Haversack over to the library at the Corners. But, I digress. I've been asked here to talk about the West Branch Bridge. I guess that's because of the body – it was really a skeleton – found beneath it recently. So

I thought I should start with some information about covered bridges in general. Did youse know that according to one website – I went to see George to do this 'cause I don't understand computers – there are close to a hundred – one-zero-zero – covered bridges in Michigan?"

An audible gasp escaped from the audience.

"I'm with youse. I didn't believe it but the majority of them are not what youse would call a covered bridge. They are small bridges, some footbridges and some for golf carts, built more for show."

At this point he reached into a back pocket and pulled out a couple of pieces of paper folded into a rectangle small enough to fit in the pocket.

"Forgive me if I cheat and use notes," he said as he unfolded the papers and then stared at them. "Oops, always forget," pulling a pair of granny glasses out of his left shirt pocket and putting them on. "Nows I want to give credit where credit is due. This information was put up on the Web by," peering at his notes, "Rickie Longfellow on a website about 'Ohio's Vanishing Covered Bridges'." There were a few boos from the audience indicating the die-hard University of Michigan faithful dislike of the team from that state to the south. "He says the first covered bridge can be traced back to Babylon in the eighth century B.C. Now that surprised me. A covered bridge in Babylon, New York, that long ago."

A groan came from his audience.

"I'm not being paid much to do this, you know," Maurice said peering over his glasses.

"I'll drink to that," Jerry Hatchett said, receiving an elbow in the ribs from Dugal McBruce that elicited an 'oomph" from Jerry.

"Anyways, according to Mr. Longfellow, the first covered bridge in these here United States of America was the Waterford Bridge in Connecticut built in 1804. It spanned the Hudson River, lasting one hundred five – one-zero-five – years. Now this surprised me cause he says that the next two was built in Oregon in the early eighteen hundred fifties – one-eight-five-zero," and the crowd recited the numbers with him. He looked up from his papers and glared at them. "Most bridges were built to replace ferries that charged people to be floated across bodies of water. People thought they should be free and so the bridges were built. Land sakes, that didn't help because tolls were charged until the bridge was paid for. Now that never happened with our bridge, but I'll get to that. Now here's a statement made by Mr. Longfellow – least I judge that Rickie is a man's name – most covered bridges were built between eighteen hundred twenty five," one-eight-two-five came from the audience and drew another glare from Maurice, "and eighteen hundred seventy five." One-eight-seven-five the audience verbalized, this time directed by the speaker. "See, now that means that between eighteen hundred twenty five," and he waved them to shut up as they started one-eight, "and eighteen hundred fifty no bridges were built because the next two was built in the early... " eighteen hundred fifties the audience roared, and Maurice glared.

"Why was they covered? Two reasons. Most people say to provide cover for travelers when it was raining or snowing and that makes sense, but also to protect the trusses of the bridge from the weather to preserve them. But because of time and weather, many are disappearing. At one time there were twelve hundred – one-two..." and when the audience started to echo he quit.

"Now to the West Branch Bridge. In the late nineteenth century – that's the one where the years start one-eight," and the audience laughed, "logging of this area started and that's when the dam was built to raise the water level of the lake so that the logs could be floated down the West Branch to the dam. And be damned if I know where they went from there. So with the logs being there and all, a group of Amish who were helping with the logging, and I think eventually settled here, decided to build the bridge. It took them eight months to build the bridge because they also had to work on logging. They got the logs for free, and their work was free, so there weren't no tolls. It was a sturdy bridge and lasted into the late nineteen hundred forties," waving off the audience's echo. "At that time it was disassembled with parts numbered, the concrete pillars put in on either side, metal girders put down for support and the bridge reassembled with parts that needed replacing replaced."

At this point, Maurice paused, folded the papers and put them back in his pocket. He turned around and picked up a bottle of water from the table where the Hibbard Pond Sportsman officers sat, unscrewed the top, and drank half the bottle.

"Man, that's good," he said. "Wish it were stronger."

"I can help with that," Jerry Hatchett said and several people chimed in "hear, hear."

And without further ado, Maurice took a seat carrying the half-full bottle of water with him.

"Are there any questions?" Ed Stockwell, Hibbard Pond Sportsman president, asked.

"How can there be?" Maurice said. "I tells it all."

Jerry Hatchett leaned over to Dugal, "Watch this," and he raised his hand.

"Yes, Jerry?" Ed said, inwardly cringing at what Jerry might ask.

"Why do some bridges have windows and some don't?"

"Cause that was how they were built," Maurice spouted. "T'was a matter of taste."

"Funny," Jerry mused. "I thought it was so you could fish off the bridge."

There was a round of laugher and a "hear, hear" from across the room.

"Any other questions?" Ed asked. There were none. "Well, before we break for coffee and a special order of pecan chocolate chip cookies from Gert, let me introduce our new secretary. As you know, Mabel Reese is seriously ill, although the prognosis is good. So without being asked, one of our new members volunteered: Jane Eyre Polli."

There were shouts of "Eyre Spy" and "hear, hear" and an enthusiastic round of applause. Jane Eyre Polli stood up, attempted a slight curtsy, and the rush for the cookies was on. However, the banging of the gavel by Ed Stockwell brought the stampede to a quick halt.

"One more thing," Ed Stockwell said holding up a stack of paper. "The body they found has been identified."

The crowd was reverently silent and many retook their seats.

"His name was Nathan Biggins. He was from the Lansing area and disappeared April 17, 1958. He had run away from home, that being his mother and her boyfriend, both now deceased. There were no other kids in the family. Police report at the time said that the boy-friend was physically abusive to the boy and was probably the reason for him running away. The mother and her boyfriend split shortly afterward. The father – they were divorced – went south, and I mean that literally because he moved to Alabama, marrying but not father-ing any more kids. He's dead also, as is his second wife. So what the sheriff has is a really cold case and he's ask-ing for help. These sheets are pictures and a description of Nathan Biggins. Take a couple, ask around, and see if anyone knows anything about the boy."

It was a somber crew that filed by the table picking up a copy of the poster and going to partake in the re-freshments.

Chapter 39

Nathanial looked into the interview room through the one-way glass in the door. The three Boswick brothers, dressed in orange Alpena County Jail jumpsuits, sat at a steel table, handcuffed with the cuffs fastened to eyebolts in the table. Burke (the oldest) was in the middle, Burl (the youngest) was to his left, and Burt (older than Burl by thirty minutes) to his right. It was difficult to believe that they were not triplets. Burl and Burt were fraternal twins, but Burke was older by two or three years. All were big, both in height of six feet four or five and weight of two hundred eighty to three hundred pounds. They looked like NFL linemen except maybe for the shaggy black hair and beards. An apt description of them was "mountain men." They were known – or at least reputed – to have served as bodyguards for Edmund Fitzgerald when he arrived and left in his plane. Rumors were they were armed during these times, but that had never been confirmed. All three sat with their heads down looking at their hands. Burke was drumming the fingers of his right hand, his left impassive. Burt had his hands folded together and Burl's were flat on the desk. They got their size from their mother, dead for many years, not their father who was small.

Nathanial was dressed in worn blue jeans, a white guide shirt, cross trainers (with socks) and a L.A. Dodgers baseball cap. He had driven his wife's sedan and parked in the visitors lot and came in through the jail's backdoor. Those had been his instructions when Alpena County Sheriff Jim Whittaker had called him approximately an hour before. "The Boswick boys want to meet with you in an unofficial official capacity."

"What do you mean 'unofficial official'?"

"They want to talk to you officially but in an unofficial manner – that's how Burke said it. You are to dress in civvies and not drive an official vehicle. Park in the visitors' lot and come in through the back door. Their lawyer will not be present."

"I'll be there in about an hour."

"I'll have a deputy waiting at the back door."

Nathanial opened the interview room door and stepped inside. All three brothers looked up and brought their hands flat on the table although Burl didn't move other than raise his head. There was a tape recorder sitting in the middle of the table. Nathanial sat down and turned it on.

He gave his name, date and time. "Also here are Burke Boswick, Burt Boswick, and Burl Boswick. I am here at their request without the presence of their lawyer. Is that correct, Burke?"

"Yes," Burke answered.

"Is that correct, Burl?"

Burl shrugged.

"Please answer verbally."

"Yes, I guess."

"Is that correct, Burt?"

"Well, duh. You're here and he ain't."

"Answer yes or no."

"Yes."

"Now that that's clear, what do you want?" Nathanial said, sitting back to listen.

Burke looked at each of his brothers who nodded in turn.

"We want to make a deal."

"I can't make deals. That's up to Clemson Mathers."

"Who's he?" Burt asked.

"He's the county prosecutor."

"I thought that was Dorothy Meeks."

"Dorthea Meeks is the Alpena County Prosecutor," Nathanial corrected him.

"Well, ain't we in Alpena County?"

"Yes, Burt," Burke said impatient with his brother's ignorance. "But the charges are from Alcona County. We're only here for our protection."

"Ha," Burt laughed. "Protection from what?"

"From my deputies," Nathanial said. "Just in case they didn't like the fact that you tried to kill one of them."

"Should...," Burt started but Burke snarled, "Shut up!" and tried to get at him but was restricted by the handcuffs. Burt didn't move and continued to sit there, hands flat on the table.

"Okay, boys," Nathanial cajoled, "let's get to this deal you want. As I said, I can't make a deal but can talk to Clemson Mathers about it."

"We want reduced sentences," Burke said.

"That was to be assumed. What are you offering?"

"The person who wanted us to derail the investigation by shooting that deputy." This from Burl.

"That isn't what he said," Burke said. "You were told to 'sideline' him."

"Well, we did," Burt snarled.

Burke shook his head sadly.

"Yes, you certainly did. But if you idiots had done what you should have – could have – done without such force, then we wouldn't be in this jam."

Nathanial sat patiently during this exchange, internally happy that it looked like the case could finally break. Another instance of dumb luck.

"Anything else?" he asked.

Burke looked at his two brothers. "Yes, we want our pappy's name cleared."

"How can I do that?" Nathanial responded.

"We'll tell you who shot that Frenchman," Burke said. "It weren't Pappy."

"Couldn't have been," Burt said.

"Pappy couldn't hurt a fly," Burl added.

"Were you there?" Nathanial asked trying not to show his excited state.

"No, course not." Burke said.

"Well, then how do you know? Did your pappy tell you?"

"He t'weren't there either," Burt said. "He told us so."

"When?"

"Later, two or three days later."

"Well, how did you know your pappy didn't shot LeBeuf?" Nathanial waited.

"He weren't the one who called and told me to deep-six the body," Burke said.

He? Nathanial thought. *Does he mean Edmund Fitzgerald? By what he said, the caller still could have been a woman. The only woman involved is Edna Fitzgerald.*

"Who?" Nathanial asked.

"We're not saying until we get the deal," Burke said.

"In writing, all nice and pretty," Burl said his right hand moving at least indicating a signature being made.

"So you'll tell me who called you to deep-six the body?" asked Nathanial.

"Yeah," Burt said. "And it wasn't Pappy neither."

"But is that the same person who shot LeBeuf?"

"Had to be, didn't it," Burl said. "Else why would he call?"

"To protect someone. Like your pappy."

"NO!" the three shouted, their six hands slapping the table simultaneously and causing Nathanial to jump. The door opened and the deputy stepped into the room, his hand on his holstered revolver.

"Everything all right?" he asked.

"Everything's fine, deputy," Nathanial said. "The boys were just being a little emphatic."

The door closed.

"If he didn't kill the Frenchman, he has to know who did, don't he?" Burke stated.

"Possibly," Nathanial said. "Let me tell you what I think. Clemson Mathers will most probably deal on reduced sentences for revealing who told you to 'sideline' Deputy Misdorf. Those sentences are the ones associated with that crime. He will probably agree to reduced sentences on the deep-sixing of the body if he knows who told you to do it. He will make a better deal on that if this person is the killer or can identify the killer."

"But we don't tell you who it is until we get the deals in writing," Burke said.

"Understood," Nathanial said. "Anything else?"

The three brothers looked at each other, and then at Nathanial, and shook their heads.

Nathanial turned off the cassette recorder, removed the cassette and stood, holding the tape where they could see it.

"I'll be back with an answer," he said and turned toward the door.

"When?" Burl snarled as Nathanial's hand grabbed the knob.

"When I have an answer," Nathanial said opening the door and disappearing as the door closed behind him.

Chapter 40

When Nathanial returned to the Alpena jail the next day, it was as though the brothers hadn't moved – all three were sitting with palms flat on the table. A tape recorder sat in front of them. The brothers looked up as Nathanial entered the room, bearing a folder filled with papers that could or could not be signed. All depended on the mood of the brothers.

After starting the recorder and introducing himself, he said, "In the room with me are the three Boswick brothers Burke, Burt and Burl. I will ask them to introduce themselves and state that they are here of their own free will without an attorney present."

He nodded at Burke who, looking straight at Nathanial, answered, "Burke Boswick and yes, I am here without an attorney."

Nathanial sat staring at him. "Of my own free will," Burke concluded.

Nathanial looked at Burt, who shrugged and said, "Burt Boswick here without an attorney cause he was no damned good."

"That may be," Nathanial said, "but you need to say you're here willingly."

"Yes, willingly," Burt snarled and Nathanial let it go.

He looked at Burl, who continued to look at his hands.

"Burl?" Nathanial said.

Burl looked up. "What?" he snarled, spittle spewing halfway to Nathanial.

"You need to state you are here of your own free will."

"I ain't," snapped Burl. "I don't want to be here at all."

Nathanial stood up and stepped to the door. Opening it, he said, "Deputy, would you please take Burl back to his cell."

As the deputy stepped into the room, Burl looked startled. "I don't want to go back to my cell. I meant I wasn't in jail because of my own free will. I don't want to be in jail. But I want to make a deal without an attorney. That's why in the hell I'm in here now."

The deputy looked at Nathanial who nodded, and the deputy backed out of the room and closed the door as Nathanial resumed his seat. He opened the folder in front of him. "Before I get to the agreements that Clemson Mathers has proposed, he and I have a question."

"How's he going to hear it?" Burl snarled.

"On the tape," Nathanial said. "The same way he heard you say you wanted to bargain."

Burl looked at the recorder. "I forgot," he said.

"Not a problem. Everyone else okay?"

Burke and Burt nodded.

"Please give an audible answer."

"Yes," they both said.

"Fine. Here's the question: 'Why are you doing this without your lawyer?' "

"'Cause he wanted us to lie," Burke said.

"Yeah," snapped Burt. "He wanted us to cop a plea."

"No, not a plea," Burke said. "He wanted us to admit to a murder."

"What murder?" Nathanial said a bit perplexed.

"That fuckin' Frenchie," Burl snarled. "He wanted us to say we killed the Frenchie and then dumped his body."

"He was your lawyer," Nathanial said aghast. "Why would he want you to admit to a crime for which you weren't charged?"

"He weren't our lawyer," Burl snapped. "He was..."

"Shut up," commanded Burke. "You say who and we can't deal."

Burl shut up and stared at his hands.

Burke sighed. "We didn't hire him. He was hired for us. He told us that if we said we had killed the Frenchie, we wouldn't get the chair."

"That's true," Nathanial said. "The State of Michigan has never executed anyone."

"That's not true," Burl snapped, slapping his hands loudly on the table. "Anthony Chebatoris was hanged in 1938."

Simultaneously Nathanial stood holding a hand up, palm toward the door as it opened and the deputy stepped into the room, hand on his holstered pistol. "Everything's fine, deputy. Burl was just making a point."

The deputy didn't move until Burl relaxed, head down, hands flat on the table. Nathanial nodded at the deputy who backed out and closed the door, and Nathanial resumed his seat.

"That guy's fast," Burt said. "Glad that gun wasn't out."

"Me too," Nathanial said. "Burl, you are correct. Anthony Chebatoris was hung in 1938. He killed someone while robbing a bank in Midland. But he was in the Federal Correctional Institution near Milan. It was a federal execution. The state was exempt."

"You mean we can't get the chair because we shot the deputy?" Burt answered.

"Not the chair, not the noose, not the drugs."

All three brothers slapped their hands on the table simultaneously shouting, "That sonofabitch Fitzgerald tried to set us up." And realizing what they had said, immediately shut up and looked apprehensively toward the door, but Nathanial, an obvious smirk on his face, had his hand up and the door never opened. Inwardly Nathanial breathed a sigh of relief. He had a name but he needed more. Unless something really went awry in the negotiations for terms, they would be able to close the case.

Looking crestfallen, Burke asked, "Do we still get to deal?"

"Of course," Nathanial said knowing he needed as much information as he could get to secure a conviction and wishing there was a death penalty in Michigan.

Chapter 41

"Now let's begin with the worst of your crimes. Your attack on Deputy Arthur Misdorf falls under Section 91 of the Michigan Penal Code: Attempt to murder."

Burl was the one who slapped his hands this time. "We didn't intend to kill him, we only meant to sideline him."

"When you assault someone with a gun, and by this I mean simply that you shot the person, the law assumes that you meant to kill that person."

"But we didn't," Burt said. "We was told to sideline him, wasn't we, Burl?" continued Burt, leaning forward to look at his brother.

"Sidetrack," Burl said. "Sidetrack, not sideline."

"Sidetrack, sideline. What's the difference?" Burt scoffed.

"Again," Nathanial slid in, "that's not the point. The point is you attacked him with a gun. You shot him three..."

"Should have been four..."

"Shuddup!" Burke yelled, simultaneously slapping his hands on the table. "Shuddup or we'll get a lawyer and then there'll be no deal."

Burt glared at him but shut up.

"Okay," Burke said. "What's the law?"

Nathanial read, "Attempt to murder by poisoning, etc.—Any person who shall attempt to commit the crime of murder by poisoning, drowning, or strangling another person, or by any means not constituting the crime of assault with intent to murder, shall be guilty of a felony, punishable by imprisonment in the state prison for life or any term of years."

"Okay. That's Burt. He did the shooting," Burl said with Burt glaring at him. "What about me?"

"No difference. You were there, driving the truck. It's the same thing."

"WHAT?" Burl's hands slapped the table. "I didn't shoot."

"That doesn't matter under the law."

"You mean that Burke is guilty also?"

"Yes, by not turning you in and by disposing of the gun, he is a party to the crime."

"A party?"

"He abetted or helped, although not as much."

Burl was quiet, hands flat on the table, almost contemplative.

"So what does Clemson Mathers want on this one?" questioned Burke.

"Life for Burl and Burt, 40 years for you."

"That much?"

"You mean for you?"

"No, for my brothers."

"Well, they tried to kill a law official. The courts do not take kindly to that," explained Nathanial.

"And what about the person who gave the order?"

"Life – for that person there will be no bargaining."

"And if we give him..." Burke responded. Nathanial looked at him quizzically, "... or her up?"

"Twenty years."

"For all of us?"

"Yes."

"But life ... for whomever?"

"Yes, no bargaining."

"Where do I sign?"

Nathanial slid a paper across to Burke who picked up the pen and signed the form.

"Give me mine," Burl snarled and Burt echoed. Nathanial complied and both signed and returned the papers. Nathanial looked at the signatures and then said, "As indicated on the form, this is contingent upon..."

"Contin-what?" Burl asked.

"It is only valid if you reveal who gave the order."

Burl sat there drumming the table with the fingers of his left hand, then he muttered something.

"I didn't catch that," Nathanial said.

"Fitzgerald," Burl snarled.

"Which Fitzgerald?"

"Mr."

"You mean Edmund?"

"Yeah, the one who flew in on that sea plane all la-di-da."

"He wasn't here, was he?" Nathanial asked.

"I don't know. I just answered the phone."

"Exactly what did he say?"

"He wanted us to sidetrack that sheriff's deputy Misdorf."

"That's it?"

"Yeah!"

" 'I want you to sidetrack that sheriff's deputy Misdorf.' And he hung up?"

"Yeah, I told you."

"No, 'Hello, is Burke there?' "

Burl looked at him, and closed his eyes. His face screwed up as though he was having trouble thinking.

"He said there is a problem and that Deputy Misdorf needed to be sidetracked. Oh, yeah, I asked what sidetracked meant and he said, 'put somewhere he cannot bother me.' I asked when?" Burl laughed. "I remember now, he said something funny."

"Funny?"

"Yeah, he said, 'Today, not yesterday, not tomorrow.' Then he told me where and when we could find him."

Nathanial smiled. That saying, "Today, not yesterday, not tomorrow' was one which had originally tied Rolli Polli to Edna Fitzgerald. Both had used it and had gotten it from a nun in their orphanage. She had gotten it when, as a novice, her mother superior had told her she didn't have what it took to be a nun and would never have it "Not today, not yesterday, and not tomorrow."

"Are you certain that is all?"

Burl's face screwed up again, his eyes shut. Then they popped open. "Yep. Definitely," and his hands slapped the table.

"The phone he used, a landline?"

"Nah, we don't have one, just cells. We had one he gave us so that he could contact us."

"Had?"

"What?"

"You said, 'had one he gave us.' You don't have it any more?"

"No, we got rid of it on the way to the Soo."

"Yeah, didn't get to see the locks either," Burt said. "That pissed me off."

Burke just looked at the table and shook his head.

Nathanial looked at his notes. He knew they didn't have a landline but had hoped they still had the phone used to make contact with the perp.

"I think that does it for that charge, at least for now."

"What do you mean 'at least for now'?" Burke asked, suddenly interested.

"Clemson Mathers may need more details."

"Oh. But the deal still stands?"

"Yes, of course."

Chapter 42

"Now to the charge about the dumping the body," Nathanial said. "That falls under Section 160 of the legal code that covers the disinterment, mutilation, defacement, or carrying away of a human body. I am going to just state the portions that apply: 'A person, not being lawfully authorized so to do, who shall willfully convey away a human body, or who shall knowingly aid in such conveying away, and every person accessory thereto, either before or after the fact, shall be guilty of a felony, punishable by imprisonment for not more than 10 years, or by fine of not more than $5,000.00.' "

"$5,000?" Burt snarled. "We just got $1,000. Where are we going to get another $4,000?"

"We don't need $4,000," Burke said. "We'll need $14,000."

"What, how you figure?"

"There are three of us, each of us is guilty of that."

"Oh," Burt said. "Can we get years instead?"

"That's possible," Nathanial said. "Clemson wants the $5,000 for each of you because of the cost in getting the body out. If you give up the name of the person who called you and if that person is the murderer, he'll give you two years each or $1,000 each."

"So one of us could get out free?"

"No," Burke said shaking his head. "There's still the attempted murder of the deputy."

"Oh, yeah," Burt said.

"Duh," Burl said, and Burt tried to stand and get at his brother but couldn't because of the cuffs. The racket caused the deputy to open the door, and Burt quickly sat down and glared at his brother past Burke.

"This is why I am in the middle," Burke said.

"Good thinking," Nathanial agreed. "Now there is one other charge that we are going to include with this deal."

"What charge, there weren't any more bodies!" Burl said.

"Well, there is a burnt truck body."

"What about it?"

"It falls under Section 75, Fourth Degree Arson."

"Arson?" Burt asked. "What's that?"

"Burning," Burke said. "We burnt the truck!"

"So, it was ours, wasn't it?"

"Yes," Nathanial agreed. "And if you had burnt it on your own property, there would probably just be the charge of not having a burn permit..."

"We need a permit to burn something?" Burl snarled.

"Outside where it could spread, yes," Nathanial explained. "However, you burnt the truck on someone else's property and Clemson says that makes it arson."

"What's the penalty?" Burke wanted to know.

"Five years each," Nathanial said.

"What, five years!"

"Yes, but we are putting it with the charge of getting rid of the body and if you give up the person who called you, provided he did the killing, Clemson will drop those charges."

"Where do I sign?" Burke said and Nathanial slid a paper across to him.

"Me too," Burl and Burt agreed.

The agreements were signed, collected and put into the folder.

"Who called?"

Burt and Burl looked at Burke, who once again sat looking at the table or his hands.

"Burke," Burl said. "You answered the phone."

"Yeah," Burt said. "It was you. You never said. Just told us what to do."

Burke sat still for a minute longer, then raised his head and looked straight into Nathanial's eyes. "You already know," he said drawing out each word as though talking was difficult.

"No, I don't," Nathanial answered.

"It's the same guy."

"You mean, Edmund Fitzgerald?"

"Yes. There's only three people who call that phone. Him, his mother, and Pappy. 'Cept Pappy ain't calling no more." Tears welled up in his eyes as they did in his brothers' eyes.

"Mrs. Fitzgerald called you?"

"Only when she needed help and Pappy and her son t'weren't around."

"So that night, Edmund Fitzgerald called and asked you to do what?"

"Deep-six the body."

"That's it?"

"No, he said there had been a shooting and he needed a body deep-sixed. I asked how and he says to get a shelter from the Loon Creek Inn. We were to use his pontoon. It had been pulled for the winter, so we had to go over and get it in the water."

"How did you do that?"

"It was on a trailer in a barn. He didn't want any noise so we couldn't use the tractor. We had to pull it in and out."

"That was a bitch," Burl said.

"Truly was," Burt agreed. "Especially out."

"You used your truck to get the shelter?"

"Yep. Same one that was burned. Hated to do that. Worked hard making it look good."

"Must have been difficult getting the shelter on the pontoon."

"Nope. We used some two-bys he had to make a ramp and just slid it over the rail."

"It wasn't that heavy," Burt said.

"It was empty," Burl put in.

"So who got the shelter?" Nathanial asked, waiting patiently to get the information he sorely wanted.

"We did," Burl said. "Burt and me. Burke got the body."

Nathanial looked at Burke.

"You got the body?"

"Yep. It was in a cottage, wrapped in a tarp. I just had to pick it up and carry it to the pontoon."

"Anybody in the cottage?"

"Just him."

"Him?"

"The guy in the tarp."

"Did you know who it was?"

"Nope, just that he had crossed Fitzgerald and he'd shot him."

"Fitzgerald shot him?"

"Yep, at least that's what he said."

This was what Nathanial had been dying to hear.

"What did he say?"

Burke closed his eyes and tilted back his head. "I knew you were going to ask and I wanted to get it right, so I've been thinking. He said, 'I need you to deep-six a rat I caught who took a couple of k's of mine.' "

He looked at Nathanial. "Then he told me about the crate, where the pontoon was, where there were hammers, nails, wood. Everything we needed."

"What about the concrete blocks?"

"They was in the shed. Stack of them. We just took what we needed. He said to use eight."

"How about the tree?"

"I cut that with a hand saw while I was beached waiting on those two to get the crate."

"What did you do with things when you were done with them?"

"What things?"

"Hammer, nails."

"Oh, back in the shed where we got them. Took the ramp apart, put the wood in the shed, straightened out the nails and put them with the others. Heck, they were still good and nails are expensive."

"What about the tarp?"

"Folded it and put it back in the shed."

"Did you clean it first?"

"Why, it just had a body in it?"

"Blood from that body."

Burke looked at him. "Shit, made a mistake," and shook his head.

Made more than one, Nathanial thought.

"Now for way of clarification, when exactly did this happen?'

"November 15, two years ago," Burl said. "I remember 'cause we each got a deer. Best opening day ever."

And that made Rolli Polli's confession null and void, once they checked with Rolli's doctor. Jane Eyre would be happy. And now he had everything. Well, not everything. He still needed Fitzgerald in person.

He gathered the papers and put them in the file folder.

"When do we know?" Burke asked.

"Know what?"

"If the deal's set."

"I'll talk to Clemson Mathers and we'll let you know." Nathanial turned off the tape recorder, ejected the tape and put it in his pocket.

"Until we get Fitzgerald, you lock those mouths up tight. Not another word. Nada. Zip 'em. Fermer vos bouches. He's in Canada and if he thinks things are blown, he won't come back. Definitely don't say anything to Mandel."

Burke smiled sardonically.

"What if we tell Mandel we'll do it?" asked Burke.

Nathanial smiled in return. "I like that."

Chapter 43

The Harrisville Municipal Marina isn't big, having only ninety-eight slips' forty-nine seasonal and forty-nine transient. But at five o'clock on a summer's morning, it is a happening place as boat captains get ready to take charter groups out trying to catch the big fish that Lake Huron has: steelhead or brown trout, Chinook salmon or a smaller pink salmon. That was exactly what Leonard Hilbreth was doing that morning when he noticed a pair of shiny black boots on the dock next to his boat "The Golly Gee." He looked up to see the smiling face of Nathanial Jefferson underneath his Smokey Bear hat.

"Morning, Nathanial," Leonard said, "or should I say 'Sheriff Jefferson' because I doubt at this time of day it is a social call."

"Either will do, Leonard, but you are correct. It is not a social call. I know you are busy getting ready for your morning charter – no, wait; this is an all-day charter, isn't it? Four men from Lansing, I believe. Two who work for the state auditor's office and two of their friends. Actually three of them are friends of the fourth who is responsible for the charter. Steven Hibbs, I believe."

Leonard stared at Nathanial and then stood up from where he had been working on some fishing gear.

"What's this about, Sheriff?" Leonard spit out the last word.

"Let me tell you a little story, Leonard. Steven Hibbs first came to Harrisville in March as part of a team of auditors to check the books and see how much money Karen Nelson had really absconded with. He was here for about a week and during that time he spent a few hours each night visiting some of our city's watering holes. In one of them he made the acquaintance of a local charter fisherman, and county sheriff want-to-be, but Steven didn't know that part. All he knew about this local charter fisherman was that he was a 'concerned citizen' who suspected that there was more going on than just the treasurer. In fact, this concerned citizen was very certain that the current sheriff was ... now what was the term? ... oh, yes, 'manipulating funds for his own benefit.' That was it."

"Lots of people have concerns."

"Yes, that's true, but most of them don't use leverage to try to get public officials to reveal secrets."

"He's not a public official."

"Oh, then you do know him," Nathanial had a broad smile on his face. "And you're right, not a public official – a state employee."

"Get to the point."

"Now don't rush me, Leonard. Let me see. Oh, yes, a deal was reached. In exchange for some privileged information, he was offered a four-hour fishing charter for him and a friend. Oh, okay, make it all day. And yes, for four. 'But the information better be juicy.' "

Leonard was growing tired of this, "If you've got a point, make it."

"Oh, Leonard, and spoil the surprise? See Steven Hibbs was basically an honest person and he knew anything he told you could not be in connection with the prime reason for the audit, so he fed you some 'juicy tidbits' about funds, but not about audited funds. It just so happened that the information was, at that time, restricted and giving the concerned citizen that information, while not illegal, did raise a question of propriety.

"So this concerned citizen had a 'juicy tidbit' and just needed to find an unsuspecting dupe to bring it to light. And that poor fellow was Jim Crenshaw of the Genesee County Herald, who was having a solitary breakfast in the Flour Garden the morning of the supervisors' press conference about the Nelsons' return to Alcona County. He was surprised when this 'concerned citizen' slid into the booth and offered him this 'juicy tidbit.'

"Now the thing is, Jim Crenshaw didn't do anything wrong. He is a reporter given a 'juicy tidbit' and what does any good reporter do with a 'juicy tidbit,' but take it and try to make headlines. Sadly for Mr. Crenshaw, he ran afoul of the local sheriff who doesn't like his privacy invaded. But to make a longer story shorter, he was only too willing to make an official statement including the identification of the 'concerned citizen.' Armed with that information, with help the sheriff was able to track down Mr. Hibbs and get his side of the story and identification of the 'concerned citizen.' What it cost him was a month's unpaid leave of absence and a year on probation under extremely close scrutiny of the state auditor. The local sheriff hates to brag, but he stepped in and stopped Mr. Hibbs from being severed from the service, so to speak.

"Now, I believe you wanted for me to get to the point. Well, here it is, Leonard. If that 'concerned citizen' tries in any way to malign the integrity of this local sheriff in the foreseeable future – and I can see a long way – this will be made public knowledge and will definitely ruin any chance that 'concerned citizen' has of being elected to any public office in Alcona County."

Nathanial brought the index and middle fingers of his right hand up to the tip of his Smokey Bear hat in the form of a salute. "Have a nice day, Leonard. Hope you find a good way to write this off on your taxes." He turned to walk back down the pier and turned back, "And taut lines."

As Nathanial walked up the ramp from the berths toward solid ground, he passed four men dressed for an all-day outing and buzzing with excitement about a day of fishing.

"Have a good day, gentlemen," he said as he passed them, recognizing one of them.

"Was that the local sheriff?" one of them asked Steven Hibbs.

"I have no idea," Steven Hibbs answered truthfully.

"Wonder what he was doing here so early," his friend responded and then the encounter was forgotten and a long day on the water began.

Chapter 44

It was two weeks after the Boswick boys had come clean and Nathanial was sitting in his cruiser pulled off the West Path about a hundred yards south of the entrance to the Fitzgeralds'. Arthur Misdorf was with him. Mitchell Webster and Bob Roberts were in Roberts' SUV similarly situated north of the Fitzgeralds'. They had been in place for about an hour and were waiting for Fitzgerald's plane to land. They had been notified when it lifted off from Montreal by U.S. Customs, and their windows were open listening for sounds of the plane. Out on Hibbard Pond was the Boston Whaler with interns Rachel Whitaker and Jeremy Bridges, and Rich Walker. They were ostensibly conducting routine patrols but always within eyeshot of the Fitzgeralds' dock.

In Misdorf's pocket were a number of warrants: arrest for the murder and illegal disposal of the body of Pierre LeBeuf, arrest for the attempted murder of Arthur Misdorf, and a search warrant for the premises. The latter was iffy because all they could look for were things related to the two other warrants, but at least they would have access to the house. Once the plane landed, Fitzgerald deplaned, and the plane departed, the Boston Whaler would take up position in front of the Fitzgerald estate and Nathanial would lead Roberts' SUV to the house. Roberts would wait outside for any potential flight (which was unexpected but must be planned for) while the other three would confront Fitzgerald.

Nathanial looked up as a purple van passed his position headed north. "Jane Polli," he muttered. "Wonder where she's going." He picked up his microphone. "Roberts, there's a purple van headed north. Let me know if it passes you."

"Roger," came back and a few minutes later, "No on the van."

"How appropriate," Nathanial mused. "Once again the gang's all here."

Nathanial started thinking about how lucky they had been to get the breaks in this case. First, the plane crash. Looking back, that was the greatest piece of luck because without it the next three pieces wouldn't have happened. Second, Zeb finding the stone head. Anyone else without diving expertise would have ignored it. Oh, maybe mention something hit them, but the plane was moving in the waves before being righted. Who knows how far it had moved. Twenty feet is a lot in an underwater search. Third, the Pickens boys finding the resin head. Probably fell out when the plane was righted and water poured out of the cockpit. And they just happened to pick the correct spot. Dumb luck. They were wallowing in it. Fourth, Edmund Fitzgerald getting nervous, maybe because he knew what was lying out in the lake. Getting Mandel to convince the boys to take a fall. That was the needed piece in the puzzle. Clemson Mathers agreed that although everything was circumstantial, putting them all together they had a strong case. All they needed to sew it up tight was a confession, a few words is all. And Nathanial knew just how to get it done.

Twelve minutes later they heard a plane pass behind them headed south. The sound grew softer, then louder and changed its tone. "It's landing," Misdorf said. "Yep," Nathanial agreed. "Looks like the quarry is entering the arena," Robert's voice came over the air. The sound died out and all was quiet for a few minutes. "Wonder who's helping with the luggage?" Misdorf said. "Probably isn't much," answered Nathanial. "It's usually just the weekend and like most people, they have clothes here." A few minutes later, they heard the pontoon plane's engine start up and shortly after they could tell that it had taken off.

Nathanial's phone rang. "Yes, Walker."

"Fitzgerald is here as is his wife."

"Good, take position."

"Let's go," Nathanial said into the mike, and pulled out onto the West Path heading north. Robert's SUV was sitting across from the Fitzgerald's driveway, left-turn indicator on and it followed Nathanial's cruiser in. At the house, the four got out, they unsecured their weapons, and led by Nathanial, all went to the front door except for Roberts who remained standing by his vehicle.

The sounds of "O Canada" had just died out when Alix, whose eyes widened perceptively when she recognized the uniformed officers, opened the door. "Greetings, Deputy Misdorf," she said smiling sweetly and somewhat seductively, Misdorf thought. "What brings you and your compatriots here?"

"I'm Sheriff Nathanial Jefferson," Nathanial said. "We want to speak to Edmund Fitzgerald."

"I don't know...," Alix began.

"We know he's here," Nathanial said, stepping forward and forcing Alix to step back and open the door wide. Misdorf and Webster followed him in. "Where is he?"

"In the Lake Room with his wife, mother, and Mrs. Polli."

They went down the hallway with Alix trailing and had just turned into the living room when they saw Edmund's back as he stood at the doorway to the Lake Room talking to someone inside. He must have heard something because he turned in their direction.

"Sheriff Jefferson," he said, a not overly wide smile on his face. "To what do we owe the honor? Could we ply you with a libation?" He had a half-full (in this case actually half-empty) martini glass in his hand, which he hoisted in Nathanial's direction. He was wearing a windbreaker so it was fairly evident that upon entering the house, his first thought had been for a drink.

"No, thank you, Mister Fitzgerald," Nathanial said as Misdorf and Webster followed him into the Lake Room with Alix trailing. Liza Fitzgerald, his wife, was standing by a glass-topped tea cart upon which were a crystal ice bucket basically full of ice, a bottle of Grey Goose Vodka, a bottle of Jack Daniels bourbon, a bottle of Martini & Rossi dry vermouth, a crystal cocktail shaker, two martini glasses, and several highball glasses. She picked up a highball glass filled with Jack Daniels and ice cubes. Edna Fitzgerald sat in her usual chair, a full martini glass on the small glass-topped table to her right. She was staring out at the lake where the Boston Whaler sat dead in the water. Jane Eyre sat to her immediate left facing them in one of the high-back white wicker chairs, a martini glass half raised to her lips, which showed a surprised smile. Misdorf walked past Nathanial and took a position in the center of the window wall while Webster stood by the door. Alix, who had followed them into the room, turned to leave.

"Please stay, Ms. ...," Nathanial said.

She stopped and turned. "Pécody. Alix Pécody." She moved to stand next to the tea cart.

After acknowledging each of the ladies, Nathanial turned to Edmund Fitzgerald.

"I have a few questions if you don't mind."

"I believe it won't matter whether I do or not," Edmund said. "Of course, I might not answer them without a lawyer present." His mouth smiled sardonically. "What are they about?"

"That will be your choice," Nathanial said. "Answering them, I mean. And they are about several different things. Let's start with the murder of Pierre LeBeuf."

"I thought that was behind us," Edmund said. He finished his martini in one swallow and turned to the tea cart.

"There are just a few loose ends to tie up," continued Nathanial. "You were here that night. November 15, two years ago."

"If that's when it was. I think we already established that I was here." He took the top off the cocktail shaker and, his hand visibly shaking, it clattered as he set it on the tea cart.

"That's strange, maybe unusual is a better word, because that was a Thursday and you usually arrive on Fridays."

"Every time is different. It depends upon business," Edmund said, eschewing the ice tongs, picking up ice cubes in his hand and dumping them unceremoniously into the cocktail shaker. One of them missed, bounced off the glass top and skittered across the narrow distance to Alix's feet. She stooped to pick up the cube, her hand closing on it just as his did. Their eyes meet briefly and she stood, handing him the ice cube, which he dumped into one of the empty highball glasses. The smile that passed between them was one for secret lovers.

"Yes, business. That's probably what brought you here. The fact that Pierre LeBeuf was – how should I say it – stealing from your business?"

Edmund had picked up the Grey Goose bottle and stopped midstream in removing the bottle stop.

"Stealing from my business? And pray what was he stealing?"

When Nathanial had asked the question, Edna Fitzgerald's head had turned almost imperceptivity toward her son, her eyes now locked fully upon him.

"A couple of kilo's of cocaine or heroin. One of the two."

A forced chuckle came from Edmund as he removed the bottle stop and poured a liberal amount of the vodka into the cocktail shaker.

"Really?" he said, twisting the stop back into the bottle's neck and setting it on the table. "And where would I get that kind of stuff?" picking up the shaker's top and putting it in place.

"Don't you want any vermouth?" Nathanial asked, a wry smile on his lips.

"No," Edmund said, picking up the shaker with his right hand, his left securing the top. "My mother is the only one who uses vermouth." He started shaking the container.

"Probably from Mexico," continued Nathanial. "In one of those resin heads you import. Like the one that fell out of your float plane as a result of the crash."

Everyone except Edmund jumped as the crystal cocktail shaker shattered on the tile floor spewing shards of fine crystal, ice, and vodka everywhere.

Chapter 45

For a moment, almost everyone was frozen in place. Alix started moving forward, as did Webster, but everyone stopped when they heard, "YOU BASTARD! Not only are you screwing the maid but you're poisoning your countrymen!"

All eyes shifted from the mess on the floor to Liza Fitzgerald who, during the momentary distraction, had picked up her handbag on the chair next to where she was standing and pulled out a Beretta Mini that she pointed at her husband. "Don't anyone move," she cautioned. "Especially you, Deputy," pointing at Webster. "I know how to use this, but I am not at all comfortable with it. I am certain you don't want a dead murderer."

With a gun around, especially if you're not comfortable with guns, you are going to obey and everyone did.

"NOW, BASTARD," Liza screamed at her husband, "IT'S CONFESSION TIME. AND I WARN YOU, EDMUND, GIVE ME A WRONG ANSWER AND YOU DIE."

"Fine," Edmund said in a calm voice, but he was visibly shaken. "Just don't shoot. What do you want to know?"

"Well," Liza said, calming herself a bit, "I brought this," waving the gun to indicate what she meant, "here to find out, and so now we will. Were you – are you – screwing that bitch?" pointing at Alix with her left hand.

"Yes, but..."

"BUT NOTHING. JUST ANSWER THE QUESTION."

Edmund nodded his ascent. What he had seen looking at her that no one else had seen gave him hope.

"Did you kill that rat-faced Pierre LeBeuf?"

Before he could answer, Misdorf, having silently moved from the windows while attention was elsewhere, grabbed Liza with his left arm around her waist, his right hand grabbing and knocking her gun hand down. The gun fired, but the bullet hit the tile floor and ricocheted into the doorjamb just inches from Webster's head. Nathanial started moving toward Liza and Misdorf. Alix tried to flee the room.

"DON'T ANYONE MOVE," this time it was Edmund who had pulled another Beretta Mini from a belt holster in the middle of his back where it had been concealed by his windbreaker. Everyone complied except Liza who kept struggling to free her gun hand from Misdorf who was squeezing her wrist. She dropped the gun and in the continuing struggle inadvertently kicked it with her right foot, and it skittered across the floor stopping halfway between Edna and Jayne Eyre, who had fainted at the gunshot.

"LIZA, STOP IT!" And she did. Now all eyes were on Edmund.

"You stupid bitch," Edmund snarled. "Why do you think we were living so well when the antiquities trade dried up? If it wasn't for the drugs, we'd be broke. You don't realize how much those two kilos that Pierre took were worth. He thought he was smart, but he wasn't. He was just a stupid thief. And yes, I'm screwing Alix. You're worthless in that department. She and I are going to leave all this behind and go somewhere warm and sit on the beach drinking martinis and eating shrimp."

"No you are not, Edmund!" All eyes turned to see Edna Fitzgerald standing in front of Jane Eyre and holding Liza's pistol. She appeared icily composed. Edmund's gun, which had been pointed at Nathanial, started moving toward his mother.

"Edmund, stop." And he did. "I know how to use this thing. After all, that gun you used to kill LeBeuf was mine. Actually it was your father's, but what was his became mine. He taught me how to use it. It was for protection, you know. This area is isolated in the winter and, being a big city boy, he was a little fearful."

"Mother, put the gun down. You don't want to hurt anyone, especially me."

"On the contrary, Edmund, you are the only person that I want to hurt. Even killing you won't hurt as much as your betrayal has hurt me."

"What I did was for your good too, Mother."

Edna laughed. "For my good? Killing a childhood friend! One of only two who meant anything to me. Now put your gun down."

"No, Mother. I can't. I won't. I am not going to go to jail."

"It's either that or the grave, Edmund. You have to pay for your crimes. I'm just sorry they can't add Rolli's death to the list. It's because of you, killing Pierre and dumping his body in the lake, that this investigation started. After so long, no one would have looked into that arson if it hadn't been for this investigation. Now put your gun down."

Nathanial's eyes were flicking back and forth between Edmund and Edna as thought he was watching a tennis ball being exchanged during a match at Wimbledon. He saw that Edmund's gun arm was starting to move toward his mother, and out of the corner of his eye he saw Jane Eyre stand up behind Edna and grab for the gun. But her arm was too short; her bulk made her too clumsy. She jarred Edna and the gun went off. The shot was echoed by another from Edmund's gun. That bullet, like Liza's, hit no one but embedded itself in the ceiling of the Lake Room as Edmund's arm went skyward. He fell backward with a bullet in his chest, the gun then falling harmlessly to the tiled floor. All three lawmen had their guns out pointed at Edna who had a look of abject horror on her face.

"Edmund," she screamed, dropping the gun and hurrying to kneel by his side, mindless of the pooling blood.

Edmund's eyes were closed but they flickered open and he looked at his mother.

"Oh, Edmund," she wept, "I didn't want..." as he said, "Mother, I didn't think..." and his eyes saw no more.

Chapter 46

In the aftermath of the shooting, Nathanial found himself with his hands full. First, of course, there was the gathering of evidence from the murder site. That was left to Roberts and Walker, the former who was let in the front door after standing outside and listening to the three gun shots and wondering what was going on inside, but standing at his post just as he should have; the latter who watched the entire incident through binoculars and therefore could be—and would be—a witness at the inquest. Still, as a police officer, he had a duty to perform, but he delegated the majority of work to Roberts so there would not be any problem with bias. The two most important items recovered were two of the three bullets. The first bullet fired from Liza's pistol had hit the tile floor and was too damaged for comparison, and therefore no material evidence. The second bullet fired from Liza's pistol had killed her husband and could be used for ballistics comparison. The third bullet fired from Edmund's Berretta Mini had lodged in the ceiling and was good enough for ballistics comparison. There was not a match for either bullet in any known database. However, they and the pistols would be kept on file just in case.

Following the gathering of evidence from the Lake Room, Roberts and Walker once again performed as an efficient team doing a once over of the storage shed where the pontoon had been kept. The evidence there was mostly circumstantial at best: a can of nails which matched the type of nails used to nail the top on the shelter, and a stack of nineteen concrete blocks of the kind used to sink the shelter. They could identify some nails that had been straightened, but there was no way to tell when and for what purpose they had been used. Also there was a stack of two-by-fours with nail holes. Walker and Roberts knew that if push came to shove, they could reassemble the ramp. The only piece of evidence that was incriminating was the tarp. It did have dried blood on it, and it matched LeBeuf's type. A sample was sent off, and a DNA test matched LeBeuf.

They then went to the spot where Burke had beached the pontoon, and waited while Burl and Burt fetched the shelter from the Loon Creek Inn. Naturally after almost two years there was no evidence of the beaching, but they did find the stump of a fir tree, which they photographed and then removed to study at their lab. After several hours of exacting study, they were 99.9% certain that the fir in the shelter had been cut from that stump.

While the forensic team was busy in the Lake Room, the search warrant was executed and Misdorf and Webster investigated the storage room where they found fifty-four different pieces of Aztec and Mayan statuary. With Misdorf's eye for detail, even though he didn't have an eye for art, he was able to identify the pieces that he felt had been removed from his sight that first day. When the forensic team was done in the Lake Room and before they went outside, Misdorf had them photograph the pieces that he and Webster then cataloged. The storage room was locked and sealed until the proper authorities could come and prepare it for shipment back to Mexico and Guatemala.

Then there were the four sobbing, and for a while, incoherent women. A doctor was called and sedatives given to Alix and Liza who were each confined to their rooms with a guard posted by Alix's door just in case. When she was questioned and her background examined in minute detail, it was determined that she had no involvement in anything other than her adulterous affair with Edmund, which had been going on several months before she came here. She had been working in his store. She was then sent back to Montreal. Liza's only crime was one of the heart, and she had not really done anything wrong and no charges were filed. She came to terms with her mother-in-law and they spent the rest of that summer together in the house on Hibbard Pond.

Jane Eyre had come to visit Edna at her invitation to hear why Edna had been so distant on that visit right before Memorial Day. They had just finished their first drinks, and poured a second, when Edmund arrived and mixed his drink. The arrival of the sheriff and his posse had shocked her. She had sat stunned listening to the questioning until Liza had pulled her gun. Things then had happened so fast and her heart was pounding so rapidly that when the gun went off, her system had overloaded, and she passed out ever so briefly. She had come to when Edna had told Edmund she could kill him and had quickly determined, based on what she had heard, that Edmund's death would leave too many questions – too many of her own questions – unanswered, and had instinctively tried to stop Edna from killing Edmund. The fact that her actions had resulted in Edmund's death did not sit well with her. She had never fired the pistol and had been trying to stop it from being fired, so she had no part in Edmund's death. It was ruled self-defense on Edna's behalf based on Nathanial's testimony and, if Clemson Mathers had wanted to pursue it, could be ruled accidental as well. She had been greatly relieved when Nathanial had reminded her that on the day of Pierre LeBeuf's murder, Rolli had been confined at home because of his severely twisted ankle. She was also given a sedative by the doctor to be taken when she got home, and she was escorted there by Misdorf driving her van, followed by Webster in the sheriff's cruiser. Once home, she made herself a pitcher of vodka martini's, stirred not shaken, with "Vermouth' whispered over the top because she and Rolli had always liked them extremely dry. She had taken the pitcher and her art deco martini glass to her lift chair, settled back, taken the sedative with a sip from her first drink, and drifted to sleep more from mental exhaustion than the sedative after taking just one more sip. She slept through until midmorning the next day, and set forward on the first day of the rest of her life with a brightly illuminated end of the tunnel.

Chapter 47

As for Edna, she was grief stricken that she had killed her only son. No consoling from Nathanial or in coming days by Liza and Jane Eyre would help, and it was a week before she came to grips with the reality of it. She, too, was given a sedative and put to bed. It was the day after the shooting when she finally talked to Nathanial.

"I called Jane Eyre that afternoon when I knew Edmund was coming with Liza. I wanted to explain to her why I was so out of sorts that afternoon she stopped in. I was in shock, I think. I had heard Alix talking to Edmund – I know it was he because she used his name. I heard her say, 'I can't wait until you are here, mon amour, and I am glad that vache stupide cannot come. We will have nothing to stop our love making.' The afternoon of the crash he called her, told her about the crash and asked her to bring the SUV. I know because she said 'Oh, mon Dieu. Are you fine?' Then she listened, said 'Immédiatement!' and went running out without a word. It was only when they came back that I got the story. That night I heard Edmund leave his room when he thought I was asleep and I peeked out and saw him go down the hall to her room near the kitchen. He knocked lightly, I think I could hear rapping, and then went in. It was well over an hour before he came back."

Edna smiled coyly. "Must have been some tryst. I can remember times like that." Then she blushed, realizing what she had said.

"I couldn't believe it when I saw you holding that gun," Nathanial said. "We all thought you had dementia or Alzheimer's."

"Oh, fiddlesticks," Edna said. "When I learned that Pierre had been shot, I was depressed because I knew that he had been killed in my own home. Well, not in my house, but on my property."

"When was that?" Nathanial asked.

"When was what?" Edna responded.

"You're doing it again."

"Doing what?"

"Acting senile."

"Oh, posh, I just don't understand when I knew what?"

"When did you learn that Pierre had been killed?"

"When they pulled him up from the lake. Edmund had told me that he had taken off in the middle of the night and nobody knew where he had gone. Honestly, I didn't suspect anything, but it didn't seem like the Pierre that I knew. People change I know but ... well, I just didn't know. I suspected that Edmund might have a part in it, and thought that the best thing I could do was to remain on the fringe of things and let them sort it out. So I acted a little senile when I had company unless I really wanted to have company.

"The biggest mistake I made, and for this I will never forgive myself, was to call Edmund after that nice Deputy Misdorf was here the second time. He was beginning to put things together and for me they began to point at Edmund. I don't think that Deputy Misdorf had any idea that Edmund was involved at that time. I called Edmund to warn him about what was happening. I didn't know – and didn't think until the very end – that Edmund had sent those two boys after the deputy. I am so sorry for that."

"Before that, though, that first day that Deputy Misdorf came to see you, something happened that he needs to know about," injected Nathanial.

"What's that?"

"Well, Briel left him standing in the foyer for about five minutes while he checked with you. On the way to see you, Misdorf noticed that some artwork was missing from the walls, and bookends from a table in your living room."

"Yes, he's right. The last weekend Edmund was here before that, he had been saying that things were getting tight in the antiquities market. That American, Canadian, and Mexican authorities were looking for artifacts that had been taken from Mayan and Aztec sites. I thought that the deputy might be part of that. People know we have a lot of that stuff. So I had Briel take it and put it in that storage room where you found it. Took a few days to get stuff to replace it. I really like the stone work though. Some of it we got before they put the law into effect. My Edmund and I brought a lot of it back from our honeymoon. We could do that then. I should have known it was wrong, but we were young and excited about it. Now it will all go back where it belongs. I'll miss it, but it's for the ages."

"What about your confession?"

"Oh, that evening when you went after Briel – I called him Butch just to aggravate him – Edmund followed you. After Briel had killed himself, Edmund came back and told us. He said that Briel had confessed to killing Pierre and gave us details. He said that it would break his kids' hearts if they thought he had. So when I thought about it and the way things were, I thought that eventually an investigation might lead to Rolli because of his history with Pierre. So that day you were here, I confessed to protect Rolli. I knew that with two confessions, you would have a problem even with one confessor dead and the other a senile old lady."

At this point she winked at Nathanial in the same way she had that day.

"When I heard that Rolli had confessed, I couldn't believe it. I knew it was just to protect me, but I couldn't say anything. I had forgotten about his twisted ankle and him being laid up and all. Then he killed himself, and I really became depressed. That's when they said I had a stroke and maybe I did. But I had gone too far and decided to keep up the charade until I could figure out who did it. I had a sickening feeling it was my son, but I couldn't believe it. So I decided that I had to discover for myself and try to gather enough evidence, word of mouth or whatever, to prove it one way or another. So when you arrived yesterday and started questioning Edmund, I knew you were right. I was furious that my son, my own flesh and blood, had killed one of my two best childhood friends. No matter that the friendship had fallen apart, my memories were destroyed. I wasn't going to let Edmund get away with it, but I didn't know what to do. Then that pistol landed just a few feet from me and everyone was looking at Edmund, so I simply picked it up. I didn't want to kill him. I don't know if I could have. I was aiming over his left shoulder. I knew that if push came to shove, I could move just a little to my left and put a bullet between his eyes."

She saw a slight smirk twitch Nathanial's lips.

"Don't believe this old lady, huh? Tell you what, let's you and me get a couple of tin cans and set 'em up outside. Then we'll see who's senile."

"Can't do that," Nathanial said. "Bullet goes through a can and ends up who knows where. Might kill an innocent bystander."

"Then take me to your range with those targets that look like people. I used to group them pretty good back when my Edmund taught me to shoot."

Nathanial held up his hands. "No, I believe you. I saw the look in your eyes and knew that, if push came to shove, you'd shoot. I just didn't know what you'd hit."

"Yes," Edna agreed, "and sadly it was a push or maybe a shove of Jane Eyre – isn't she a sweet lady – trying to stop me." She stopped talking and her eyes got that distant look.

Chapter 48

Late the Saturday afternoon after the shooting, Jane Eyre heard the "Hymn of Victory" ring out announcing a visitor. It took a minute for her to get up out of her lift chair and hurry barefoot to the door dressed in dark purple silk pajamas with a pattern of red crowns. Standing on tiptoe and looking through the peephole, she saw a man wearing reflective sunglasses and a Detroit Tigers baseball cap. There was someone else with him, but she couldn't make out who it was.

"Yes?" she said opening the door. The man in front had on a white Alcona County Sheriff's Department tee shirt, blue jeans and topsiders. The man behind wore reflective sunglasses, a New York Yankees baseball cap, a blue Alcona County Sheriff's Department tee shirt, blue jean shorts with a frayed bottom hem and sandals, not flip-flops. In the driveway behind them was a dusty blue Chevy pickup truck.

"Afternoon, Mrs. Polli," both men said raising right hands to their caps brims in a two finger salute.

"We were in the neighborhood and thought we'd stop by to see how you are doing after the shooting yesterday," Arthur Misdorf said, half cringing at the little white lie about being in the neighborhood. They had driven forty minutes from Mitchell Webster's place in

Greenbush, but they had come to see how she was doing.

Jane Eyre squinted at both men trying to recognize them because she knew she should. Realizing this, Arthur and Mitchell removed their sunglasses.

"Arthur! Mitchell! Land sakes. What a surprise. Come in, come in," Jane Eyre said holding the door open for them. As she led them into the great room, she offered, "Can I get you something to drink? Beer, a martini? I can tell by your dress that you're not on duty."

"No, ma'am. Not today," Arthur replied. "I would like a glass of water."

"I'll have the same, ma'am," Mitchell added.

"But it's five o'clock somewhere and I'm having a martini. Won't you join me?"

"No thanks, ma'am. We both have to drive home."

"I have some good iced tea, Arthur," Jane Eyre said demurely. "Not that wretched stuff from last time."

"Okay," Arthur said. "I'll give it a go," nudging Mitchell.

"Me too, Mrs. Polli," Mitchell said.

Jane Eyre bustled into the kitchen while the two men walked to the glass wall and looked out at Hibbard Pond, still busy on a beautiful June Saturday afternoon.

"Here you go," Jane Eyre said holding out dewy glasses of iced tea, a slice of lemon on each rim. The men took the glasses and seats she indicated as she settled back in her lift chair.

"So, did you sleep alright last night?" Arthur asked, not daring to test the tea.

"Did I? I fell asleep right here and didn't stir until 10:00 a.m. this morning. That's late for me. How's the tea?"

There was nothing for it, but to try it and both men did. "Great!" they said in unison visibly relieved that indeed it was.

"Good. I've been learning. Has everything been cleaned up?"

"What do you mean?" Misdorf asked.

"I mean, have you worked out all the explanations about who did what?

"Yes, ma'am," Misdorf said. "That's one of the reasons we're here. Edmund Fitzgerald was pretty much involved in everything. He got into trouble when Central American countries made possession and/or export of artifacts illegal. That was a lot of his business. So he went into making replicas, set up a small factory in Mexico. But that trade didn't match what he had before and his lifestyle suffered. He was approached by a Mexican drug lord about smuggling his product into Canada and they came up with the idea of putting it in resin heads. He had Pierre LeBeuf down there handling things, but Pierre got greedy and snitched a couple of kilos, which he sold on the street in Montreal. We know this from the Montreal police who at that time had a close watch on him. They were going to shut him down and learn his source when he disappeared. Edmund had 'invited' him for a getaway at his Michigan home."

"Here on Hibbard Pond," mused Jane Eyre, sipping on her martini.

"Yes, ma'am. Apparently when they got here, Edmund escorted him to his room and out of this life. The Boswick boys weren't available at that time—being in the woods—so he wrapped the body in a tarp and then proceeded in as natural a manner as possible, saying that Pierre had been taken ill. When it was dark and the boys got home, he called them and got them to dispose of the body. That's when things went wrong as we know, and eventually led to the discovery."

"And that was the investigation that brought my Rolli's activities into question and led to his death," a big swig of the martini by Jane Eyre following this statement.

"Yes, ma'am," Mitchell injected. "I'm sorry about that."

"Don't be," Jane Eyre said. "You were doing your job, and you did it just fine. Maybe a little too fine, but that just shows what a good cop you are. I blame Edmund and no one else. Of course, Briel's confession started the ball rolling and eventually brought about Rolli's confession."

"Yes, ma'am," Misdorf said. "About that. We know that the shooting was on November 15, the first day of deer season and we know that your husband was incapacitated at the time and couldn't possibly have shot Pierre. So we have closed our books on that."

Jane Eyre sighed. "Thank goodness for that. Now there's just that arson bit."

"Yes, ma'am. That's the Montreal police's problem. From what I understand from my contact there, they can't determine what was used to make the chemical timer."

"Well, don't come asking me. I have absolutely no idea. My knowledge of chemistry is that H-two-O is water and NaCl is salt. Nothing beyond that."

"Yes, ma'am. They realize that and have closed the books."

Another big sigh and big swig of martini by Jane Eyre.

"So it's done. Closed. Over."

"Yes, ma'am. That's what we came to tell you. Hope you don't mind the informality."

Jane Eyre waved, indicating it was fine. "So other than that, what brings you by?"

"Excuse me?" Misdorf said.

"I know you weren't 'just' in the neighborhood, and it was good of you to do it on an off day, but there must be something else."

"Yes, ma'am," Mitchell Webster said, looking down into his half-empty glass of iced tea. "We've been running around this afternoon looking at motorcycles."

"Really?" Jane Eyre said, one eyebrow raising.

"Yes, ma'am. I'm from this area originally. Grew up in Au Gres. My parents struggled making a living and we didn't travel much. Had 'stay-cations' as they say now. I want to travel and see this great state and the wonders it has to offer, but what with gas prices, I just can't afford to do that. So I am thinking about getting a motorcycle. There's just me, no one else in my life at this moment, and a motorcycle would be a way I could do it, camping as I go. So I asked Arthur to go looking with me today and we didn't find anything I liked or could afford. Then Arthur reminded me about your husband's Harley."

"Yes, ma'am," Arthur said. "I have seen it in the garage."

"So," Mitchell said gaining confidence, "I would like to see if you want to sell it."

"I hadn't thought about it. You know it was underwater for a couple of hours."

"Yes, ma'am. There shouldn't be too much damage. Maybe some of the leather. I'm pretty good with machinery. My dad was a good mechanic and taught me about engines, so I think I can rebuild the engine and whatever else needs to be repaired."

"So you're not talking about riding in the woods or over sand dunes?"

"Oh, no, ma'am. That hog is a street bike, not a mountain bike. I may take dirt roads. Up in the UP, they're everywhere."

"I don't know how much I should charge."

"Well, Mrs. Polli, I thought about this on the way over. Let me take the bike and repair it, my cost. When I get it fixed, I bring it back, tell you what I put into it and give you an equitable sales price. Then you can make a decision."

Jane Eyre thought for a moment. "I accept your offer. That's fair and it will just get worse sitting there."

"Yes, ma'am."

So the two men loaded the Harley into Webster's truck, rolling it up a two-by-eight Webster had thoughtfully brought along. They secured the hog in position with heavy bungee cords. They waved to her and started to get into the truck. "Don't forget the helmet," Jane Eyre yelled. Mitchell ran into the garage and retrieved the helmet, putting it in the front seat. After thanking Jane Eyre again, Mitchell and Arthur headed back to Greenbush, where they unloaded the Harley into Mitchell's garage. Then Misdorf went home and Mitchell started reconditioning the motorcycle.

Chapter 49

Nine o'clock Monday morning, Nathanial strode into his conference room carrying ten sheets of paper, one
for each of the eight news people in the room, eleven if
you counted the television cameramen for Alpena Channel 11 (local CBS affiliate), Detroit Channel 7 Action
News (ABC affiliate), and Fox 66 from Flint (Fox affiliate). The news reporters were from the Detroit Free
Press, Detroit News, Lansing State Journal, The Alpena
News, and the Alcona County Review.

After doing a headcount despite the fact that
Misdorf, standing at the back of the room, had personally identified each of the attendees, Nathanial began.
"Good morning. You are here by special invitation because you have not caused any problems in previous
news conferences, and I am sick and tired of inconsider-
ate and/or non-professional members of the press. That
said, if any of you, and that includes the cameramen,"
and he pointed at the three individually, "step out of
line, your publication or station will no longer attend
further conferences. Is that understood?" There was a
unanimous affirmative reply. "Good, you may now start
your cameras and tape recorders. I will furnish you with
a copy of my statement."

He looked down at the statement, then up at the reporters. "This is not about Nathan Biggins, although I wish to hell it was.

"Friday afternoon, acting on evidence gathered through a variety of sources, my deputies and I went to the Hibbard Pond residence of Edmund Fitzgerald for the purpose of arresting him for the murder of Pierre LeBeuf, known to you as 'The Body Under the Ice.' When confronted with our evidence, his unsuspecting wife pulled a gun she had brought for another purpose and for which no charges have been filed. While Deputy Misdorf was wresting the Beretta from her grasp, a shot was fired but no one was hurt. The pistol fell to the floor. During this confusion, Edmund Fitzgerald pulled another Beretta, which he held on me. His mother, Edna Fitzgerald, picked up the first pistol and pointed it at him, warning him that even though he was her son, she would shoot him. Apparently he didn't believe her and was swinging his gun arm toward her when Jane Eyre Polli tried to stop her from shooting Edmund. The gun went off and Edmund was struck fatally, his gun firing harmlessly into the ceiling. No charges will be filled against Edna Fitzgerald, Jane Eyre Polli, or Liza Fitzgerald and all have asked not to be interviewed."

There was a low murmur among the reporters and Nathanial knew that this was a complete surprise to them, and he was baffled that the word had somehow eluded the Alcona County Grapevine. *Boy, will Gert be upset,* Nathanial thought.

"A subsequent and legal search of the house brought to light the fact that Edmund was in possession of illegal artifacts of Mayan and/or Aztec origin as well as a considerable amount of illegal drugs – Mexican heroin. Believing that the drugs at least had been imported from Mexico by his import/export company, the Montreal police were notified. Saturday night a raid was made on Fitzgerald's main store and warehouse. More illegal artifacts were confiscated as well as twenty-one kilograms of pure heroin. The heroin had been hidden inside resin replicas of Mayan and Aztec stone statues."

Nathanial then explained why Pierre LeBeuf had been shot, how the body had been disposed, how the two heads had been found in Hibbard Pond, and how the Boswick boys had turned state's evidence. He asked that the Pickens boys' parents be contacted before interviewing the two brothers, and that Zeb had asked not to be interviewed. "He said he was just doing what anyone would have done in his place."

Nathanial had spent the entire day Sunday preparing his statement and there were no questions, except wanting to know if anything new had happened in the case of Nathan Biggins. "Sadly, no," was his answer.

***

While this news conference was being held, Alpena County Sheriff Jim Whittaker paid a visit to Alfred Mandel.

"Sheriff," Alfred Mandel said, rising from the chair behind his desk strewn with papers, "to what do I owe this visit?"

"It's not official," Jim Whittaker said, taking a seat in one of the office's visitor chairs as Mandel settled back in his. "It's about those three clients of yours, the Boswick boys."

Mandel's interest was raised because he had met with the boys and they had told him they would cop a plea to the murder of Pierre LeBeuf, but would do it personally only to either Sheriff Whittaker or Sheriff Jefferson.

"You probably know they're not the brightest bulbs on the tree."

Mandel nodded in agreement.

"Except for Burke," Jim Whittaker continued.

Mandel straightened up in his chair.

"He's got some good sense. Thought that maybe they could do better dealing with Clemson Mathers. Now, ordinarily they'd do this with you present but, I don't know, for some reason they don't trust you."

"What?" Mandel sputtered.

"I know, responsible lawyer like yourself," Jim Whittaker said, a wry tone in his voice. "So they made a deal with Mathers through Sheriff Jefferson. Now how's that for a turnabout?"

Jim Whittaker leaned toward Mandel, hands on his knees.

"Accepted deals on all charge counts. That'll save a lot of money for the county, won't it? No long trial even though their guilt is pretty obvious. Of course, to make a deal they had to offer something and they did. They offered the killer of Pierre LeBeuf."

"Really," Mandel said, pleased with himself. "They admitted to killing him?"

"No, that's not what I said," Jim Whittaker said smiling. "They gave up the killer."

Mandel seemed perplexed.

"Yep, and Friday evening Sheriff Jefferson went to make the arrest. Now this doesn't seem to involve you much on the surface other than lowering the cost of your fees, what with the shortened trial and all. But here's what does involve you...."

If Mandel had been a dog, his ears would have perked up.

"They've filed a grievance against you with the Michigan Bar Association. Seems that the Bar doesn't think it's very ethical for a lawyer to attempt to get his clients to plead guilty to a crime, especially murder, that they didn't do."

Jim Whittaker stood and turned to leave, stopped, and turned back.

"Two other things. I don't think that your costs for the defense of those boys will be paid. Seems that Edmund Fitzgerald was killed during the attempt to arrest him and I don't think the family will be honoring your bill. Again something about ethical practices. And one last thing, even though the Boswick boys have accepted a plea, they deserve legal representation. Don't know for certain, but the Bar might look a little more favorably toward you if you did the defense pro bono. Have a good day."

Jim Whittaker turned and left the office leaving a defeated Alfred Mandel slumped in his chair.

Chapter 50

"Welcome," Michal Paul said opening the big door. "Come in but ignore the mess."

It was 5:05 p.m. on a Wednesday six weeks after Memorial Day, and the McBruces had answered an invitation to come for cocktails and appetizers with a warning that the appetizers were intended to serve as dinner. They knew that the Pauls had just arrived the day before, having gotten possession of the house the previous week, and Earleen had questioned whether they were really ready for company.

"No," Kathy Jo had responded, "but we need to relax and we don't know anyone else."

"So it's us or the highway?"

"What?"

"It was a stupid play on 'It's my way or the highway.' The old ultimatum ploy."

Kathy Jo laughed. "You go flag someone down and say, 'Want a drink?' Who the hell knows whom we'd get. Say, now that you mention it...." She laughed heartily. "Don't dress up, we're going to be cleaning all day."

"So grubbies?"

Kathy Jo laughed. "No, we'll clean up, but it's shorts, tee shirts, and bare feet for us."

"I can go for the bare feet after we get there, but not on the gravel road walking down. See you five-ish."

After exchanging pleasantries, Michal offered drinks. "Don't have any Lumber Logger Red but got some Yuengling."

"Could I have red wine, please?" Earleen said.

"Not a problem," Michal said, handing her a glass while Earleen looked amazed.

"Oh, Kathy Jo said you'd want a red wine, so I had one ready. For the ladies, she's not often wrong. Dugal?" Michal said as he reached back to the bar. "Beer or Absolut on the rocks?"

"I think the Absolut tonight," Dugal said, taking an Old Fashioned glass that Michal handed him. "Wow, two for two."

"Not really, that's mine but I'll make another. Don't worry, I haven't started it."

The two ladies wandered into the kitchen and Dugal and Michal migrated to the porch, which had the sliders open and a warm breeze coming in through the screens.

"Too much air and I can close the sliders."

"Nope, that's fine," Dugal said, choosing a seat on a couch that had a low wooden table in front of it. Michal took a seat in a chair to his immediate left. "I was down in the boathouse today giving it a once over to see what needed to be done before we offer it to guests for the wedding – date not established by the way, but we're thinking in two weeks. We want to get everything ship-shape first. Anyway, I pulled out the drawer in the desk and it stuck. Something holding it in. The fit is so tight, I couldn't tilt it and get it out like you can sometimes. So, I reached in and in the middle of the back's top, I felt a ridge of metal. I can say that now, because that's what it is. I managed to lift it out, came easily, and found this."

Michal reached to a small glass table to his right and picked up a metal object. It was basically a flat gray strip of metal about an eighth of an inch thick, three-eighths of an inch wide, and four inches in length. At the ends were two extensions about half an inch long and at one end another about a quarter of an inch from the first but shorter by about an eighth of an inch. He handed it to Dugal and sat back.

"The slot in the top was wide enough so it goes in and out easily, so it was not meant as a stop. I'm a bit clueless about what it is."

"I'm with you," Dugal said turning it over in his hand and looking at it closely. "Handmade, I would guess. If it was to serve as a stop – it did, but that's not its primary purpose. As a stop, it would be a solid piece. This took some time to make. I don't work with metal, but I can see that."

He set the object on the wooden table in front of him and picked up his drink. Taking a sip, he sat back cogitating just as Kathy Jo and Earleen walked out onto the porch, each carrying a tray and a glass of red wine. Kathy Jo's tray, which she sat in front of Dugal, was filled with vegetables and several bowls with various dips in them, Dugal assumed. The tray Earleen set down contained some tasty looking meatballs, boneless Buffalo wings, and what Dugal judged to be light-colored chicken tenders and dark-colored chicken tenders.

Kathy Jo could tell he was confused. "The darker color ones are whitefish sticks, the others are chicken. Sorry, I haven't had time to make sauerkraut balls."

"Gotcha," Dugal said, picking up a Buffalo wing and popping it into his mouth. It was spicy hot but not overly. "Tasty."

Earleen handed him a paper napkin and at the same time spotted the metal object and picked it up. "What a funny looking key. What's it for?"

Dugal and Michal looked at each other and said, "A key!"

"Have no idea what it's for," Michal said.

"Where's it from?" Earleen asked.

"The boathouse. Found it today."

"Fun," Earleen said. "Let's go find the lock."

Kathy Jo and Michal looked at each other.

"Why not," Michal said. "It is a nice night, there's a table and chairs on the deck, let's investigate. Dugal and I will carry the trays and our drinks; you ladies bring your drinks, the wine bottle and the vodka. There's ice in the trays in the boathouse fridge."

And so the happy hour party migrated to the boat-house deck.

And that's where they were, a little the worse for wear, when Nathanial arrived an hour later.

Chapter 51

"So, before I see your booty, tell me the story," Nathanial said when he encountered the four on the deck at the front of the boathouse.

So with Dugal narrating and the other three chiming in as needed, Dugal told the story from their arrival at the boathouse. He and Michal had set the trays on the table and Michal had gone back to unlock the boathouse door and open the slider, which he had just accomplished when the ladies arrived with the liquid supplies. It was a beautiful summer evening and, being mid-week, the lake was fairly quiet, although there were several fishing boats to be seen and an occasional pontoon on a cocktail hour cruise coming by. The four sat there for a few minutes enjoying the evening and getting sustenance from the appetizers.

"Well, let's go key-holing," Earleen said.

"Yep," Michal said standing, drink in hand. "Get a drink and let's go."

Naturally the initial area of interest was the desk where the "key", if that's what is was, was found. Michal pulled the drawer out and showed them where the "key" had been and how it fit.

"Surprised that none of the previous owners found it," Kathy Jo said.

"Maybe they were not as curious as I was," Michal said.

"Or," Earleen said, "maybe they didn't recognize it as a key," and got an affirmative response from the others.

Dugal did a cursory look of the desk, spotting nothing that resembled a keyhole or slot into which the metal key would fit. He looked around the room and saw nothing that would appear to be a door, so he turned back to the desk. He took hold of it and pulled, but it was solidly fixed to the wall. Then he started looking at the wall, which had been paneled with wood from an area barn, or so he had been told. It was all tightly fitted with no visible spaces between boards. Everyone was wandering about the room looking for a keyhole and Dugal looked at a picture frame hanging above the bed. It contained a hand-drawn map of Hibbard Pond.

"That yours?" he asked Michal.

"It is now," Michal answered. "It was here though. I looked at it this afternoon. It was drawn in the mid-1940s and shows the roads and such as they were then."

"May I?" Dugal said, indicating the map.

"Be my guest," Michal said. Dugal handed his drink to Earleen. "If you would, my lady," he said with a bow.

"Of course, my lord," Earleen answered with a partial curtsy and Dugal started to get on the bed. "But take your shoes off first, ruffian," she said.

"Oops," Dugal said. "Showing my lack of breeding, I guess."

Earleen looked at Kathy Jo. "Men," she said. "No couth at all." They both laughed.

On the bed, Dugal took the map down and looked at its back, seeing just brown paper. He handed the frame to Michal who set it out of the way. The "hook" which held the picture was a sliver of wood about an eighth of an inch thick, half an inch long and protruding from the wall about half an inch.

"Now if this was a murder mystery and we were in a haunted castle, I'd push on it and a door would open," Dugal said and pushed on it. Nothing happened.

"Wrong scenario," he said. Grabbing it with thumb and forefinger, he pulled and the piece of wood came out, revealing that it was about two inches long. What was left was a slot, half an inch high by an eighth of an inch wide. "Behold," Dugal said, "a keyhole."

"Try it," Michal said offering him the key.

"Maybe you would like to do the honors," Dugal said. "It's your house."

"But it's your discovery," Michal said. "I already did the hard part."

"Buying the place?" Dugal sniped.

Michal laughed. "No finding the key. If I hadn't done that, that wouldn't be a keyhole, but a strange way of hanging a picture."

"True, true," Dugal said accepting the key.

He slid the end with the two tines into the slot, which accepted it with no problem. He pushed it all the way in and peered at the onlookers. "Ready?" he asked and they nodded, each taking a sip of his or her drink. Holding the end of the key so that he could turn it, he tried clockwise but it wouldn't move, then counter-clockwise with the same result.

"You don't suppose, it's the other end, do you?" he asked.

"Doubt it," Michal said. "Maybe just not all the way in."

Dugal backed it out about an eighth of an inch and tried clockwise, then counterclockwise. It wouldn't budge. Another eighth of an inch, clockwise then counterclockwise.

"Something's wrong," Dugal said, and then hit his forehead with the palm of his hand. "I could have had a.... This won't turn because here is no room for the shaft."

Putting the key back in all the way, he tried sliding it out with a downward pressure. Nothing until the key was all the way out.

"Too easy," Michal said, "Turn it over. Try up."

Dugal did so, pushing the key all the way back and then holding the tine with one hand, pushed up with the other. The key went up, and there was an audible click, and a three-foot long section of the wall, two pieces of barn wood in width, one on either side of the slot, popped outward at the top where the wall met the ceiling. There was an audible gasp from Kathy Jo, Earleen and Michal.

"Bravo," they exclaimed.

Putting a hand on the wood panel lest it fall, Dugal lowered it, backing down the bed and grabbing it as it came down. As it did, a thin blue book affixed to the back of the panels with tape became visible. Dugal laid the secret door on the bed, got off, bowed slightly to Michal and said, "You may do the honors, my liege."

Michal reached across the bed and pulled the book loose from the panel. As he did so, a square piece of paper fell out and landed upon the panels, right in front of Dugal. It was a Polaroid photograph faded with time and with the top closest to Dugal. Even upside down, Dugal knew instantly what it was.

"Put the book back on the panels, Michal, and let's all get out of here."

It was the kind of situation where nobody questioned him. He was the last out, and he closed the door.

"What was it?" Earleen asked breathlessly.

"I may be wrong, but I don't think so," Dugal said pulling out his cellphone. "That's a picture of Nathan Biggins."

***

By the time he finished telling Nathanial the story, Rich Walker and Bob Roberts had showed up, followed closely by Mitchell Webster. The four sheriff's officers went into the room, Mitchell Webster standing by the door. The other three pulled on pairs of latex gloves. Nathanial stepped to the side of the bed where he could get a good look at the picture and then stepped back so that Walker and Roberts could do their crime scene duties. Stripping off the gloves, he stepped out onto the deck.

"Drink, Sheriff?" Michal said knowing the answer.

"I would like one but can't. Sometimes that 'duty calls' stuff sucks."

He looked at Dugal.

"Good eye. I agree, but we'll have to let the experts do their jobs." Then turning to Webster, "Looks like a big step in this case, Webster."

Half an hour later, Rich Walker and Bob Roberts stepped through the slider on the porch of the Paul's house where the party had moved. "All sealed, Sheriff," Walker said. "Had to put the yellow tape on the sliders, regulations. Know that will draw a crowd of gawkers, but that can't be helped. That hiding place is damn ingenious. Took a long time to make that secret panel. If this," and he held the thin book up, "is to be believed and I just skimmed it, it was built in the fifties. Also I think that we're going to be able to put the Nathan Biggins case to rest. That's definitely him in the picture. The book is a confession, but I won't say by whom until we get handwriting analysis, which because of the age, might be a problem. The problem will be finding samples for comparison. Fingerprints aplenty on the inside, and we will have to find a match, but that shouldn't be hard if the person who wrote this is the one signed it. We'll finish up back at the lab and get you a copy in the morning. Want to post a guard on the boathouse?"

"No, don't think it's needed. No body or anything and you've done your job. Thanks." Nathanial stood up and put his hat on. "Thank you for your hospitality, Mr. and Mrs. Paul. The coffee was delicious." He bent over and, using a toothpick, skewered a meatball, the second plate set out that evening. "These meatballs are to die for. Hey, put them with some sauerkraut balls and you'll kick ass," he said to Earleen. "Oops, got into party mode there. You'd think I'd been into the joy juice. We'll be in touch."

Nathanial shooed the forensics team out despite their drooling at the sight of food. "Webster, pull it in and go home," he shouted to the boathouse.

Chapter 52

First thing the next morning, just after he finished his first cup of coffee and was settling in to look at reports from the previous day, Nathanial looked up when he heard a rap on the door. It was Bob Roberts and Rich Walker who stepped into his office. Walker set a stack of photographs in front of him. "Those are copies. All of the same kid. Definitely Nathan Biggins, and the diary – don't know what else to call it – confirms that. Apparently it was written by Stephen Fisher Thompson, the guy who built the boathouse and that mausoleum of a house. Goodness but it is dark in that place. Thompson was one sick dude, but he explained why the body was buried beneath the bridge. We have fingerprints coming from the Navy because he was in the big war. They also have some handwriting samples, forms signed, etc. which should be sufficient to confirm identities. Once we get that, it's a wrap."

Roberts placed a sheaf of paper on the desk beside the pictures. "Oh, yes," he added, " just in case you're wondering, there aren't any more bodies. At least not around here. There's one possibly in the Detroit River, but no clue as to where."

"By the way," Walker said. "that panel was ingenious. The bottom was cut at a forty-five degree angle so it wouldn't pop out and the top had just a sight bevel so it could close. There was a metal plate screwed into the top with two holes in it. There was a recess in the ceiling covered by another metal plate that had two pins with rounded ends pushed down by springs. When the panel was inserted and pushed back at the top, the pins pulled up and then were pushed down by the springs into the holes so the panel was secure. The inside fob of the key pushed up a metal rod with another metal plate and matching projections that pushed the ceiling pair back up so the plate could be pulled out. Never seen anything like it."

When the door closed behind them, Nathanial picked up the pictures, shuddering at the graphicness of some of them. Then he picked up the photocopies of Thompson's diary and started to read:

I joined the Navy in 1941, not because of any sense of duty or love for my country, but because in a fit of sexual desire I had abducted and killed a young Negro boy in Detroit on December 5. He wouldn't do as I wanted despite the promise of money, which I would have happily given him. When I tried to force him, he started to scream and in my attempts to silence him I choked the life from him. I wrapped him in a blanket and using some chain and concrete blocks, sank his body in the Detroit River where I hoped it never would be found, and to my knowledge has not.

I do not know his name and cannot remember exactly where I found him.

I had hoped that by being in the company of men, for whom I had no sexual desire, I would grow into manhood and rid myself of this heinous sexual predilection. And it worked! At least until the war was over. Then we had liberty in Manila and upon seeing a young Filipino lad, my sexual desire was once again raised, but this time without dire consequences. He was a beggar, wearing filthy rags and willing for a pack of cigarettes and a candy bar to give his body to me in a dark alley.

When my enlistment was over, I returned to Michigan, but knew that my perversion would rear its ugliness whenever I saw a young boy. Therefore I sold the family estate, which had been left to me when my mother died, and bought property on Hibbard Pond. The area was basically isolated and at that time not heavily built up, but things always change. In an attempt to avoid any problems, I surrounded myself with adult friends who liked to party. We would spend wild weekends drinking and gambling amongst ourselves, and to my knowledge there was no sex of any kind. Some of them wanted to bring women but I forbade that, explaining that in my status as a legislative supporter, I was not willing to risk anything that might cast any darkness upon my reputation. Although in truth they would wonder why I didn't participate and I didn't know if a woman could arouse me.

All went well until mid-April of this year when I was in East Lansing on a visit to a doctor, and afterwards went for a walk in a park where there was a playground with swings, a slide, a jungle gym and a sandbox. There was a young boy playing there, unattended and wearing dirty clothes. My initial thought was, "What mother would let her son go out like that?" I noticed that he was not friends with any of the other children and actually seemed to avoid them. When the area was virtually deserted, I approached the boy and asked where his mother was. He shrugged. I asked if he had a home, and again he shrugged. I asked him his name and he answered, "Nathan." "Would you like to come home with me, Nathan?" I asked. "Where?" he answered. I told him, "Far away on a lake." "Really?" he said. "Yes," and he took my hand.

At the lake, I took him to the boathouse and told him this was to be his new home. He was overjoyed. That first night, as many nights in the future, we shared the bed there, both enjoying our new found companionship. Over the next several weeks I learned that he had run away from home. His parents were divorced and his mother's boyfriend didn't like him and beat him. So he had run away and had been living around the park for a couple of days.

For several months we were happy, but then he became sullen and despondent. Part of it was because I would only let him out at night when we would swim in front of the boathouse. Occasionally we would go for nighttime boat rides in my powerboat or the small rowboat with its five-horsepower motor. He seemed to enjoy these outings. He didn't like being locked in the boathouse when I wasn't there, but I explained it was for his own protection because there were wild animals around - bears, coyotes and cougar.

Then one evening late in the summer, I unlocked the door and entered the boathouse and he was waiting, and he hit me hard on the head with the cast iron skillet we used to make our meals. When I regained my senses, he was gone. I turned on the boathouse lights and went looking for him. I discovered that the rowboat was gone. I got into my powerboat and went searching for him. It had a big spotlight and I used it to search the lake. I went south because more lights were showing there. I didn't want to use the light along the shore as that might arouse suspicion and went slowly along looking for the rowboat. Then I remembered that the previous day we had been talking about the lake and I had mentioned the covered bridge at the south end. When I reached the mouth of the West Branch River, I went up it and near the bridge, I discovered the rowboat sitting unattended and not tied up. I called his name but there was no answer. Using the spotlight I started searching the shoreline but could see no trace of him. I started moving further up the river and just under the bridge, I saw his body in the water. I used a boathook to get him close to the boat and then pulled his limp body in. I don't know what happened and how he had died but I was distraught and cried uncontrollably for several minutes.

When I regained control, I knew I had to do something. I didn't dare take his body back to the cabin, so I decided to bury him under the bridge since that is what he had come to see. I carried his body up and put it as high as I could get, knowing that it would only be for a little while. Then I returned to the cabin towing the rowboat behind. I got a shovel and returned to the bridge in the power-boat, not daring to have someone see my car. I tied the boat up under the bridge and then dug a grave. The ground was hard and I couldn't get it as deep as I wanted and as dawn started to break, I put his body into the hole, tamped the dirt down over it, and threw the excess into the water. It wasn't perfect but I didn't think that anyone would come under the bridge anyway. Then I returned home and collapsed in the bed we had shared for those wonderful months.

The next day I thoroughly cleaned the cabin removing any trace of him except for the pictures. I couldn't bear to throw those memories away. I decided that I would make a cache to keep them in so that I could look at them. Over the course of the next several weeks, I became *despondent as he had been and made the decision that the best catharsis I could have was to write about what had happened and put this with the pictures. If anyone finds it, I will be gone as I am ill and the doctors don't know what is wrong. It will be a black mark upon my life, but the only person who might care is dead and buried under a bridge. Maybe Nathan - he never told me his last name and I don't know if his first name was really Nathan - has family who would like to know what happened to him and this might bring some closure for them.*

May God forgive my sins and grant me absolution,

Stephen Fisher Thompson

August 18, 1958

When the story hit the media, the state's political machine went into turmoil for several weeks. Fortunately, or possibly unfortunately, all members of Stephen Fisher Thompson's party cadre were dead and there was nothing in any of their legacies that could gain substance from this revelation. Of course, the Pauls' 'Spruce Lodge at Hibbard Pond', as a sign at the walkway leading to their main entrance proclaimed it, became a subject of gawkers. The first week it seemed as though a steady stream of cars came down Spruce Drive despite a "PRIVATE PROPERTY NO TRESPASSING" sign twenty feet in from the East Path. Finally, two days of parking an empty cruiser near the sign scared off the sightseers. There wasn't much to see anyway. The boat-house was the center of curiosity and all that can be seen from the road is the roof. There was more boat traffic in front of the place and, of course, that couldn't be stopped. It was big that first weekend and took several weekends before it ceased to be obvious. Elsewhere around the lake, life went on unscathed by the events of the past six months.

Chapter 53

It was a warm but not sultry late Saturday afternoon in mid-July one week after the discovery of Thompson's diary, and six weeks after Mitchell Webster had taken Rolli Polli's Harley Davidson hog home. Jane Eyre had windows open enjoying an afternoon breeze, when she heard the roar of a motorcycle outside. Curious, she opened the front door and was surprised to see a familiar Harley sitting on the driveway, kickstand down. Mitchell Webster, helmet off, was coming up the front walk.

"You got it running!" Jane Eyre said excitedly.

"Yes, ma'am, a week ago I finished it. Just got my license yesterday. Been out riding and thought I would like to take you around the lake."

Jane Eyre put her hand to her breasts. "Oh, not me. I couldn't."

"Why not?"

"Well, I'm," she waved her hands at her heavy body, thirty pounds lighter but still rotund to put it nicely, "fat."

"Don't worry, that hog can handle us both."

"But I don't have motorcycle clothes," she said indicating his leather boots, chaps and vest over a white tee shirt and jeans.

"Don't really need them. I won't go fast, just a leisurely ride. I think you'll like it."

"What should I wear?"

"Something comfortable."

"Just a minute." Jane Eyre disappeared inside and then returned ten minutes later wearing the bib overalls and denim shirt she had worn building shelters. She had purple tennis shoes on her feet, no socks. She found Mitchell squatted down beside the hog tinkering with something.

"I'm ready," Jane Eyre said trepidatiously. "But I don't know if I can get on. My legs are so short and fat."

"Just a minute," Mitchell said. "I remember seeing just the thing in the garage." He disappeared into the dimness and returned a minute later with two paving bricks cradled in his left arm and carrying a concrete block with his right hand. Putting the concrete block near the cycle and then the two paving bricks, he made a small stairway. He put his helmet on, got on the hog, started it and motioned her to get on, holding out Rolli's helmet to her. "It's too big for me but should fit you." Jane Eyre put it on and then before climbing aboard, had one request. "When we go through the covered bridge, could you stop in the middle?"

"Traffic permitting."

She got on the cycle, the makeshift steps working beautifully, and wrapped her arms around Mitchell the best she could. He turned the cycle around and at the end of the driveway turned left. A short ten minutes later, he stopped in the middle of the covered bridge and shut the Harley down.

Jane Eyre said, "When Rolli and I first came up to this lake and drove around it, he stopped in the middle of this bridge and looked up the lake. Then he turned to me and said, 'I think we've found a place we can abide, my love,' and I agreed and he kissed me. I think he wanted to do more right then and there, but we're so big we couldn't. Anyway he kissed me again, and said, 'Once more into the breach, my love. Now to find an abode'."

"I didn't realize he was a romantic," Mitchell said.

"Most people didn't," Jane Eyre said. "But every year, on the day we met, he gave me a dozen roses. And you know what?"

"No, ma'am."

"Quit 'ma'am'ing me. We're friends. You call me Jane Eyre and I'll call you Mitchell."

"Yes, ma... Jane Eyre."

"Anyway, that day was last week. In the morning my doorbell rang and there was a florist truck sitting in the driveway. All the way from Alpena. The guy gave me a dozen red roses. There was a card in the box and it said, 'Every year as long as you live so you won't forget me'." Mitchell sensed she was crying.

"Oh, fiddlesticks," Jane Eyre said. "Let's go on."

They resumed their ride and for a while Jane Eyre cushioned her head against his shoulders. About halfway up East Path they encountered another Harley southbound. It was ridden by a small person, obviously a woman, wearing a black helmet with flames leaping out of the visor matching the flames on the front and back fenders. She was wearing an old sleeveless denim shirt and a new-looking long denim skirt underneath which Jane Eyre could see black motorcycle boots. The three waved to each other as they passed and Jane Eyre turned to watch the other Harley go up the hill they had just come down. The sun was low enough in the western sky that it looked like it was sitting atop the hill and Jane

Eyre could swear, although she never voiced it, that upon reaching the top of the hill the other Harley seemed to leap into the solar orb.

Half an hour later, Mitchell pulled into her driveway and stopped perfectly by the small stone stairway he had made, and Jane Eyre dismounted. After putting the bricks and concrete block back in the garage, Mitchell took off his helmet and put it on the cycle's seat. Jane Eyre was holding Rolli's.

"Our deal was that when this was running, I would come back and we would see if we could come to an agreeable price."

"Yes, we did," Jane Eyre agreed. "How much did you put into the repairs?"

"About twelve hundred dollars," Mitchell said.

"And I am certain a lot of hours."

"Yes, but I didn't keep track."

"I've been talking to Rolli," Jane Eyre said and Mitchell's mouth dropped open. "While we were riding, when I had my head against your shoulders."

Mitchell nodded that he understood.

"We were talking, Rolli and I. He didn't say anything. It was really all me. I told him what I wanted to do and he didn't say no." She reached into a pocket in the bib overalls and drew out the title for the motorcycle handing it to Mitchell Webster. He looked at it where the sale is indicated. She had signed it and the price was, "One ride around Hibbard Pond."

"I don't know what to say," Mitchell said.

"Don't say anything. Do you name your vehicles?"

"Sometimes."

"Well, this one is 'Rolli's Beast.' That's part of the deal."

"Done," Mitchell said and they shook hands.

Jane Eyre turned and started for the house, stopped and turned back holding up Rolli's helmet. "I get this too."

"Of course," Mitchell said. He put on his helmet, got on the Harley, started it, and waved to Jane Eyre who was at her door. He said, "Let's go, Beast," turned around, went left out of the driveway and roared southward.

Jane Eyre entered her house, suddenly very quiet as the roar of Rolli's Beast died away. She put the helmet on the seat of his recliner, the Greek flag in the background. "That was a nice thing to do, Rolli," she said and went to change her clothes.

Chapter 54

It was the second Saturday after the discovery of what happened to Nathan Biggins, and you couldn't have asked for a better day for an outdoor wedding. The temperature was predicted to reach a high of 81 and there was not a cloud in the sky. Early in the morning there was the sound of hammering from the Pauls' as a crew from Alpena put up a tent to shelter the bar – just in case. The wedding was scheduled for 4:00 p.m. to be followed by a barbeque dinner catered by JJ's from Alpena and the big red cooker arrived mid-morning to get things started. The invitation said that the bar was open at 2:00 p.m. and guests were welcome to arrive then. Cars started coming down Spruce Drive as early as 1:15 p.m., but that was to be expected for guests coming by car from as far away as East Lansing and Detroit. The early arrivals had the pick of the parking and by 2:00 p.m. cars were backed up close to where Spruce Drive turned toward East Path with the backyard of the Carolina bungalow (used with permission) filled. Dugal had permitted parking on the lake side of his driveway (really an extension of Spruce Drive.) The non-lake side was a drainage ditch and he didn't want to risk anyone getting stuck. So when he and Earleen left the cabin at 2:45 p.m., that stretch was as full as it could get and cars were beginning to line the portion of Spruce Drive that connected to East Path.

"Big crowd," Dugal said.

"Must be half the state," Earleen agreed.

When they walked into the front yard, they saw a line at the top of the stairs going to the boathouse. Kathy Jo and Michal had known they were not going to get by without the 'curiositors", as Kathy Jo called them, and so they decided to help themselves. They had someone who appeared to be a female member of the hired bar staff standing at the top of the stairs collecting $10 for each person who wanted to investigate. The path led down to the landing and into the living area door (bathroom locked and cupboards basically bare) where there was another apparent bar staffer. He was in possession of a cooler of beer for the thirsty for only $20.00 a bottle – it was good beer from Fletcher Street Brewery but with specially printed labels: Boathouse Lager emblazoned over a picture of the boathouse taken from the water and the date of the wedding underneath. Below the date was a graphic of the key. Four cases had been made and they sold out quickly. The bed and desk were roped off (yellow rope and orange traffic cones.) The panel was off and lying on the bed with a fake diary in place. The drawer of the desk was out so that people could see where the key had been.

The McBruces sought out Michal and Kathy Jo who were circulating sans drinks. Michal was dressed in a short-sleeved tuxedo shirt and pale green bow tie (the color of love, Kathy Jo proclaimed) and she in a pale green long dress (same material used to make Michal's tie), no sleeves but no cleavage (have to marry me for that, she explained to anyone who asked.) At 3:30 p.m.

Kathy Jo disappeared inside the cabin and Michal picked up the microphone.

"May I have your attention, please. Conversation about anything that happened in our boathouse prior to three thirty today is henceforth taboo on this property." There was a loud murmur among the crowd. "And we mean it."

Then Michal went into the cabin to finish getting dressed. The best man, matron of honor, two brides-maids and two groomsmen circulated trying to get the people organized to see the wedding – there were no seats. At the boathouse, the last of the curious were ushered out and up the steps with the slider locked behind them, and the woman at the top permitting no one else down.

In the boathouse living area, the bar staffer opened a kitchen cupboard and removed a plastic box. In it were tubes to mix epoxy and three small pieces of wood. Moving to the desk, the man removed the contents of the box and using one piece of wood, mixed a small amount of epoxy. Picking up one long narrow piece of wood, he put epoxy on one long narrow side and then inserted the piece glue side down into the slot of the drawer. The slot virtually disappeared but then, in reality, the man was a first-class woodcraftsman. He put the remainder of the epoxy on one end of another piece of wood and, stepping to the bed, turned the panel over and inserted the piece into the keyhole slot. Just as with the drawer, the slot disappeared. He removed his shoes, picked up the panel, stepped onto the bed, and inserted the panel into its place with a satisfying click. It would be next to impossible to remove it because the T-shaped unlocking mechanism activated by the key had been re-

moved. From under the pillow of the bed, the man retrieved a tack hammer and picture hook that he fastened
to the wall in just the right spot. Then he hung up the
framed map. He put the tack hammer and plastic box
into the desk drawer, which he closed. Picking up the
orange cones and the connecting yellow rope, he exited
the boathouse through the door. At the top of the stairs,
the two bar staffers arranged the cones and rope to block
the stairway just for looks, wended their way through
the crowd until they found Michal, and gave him the
money. Then they walked to their car parked on Spruce
Drive and went home.

At four o'clock, "When the Saints Come Marching
In" blared over the speaker system, and preceded by her
bridesmaids and matron of honor, Kathy Jo joined
Michal, his best man and his groomsmen at the chosen
site near the edge of the bluff. The ceremony proceeded
and when asked if Michal would take Kathy Jo as his
wife, the women shouted, "Say 'I do' and make an honest woman of her," which, although a little nonplused,
Michal did. When Kathy Jo was asked if she would take
Michal as her husband, the men shouted, "Say 'I do'."
The minister, all agrin and in on the conspiracy, pronounced them husband and wife and the crowd yelled,
"At last." When Kathy Jo and Michal shared their first
married kiss, there was a cacophony of New Year's Eve
horns, showers of confetti, and popping of champagne
corks. The best man yelled, "Let the party begin," and it
did.

***

Across Hibbard Pond, two women sat looking at the
lake. Jane Eyre was in her lift chair positioned to face

the lake and next to it was Rolli's chair. On the table beside her were a small pitcher of Rolli dry martinis and her art deco martini glass filled with her first martini of the day. Up the lake, Edna Fitzgerald was in the Lake Room, the sliders all open and the late afternoon breeze filling the room with fresh air. The broken floor tile had been replaced, although it had to be specially ordered. The hole in the doorframe, punched by the same bullet, had been patched. She had left the hole in the ceiling from Edmund's errant shot untouched as a reminder. From out on the lake, laughter and music could be heard as an idyllic Saturday began to draw to a close. There were the sounds of people trying to forget what evil had transpired under, on, and around the lake in the past five or six months, or in the late 1950s. Edna was alone because Liza had gone off with some new acquaintances – she was once again beginning to enjoy life. Simultaneously, Edna and Jane Eyre each picked up her martini glass, raised it in salute and took a sip. The future was looking bright and inviting, and they were happy to be a part of it.

Meet our Author

Douglas Ewan Cameron

Douglas Ewan Cameron is a retired professor of Mathematics from The University of Akron, Akron, Ohio. He grew up in Oak Ridge, Tennessee, attended Miami University (Oxford, Ohio) and The University of Akron and received his Ph.D. from Virginia Polytechnic Institute and State University (Blacksburg, Virginia). Upon retirement, he and his wife Nancy spend their summers on the shore of Hubbard Lake in the part of Michigan's lower peninsula known as "Up North" and winters in Copley, Ohio. Douglas loves to fish and spends many summer days out on the lake fishing for walleye and smallmouth bass. Retirement has also afforded him and his wife time to travel and they have visited all seven continents. When not traveling or fishing he has been able to return to his writing, something that he was not able to do while working. The stories he writes are those that have occurred to him while either fishing or traveling. Visit the author's website at:

http://books.dragonweir.com

Douglas Ewan Cameron

Also by Douglas Ewan Cameron

*****

Payback is a Bitch

Chapter 1

They were leaving. I didn't wave. They didn't wave. They didn't even look back! I guess you don't if you've just killed someone. Especially if that someone is your brother-in-law.

I got all this information as I momentarily crested a wave and chanced a quick look through half-opened eyes. Even opening my eyes just a slit and quickly closing them made my head throb.

I tried to relax and float but my clothes were getting heavy – especially my shoes. I mentally kicked myself for wearing sneakers and not boat shoes or sandals. But how was I to know that Howard was going to kill me – okay, make that "try to kill me?"

I felt the next wave carry me to its crest and snuck another peek. The boat was definitely moving away and I could hear the low rumble of its twin Yamaha 150s that suddenly turned into a roar, as Quentin must have pushed the throttles full bore. I just hoped that they wouldn't come round and try to run me over to be certain that the job was done. I didn't think Howard had it in him but maybe Keith did. I didn't know much about Keith – or Quentin for that matter.

Trying to relax, I thought about what had happened to get me into this predicament.

My wife Elise and I were on a Caribbean cruise and headed for Aruba for a week in the sun – a second honeymoon so to speak. Several weeks before, at the suggestion of my wife, I had used the web (a favorite tool of mine) to find a charter captain on St. Nantes. He had picked up Howard, Keith and me at the pier after we were dropped off from the first tender ashore from our ship, the Caribbean Isle, the flagship of Caribbean Cruise Line. Howard is my brother-in-law – rephrase that – my no-good brother-in-law. Keith is a guy to whom Howard had introduced me on the ship and I asked if he wanted to join my little excursion. He had immediately jumped on board – looking back on it, much too quickly.

We had headed out deep-sea fishing for mahi mahi and anything else that came along in Quentin's thirty-six foot boat. A fast run of forty-five minutes south through two to three-foot emerald blue swells had brought us into the area that Quentin had selected.

"Zere are a lot of fish here," he had said as he baited both lines and set them out and then got the boat slowly up to trolling speed.

We had been offered water, beer, or coke and all of us had selected beer – Heineken in 250 milliliter bottles bearing no regional brewery notation, which I had found strange. Quentin had expertly used his knife pulled from the sheaf in one of the rod holders to remove the caps. Even at 11:00 in the morning, the first draught was welcome. The three of us had touched bottles and wished each other "Taut Lines" and settled in to wait for the first strike that we had decided would be mine as I had organized the excursion.

The sun was high in an azure blue sky and infrequent seabirds crossed our vision as we questioned Quentin about the island and his life. He was a seventh generation island resident and had been fishing all his life, twenty years taking out charters for either inshore (barracuda and an occasional mahi mahi) or deep sea like today. I had chosen the latter, even knowing that its five-hour length would push the envelope getting us back for the last tender to the ship, but that was a chance we were all willing to take. We knew that the Caribbean Isle would not wait for us if we were late since it was not a ship-sponsored excursion. You pay your money and take your chance.

Suddenly the reel to my immediate left began to whine and the rod rattled heavily in its holder. Before any of the three of us could shout "Fish on!" Quentin had throttled back and was halfway to the rod holder. I stood up from my seat in the stern moving starboard to get out of his way, clutching the fighting belt and frantically searching for the snap buckle. "Don't put et on until we have a fish," he had said in his heavy French accent as he explained the technique, "et's bad luck!" Little did he know! Or, on second thought, maybe he did.

I settled back against the rod rack (no fighting chair on this boat) and Quentin brought the rod and snapped it into the holder. I gripped the rod above the reel with my left hand, moved my thumb against the line and starting winding, pushing the line to the right as I did so. Pulling the rod up and cranking it down to keep the line tight, thumb moving left or right guiding the line. Well, at least that is what I tried to do but the fish (mahi mahi, hopefully) had other ideas. The line went out and there was no way to stop it. Then I started reeling line and worked at it, pumping the rod and keeping the line going from side to side. I remember thinking that it would make more sense if these huge Penn reels had a line guide like my freshwater reels did.

The fish was huge and kept taking the line out, erasing what little progress I seemed to make. However, little by little the battle was won and at last, after what seemed like hours because of the adrenaline pumping through my veins but was actually mere minutes, Quentin told me to stop. That was an easy request to obey. Quentin wrapped the line around his hand and started pulling the fish up.

"Get over by the fish for a good picture," Keith had shouted as he had volunteered to be the cameraman on the first fish and I had given him my camera.

I moved a few feet toward the port side where Quentin was at work.

There was a flash of green ...

*****

Payback is Time to Die… Again

Chapter 1

"Daws, someone is coming."

"I know, Tres," I replied, "Thanks."

I released the intercom button on the remote I carried and looked at the picture. The car was proceeding toward The House at the End of the Road at a normal speed. My backside motion detector system had been first to acquire the intruder, but the camera would have captured him a few seconds afterward. I had two motion detector units (one on either side of the road) at the far extremities of my property that communicated with the house wirelessly and were solar powered.

I had been living here about six months and the first thing I had done after moving in was to install a security system. It wasn't mine by any means, but I knew how to run it. The system was super high tech, some of the stuff I don't even know if the military had. The windows and doors were all equipped with sensors that would detect them being opened. The windows all had glass breaks. I don't know why I put the glass breaks on because all the glass was bulletproof. All the locks were armed with pick sensors. My keys had chips in them and if the wrong key or a lock pick was inserted, then the alarm would sound. I had given up my landline four months ago and all my communication was done by satellite. A security station in the states would pick up the signal and call me. And if I did not respond, they would contact the St. Nantes gendarmes at the same time as Beecher McFalls, my security man who lived on St. Martin. He was an hour away by private plane but I could not do much better, at least in what he could do for me. The plane could land on the road and he would be at my door in sixty-five minutes tops. We know because we tried.

I had four motion detector systems at the house to pick up any intruders, one under the front deck that watched the front yard down to the slope which dropped down to the Caribbean, one on each end of the house concealed in vegetation and one on top of the carport on the back of the house. But it was the backside motion detector that had found the current intruder – I don't know what else to call him. I am a semi-recluse – except for Tres. I don't get mail delivery and my housekeeper Lynette Duprey had been here only yesterday. "Why no mail delivery?" you might ask. Because there wasn't anyone to write me. All my bills I get on line so all that could possibly arrive by snail mail is crap.

I had an automatic backup generator run on natural gas backed up by a fifty-gallon underground gas storage tank. A wind turbine in the front yard generated the majority of my electricity. It was over to the right side where it couldn't be seen from the front windows or from the deck unless you leaned over at the right end and craned your neck. Anyone who wanted to knock out my security would have to start in the house. I still had landline power but if that supply was severed, I wouldn't even have known it except for the alarm which would sound on my monitor remote which I always had with me, even when I was not home.

I was in the basement exercise room when the current alarm sounded and had just completed my workout. As usual it had started with the weights and ended with the treadmill. Treadmills are basically boring. Well, let's face it, all exercise is basically boring. I had a flat panel TV on the wall and watched CNN International when working with the weights but the treadmill I had in front of the slider and I looked out across the front yard at the beautiful Caribbean, which is basically all I could see from my house or at least the front of my house. I owned seafront property and, as with most of the people who own such, my front yard was between the house and the Caribbean. My "front" door (where any of my few and far between guests showed up) was in the middle of the back of my house.

My exercise room was under the laundry room that was at the far west side of my house, accessed by a staircase that came out at a semi-concealed door next to the kitchen on the front side of the house. I had missed it the first time I was in the house over a year ago but I was not in any shape to really notice hidden passages. I had just survived a grueling, tortuous, unending, terrifying (you pick the adjective) sixteen hours in the water after being "drowned" and left for dead by my no-good brother-in-law Howard and his equally no-good friend Keith. Fortunately, I wasn't drowned and I managed to survive.

Wondering whom the visitor was – let's call him or her that until we know more – I ran up the stairs and almost knocked down Tres, who was coming to get me.

"It's a man. He's driving a Porsche. I don't recognize him."

"Okay, then I probably don't either because you know all the people on St. Nantes that I know. Get your pistol and get down to the control room. If there is any shooting, get into the safe room. Lock it and don't come out until I tell you to."

She didn't question me, just stood on her tiptoes, threw her arms around my neck, gave me a big kiss, turned and ran toward the great room. I was right behind but not at a run. I had a towel around my neck that I had used to wipe the sweat away from my workout. Entering the great room and turning left, I stepped behind the bar, dropped the towel on it and hit a panel on the wall. The door popped open to reveal a safe door about the size of a safe deposit box. I pressed my index finger of my right hand and then the thumb of my left against the security panel, which turned blue, and the door popped open and the drawer slid out. I took the Beretta and its magazine out of the drawer and slammed the mag into the gun with the heel of my hand. I closed the door to the safe and the panel door. There was nothing else in the safe. I racked the slide back, seating the first shell in the chamber.

Thus armed, I went through the great room into the foyer. On my left was the stairway entrance to what was now my control center, formerly a theater. I crossed the foyer and looked at the flat panel screen to the left of the door. I could see a man out there, pacing. He was wearing sandals, white tennis shorts, a black emblemless tee shirt, a matching black baseball cap and reflective sunglasses. I was about to press the talk button to ask what he wanted when he stopped, looked up at the camera, and removed his sunglasses.

I stared in disbelief. I had been wrong. Tres didn't know everyone on St. Nantes that I knew.

The man was Judge Michel Villar.

The Body in the Perch Pond

Prologue

The cold wind whipped the snow in small torrents, dashing it against the ground, the tire, the lantern, his hands, his face – especially the light. Coming in brief gasps; the wind caused eddies in the falling snow and whipped the already fallen back into the air obscuring his work. If it wasn't the snow obscuring the wheel lugs, it was the snow whirling in front of the lantern's lens and dimming the light. He cursed his luck. He cursed his lack of electronics. He cursed his hands crippled both by arthritis, the cold and old injuries. If he had a radio – a simple radio – in the truck, he would have (could have) heard about the storm. That is, if he had been able to get a signal but this area was so remote that most signals were difficult to get even in the best of times. But it probably wouldn't have mattered. He still had to get her help.

His half-frozen fingers of his left hand could not control the lug wrench adequately and the half-frozen fingers of his right hand couldn't hang on to the lug nut, which dropped into the snow under the tire.

It wasn't the storm really, he knew, as he groped under the tire for the nut. It was really the tire – bald, over used – it had given out as he hit the last pothole. He knew it was there because he drove the road once a week and he had watched it develop through the long winter.

His groping fingers felt the nut – or a pebble – and closed on it. "Thank goodness," he thought. He had already lost two and losing a third would leave him only two on the wheel. In such treacherous weather, two lug nuts holding on the wheel that helped to power the truck would not have been good.

He put what he hoped was the lug nut into his mouth and sucked at it to clean the snow and ice. It was bitterly cold but there was no alternative. As the snow melted his tongue felt the hole in the object and could discern the sharp corners. His luck was beginning to turn. Spitting the nut into his palm, he turned his head, spat the water and remaining debris into the snow. With his other hand, still holding the lug wrench, he wiped the snow off the lantern's lens and then tried to start the nut onto one of the lugs.

He breathed a sigh of relief as the nut caught and he gave it several turns. He fitted the lug wrench to the nut – easier than the nut onto the lug – and started turning it.

"Need any help?"

The voice from nowhere startled him and he dropped the wrench into the snow. Turning to his left he could make out a form behind a bright beam of light. Beyond that were flashing red lights.

"What?" he stammered but "Cops!" he thought.

"Didn't mean to startle you," the voice said. "We thought you would have heard us stop. My wife and I are on HPCP" – "Hip-Cip" he pronounced it – "patrol and saw your truck at the side of the road. You should have used a flare and had your flashers on."

His mind raced. Things were cloudy, disconnected. Then something clicked and a semblance of understanding formed.

"No – I'm sorry." His eyes returned to the wheel as his hand retrieved the lug wrench and fitted it once again to the lug. "My flashers don't work and I have no flare – didn't mean to be out in this storm."

"Well, none of us should. Can I give you a hand?"

The Samaritan was now crouching at his side. A red and black jacket, red and black balaclava, making his face indiscernible, topped by a HPCP baseball cap. The man's right hand held a powerful lantern the beam of which he directed at the wheel.

"Just finishing," he responded. "Blew a tire on the chuck hole. Had to get my granddaughter home."

Damn! Shouldn't have said that. Too confused. Too cold. Too many things all at once.

The Samaritan's powerful beam moved from the wheel toward the front of the truck.

"We can take her in our truck if you want."

The Samaritan was up and moving toward the cab.

"No." A final twist and the lug was tight. He stood up and put out a hand to arrest the other's movement. He couldn't take the chance – he couldn't let the Samaritan see her. Even after so long, who knew?

"She's fine. The cab's warm and we'll be on our way in just a minute. Thanks anyway."

"You're certain?" the Samaritan said. It wouldn't be any trouble. We have four wheel drive."

"You're mighty kind," he said. "But with the tire fixed, we'll be fine."

The other retreated and he moved to the back of the truck, inserted the tire iron in the jack and started lowering the car.

"If you certain..." the Samaritan said.

"Yes, thank you," he said wishing the other would leave.

"Alright. Be careful. This storm is supposed to hang around for a while and the roads are icy."

"Right. Thanks. We'll be fine. Her home is very close and I'll stay the night."

"Okay - be careful."

The Samaritan turned and focused his light on his truck parked on the other side of the road and made his way to it and opened the door.

******

John got back into his vehicle, luxuriating in the warmth. Glad to be out of the storm. In his rearview mirror he saw the lights of the truck come on as the exhaust belched a plume of black smoke.

"Is everything alright?" his wife Myrna asked.

"Yeah," John said. "Some old guy blew a tire in a pot hole. Says he's taking his granddaughter home. Must not be from around here. Didn't recognize the truck – an old Ford 150, must be one of the first."

John watched as the other vehicle pulled off the shoulder and disappeared into the blinding snow.

"Should we log it?" Myrna asked as she picked up the microphone to the CB.

"Nah," John said. "We've already clocked out. Herb's probably shut down his base. We need to get home ourselves."

"We should never have gone out," Myrna said. "We knew there was a storm brewing."

"Well, we didn't know it was going to hit here or hit this hard," John responded as he pulled off the shoulder. "Who would have guessed that the storm would hit with this fury when we were completely on the other side of the lake. We should have gotten a room at the Dew Drop anyway instead of coming all the way back."

Some fifteen minutes later and not much more than two miles down the road, his headlights picked up the sign at the end of their driveway and he turned into the protection of the evergreens.

"We're safe now, just a quarter mile to home."

"Thank goodness," Myrna said and they smiled at each other.

******

He was anything but safe as the savage winds of this late winter storm whipped the snow against the windshield and caused the light from the headlights seemingly to flicker in and out of existence. He glanced at the blanket wrapped form on the passenger side. "How close that was," he thought. His eyes moved quickly back to the windshield.

The snow seemed to be coming down harder, his windshield wipers could scarcely keep up with it. He was traveling slowly, not more than ten miles an hour when he hit a second pothole. This one was deep and the front

wheel bounced in and out and he wrenched the wheel, trying to keep the rear wheel out but it was to no avail. The
turning of the wheel started the truck sliding and the rear
wheel plunged in, the torque of the slip whipping it against
the outside lip putting such a strain on the three poorly
tightened lug nuts that one of them striped almost to the
end and the wheel began to wobble.

He managed to get the truck stopped sitting broad side
on the road and knew that something had happened to the
wheel but he didn't know what. He thought about getting
out to look at it but knew that it wouldn't make any difference. He should have let the Samaritan take them ... no,
that was impossible. The fewer who knew, the better. He
checked the form wrapped in the blanket to his right, opening the fold and feeling her forehead. Hot and damp – hot-
ter than before. The fever was getting worse. He had to get
help.

Despite its age, the truck had continued running because instinctively he had never removed his foot from the
clutch. He oriented himself the best he could, backed the
truck up a few feet, turned the wheel and slowly started
forward. The knowledge that she needed help – more than
he could give – urged him on and once the truck was moving, he started increasing the speed. He could feel the
wobble in the rear wheel and knew for certain what had
happened. Something bad but there was nothing he could
do about it. There was no choice but to continue on his
way – she need help, help that he couldn't give her.

He knew that he was coming up to Comrock's Point
and its infamous S-curve, called Dead Man's Turn by
many of the locals. It had taken several lives over the
years. The most recent, two earlier that year when a couple
of young men heading home from a night at one of the local bars, had misjudged the turn in the snow and flown
thirty or forty feet, smashing into a huge oak that now had
two white crosses at its base.

He knew the road even in the whiteout having lived in
the area all his life – except for those three years in that

godforsaken jungle hell hole. He was getting close and would have to … what was that? Something in the road! Something big! His right foot moved from accelerator to brake as his left foot moved to the clutch. The truck immediately started to skid to the left. Ice! He turned the wheel to the left but no – the skid stopped as he felt the tires get traction and he released the clutch and spun the wheel to the right. Immediately, once again under power, the tires spun, the wobbly one gripping for traction but finding only ice. The truck swung to the right in another skid, he released the brake, cursing himself for his foolish response. Even as he turned the wheel the right rear tire caught another pothole, the poorly fastened lug nuts gave, and the right wheel buckled. The remaining lug nuts stripped and the wheel came off, falling and catching the brake housing and turning into a sled. The skid turned into a sidewise slide taking the truck off the road, across the shoulder – into the nothingness at the south end of Comstock's Curve. The right rear wheel spun, catching only air and swirling show. The truck seemed to teeter momentarily, then disappeared from view.

The sixteen-point stag hadn't moved from its position in the middle of the road since it was first caught in the glare of the truck's headlights. Even the sounds of the final crash as the truck came to its resting place at the bottom of the fifty-foot embankment hadn't bothered it.

Stillness pervaded the air. The snow whipped wildly about the stag as he slowly continued his journey across the road and into the shelter of the woods. Within minutes the winds and snow of the late winter storm had obliterated all signs of the stag and the truck. Nature was in control.

Muddy Waters

Chapter 1

To anyone watching, the cloud of dust on the gravel and dirt road would have announced the arrival of some vehicle. Or if someone wasn't watching but listening, the crunch of heavy tires on gravel and the squeal of brakes covered with road dust would have made known that something big had stopped. Through the haze of light dust, one could see the vintage yellow school bus with its red lights flashing and stop signs sticking out from its sides. As the dust settled, the door to the bus opened with an audible swoosh and, after a brief moment, a tow-headed thirteen year old boy wearing a yellow tee shirt, cut-off jeans and flip-flops jumped from the last step. He stumbled as he landed, as he often did, and his backpack went flying into the drainage ditch, narrowly missing the mailbox post that would have retarded its progress. Fortunately two weeks with no rain had left the drainage ditch dry and no harm came to the backpack. Recovering from his near fall, the boy turned to the bus and waved.

"Bye, Lucy," he said to the driver. "Have a good summer."

"You too, Chris. And be more careful."

Lucy, the driver, was a matronly woman in her mid-fifties who drove the bus more to get out of the house then to earn money. She mothered the kids on her routes mainly because some of them, like Chris, were on the bus for almost an hour. This year Chris, whom his friends called by his nickname of "Muddy," had been first on the bus in the morning and last off the bus in the afternoon. Lucy grabbed the handle to close the door, pausing a moment to watch Chris clamber into the ditch to retrieve his bag. Satisfied that all was well, Lucy pulled the handle closing the door and checked her rear view mirror. Seeing that no one was coming from either direction, she turned off the flashers, retracted the stop signs, turned on her left-turn indicator, shifted from neutral into first and stepped on the gas. The old bus seemed to groan expressing discomfort at the request to get moving again at its age and slowly moved away from the dirt road leading to the farmhouse set back from the road. Situated about a quarter mile from a wood copse by the road, the old house was surrounded by fields, which were already beginning to show the green of summer crops. Lucy shifted into second glancing in the right-side rearview mirror to see Chris opening the mailbox, backpack at his feet. *Kids these days*, she thought shaking her head, *wearing flip-flops to school instead of something sensible for foot support.* However, to her knowledge that was the only fault Chris Waters had and she knew him pretty well, as it was fifteen minutes to or from her next pickup on this route this year. The routes changed every year depending on who was going to school and this had been her first time on this particular route. The kids were well behaved for the most part although unduly rowdy today but with it being the last day of school, and a half-day at that, it was to be expected. She would miss them during the summer and she made a mental note to ask for this particular route again or whatever route Chris was on.

Muddy sorted through the mail as he always did hoping that he would get something but he never did. Of course, he never wrote a letter to anyone or at least not a hard copy letter, preferring email or texting communication as most young people did. The mail was catalogs, which his mother enjoyed, a bill or two he supposed, and some advertising circulars. He stuffed the mail into his backpack, slung it over his left shoulder and was about to start his walk home when the distant squeal of brakes announced the fact that Lucy and Alcona County School bus number 14 had reached the end of Creek Waters Road. He looked and saw the bus sitting at a stop, right turn indicator flashing. Lucy would turn onto Black River Road and follow it several miles to F41 where she would turn south and follow the road into Lincoln, proceeding south on Barlow

Road to the school bus garage across the street from the high school and middle school building. There she would leave it, sign out the last time until fall and then go home to … Muddy didn't know where home was or what it was. Lucy was closed mouthed about that but pretty much open about everything else.

Muddy waved and, to his surprise, heard the distant sound of the bus's horn and saw the yellow warning lights flashing. Then the lights were shut off, the bus turned onto Black River Road and soon disappeared. Turning toward home, Muddy started his walk to the farmhouse he shared with his parents and younger sister Katie who was only five, eight years his junior. His parents never talked about why the age difference and he hadn't asked because, he felt, some things are private. Maybe someday when he was older he would. The road was gravel, well packed down with the many years of travel by farm vehicles, but the sand and dirt still accumulated and as he shuffled along so that he wouldn't lose the flip-flops, he grinned at the warmth of the dirt that settled briefly between his toes. There was the occasional stone but those he easily shook out, hardly breaking his stride. After about a hundred feet, he turned off into the woods, stopping near the stump of an oak that had blown down several years before and been used to heat the house the following winter. Reaching behind the stump Muddy retrieved a two-gallon zip lock freezer storage bag in which he stashed his sneakers while at school. He exchanged the flip-flops for sneakers and socks and started to put the bag back behind the oak stump. Then his brain, already on summer holiday, kicked in and he put the bag with the flip-flops in his backpack. He really didn't like wearing flip-flops to school but it was the "in" thing. Not wanting to be totally ostracized, he had chosen to change before boarding the bus knowing that his mother would have objected stringently to that choice of foot apparel. He could hear her, "I don't care what other kids wear to school; no son of mine is wearing flip-flops. Now go change to sensible shoes."

"Hi, Dad," Muddy shouted entering the house as he knew that his mother was still at work and his sister in daycare. There was no answer to his shout and Muddy hurried up the stairs to his room. Removing the storage bag from his back pack, he put the flip-flops under the bed with two other pairs, folded the bag and put it in a pocket of the back pack, which he then put on the shelf of his closet. Now to get down to the business of summer vacation – first on his list was fishing at Hibbard Pond.

The Body Under the Ice

PROLOGUE

A light autumn wind blew dry leaves across the vacant parking lot as a pickup truck rolled quietly into the lot and, with its lights off, coasted beside a six-foot tall wooden fence on the far side. A man wearing night vision goggles standing in the pickup's bed was able to look over the fence and rapped once on the roof when the truck came alongside what looked like several stacks of large packing crates. The truck stopped and the Spotter hopped out of the pickup's bed carrying a portable drill. He quickly removed screws from both ends of a section of the fence and was joined by the driver who was also wearing night vision goggles. With the screws removed, the Spotter put the drill into the bed of the truck. Then he and the Driver moved the fence section from its spot and carried it down the fence until the opening was clear and they leaned the section against the fence. Both men were big and could easily have been mistaken for NFL defensive linemen but neither of them was or had been.

Moving through the opening, the men surveyed the stacks. What seemed to be large packing crates were boxes of slats about eight feet long by three feet by three feet. They were stacked in four rows, each three boxes high and each row four deep. The last was actually five wide with the last row only two high making a total of fifty boxes. The men moved purposely to the next-to-last row and, grabbing the top box at each end, they moved it and set it out of the way. They did the same with the preceding row and then reached over the first row of crates, all of which had open tops. Securing the second crate in next to the last row, they pulled it out to the edge. Then they picked up the second crate they had removed and put it back. From the ground you couldn't tell there was a missing crate. They picked up the first crate they had taken out and carried it outside the fenced area and set it behind the pickup. The Spotter lowered the tailgate of the pickup and the two of them picked up the crate and slid it into the extended bed of the truck. The men moved the fence section back into place and the Driver held it while the Spotter got the drill from the truck and proceeded to put the screws back in. Then the two men climbed into the truck and covered the crate with a tarp and secured it with bungee cords. They got out of the bed, closed the lift gate and got into the truck's cab. Both men removed their night vision goggles and the driver started the truck and drove quietly out of the parking lot.

Twenty minutes later the truck turned off West Hibbard Pond Path onto a private paved road and passed under an entry sign that read Timber Point. They turned off the main road onto a dirt road and drove until it ended at the lake where a pontoon boat was sitting nudged into the shore. The two men got out of the truck, lowered the lift gate and the Spotter got into the pickup's bed, removed the tarp and then slid the crate out onto the lift gate where the Driver could grab it and help pull. Joining him on the ground the Spotter helped pull the crate out of the pickup's bed and set it on the ground. Each grabbing the crate in the middle of a side, they carried the crate to the pontoon, lifted it up and over the rail and, guided by the pontoon's Helmsman, slid it into the pontoon on an inclined ramp made of two by fours.

The Helmsman, who was virtually indistinguishable from the other two, size-wise, started the pontoon's engines while the Driver and the Spotter lifted the front end of the pontoon and slid it off the shore before hopping aboard with an agility that their sizes belied. The Helmsman turned the pontoon around and headed out into the lake while the two men removed wooden slats from inside the crate. Then they removed a tarp covering a naked body lying on one of the pontoon's bench seats, picked the body up and unceremoniously dumped it into the crate. Picking up a six-foot fir that was lying on the deck, the two shoved it into the crate on top of the body. Then they added eight concrete blocks weighing sixty pounds that had been sitting along the sides of the pontoon, four to a side, handling them as though they were papier-mâché. Each grabbed a handful of nails from a coffee can and put them in a pocket of their jackets. The slats that had been removed from the crate earlier were set on the crate's top. Picking up hammers and getting a few nails from their pockets, each moved to a side of the crate where the Spotter positioned one of the slats and they each fastened it into position with two nails. The worked quickly and effortlessly and soon the top of the crate was covered with slats about two inches apart. Extra nails from their pockets went back into the coffee can and it and the hammers were put out of the way. The two took positions on either side of the crate and stood silently looking ahead of the boat as though on lookout but seeing only the blackness of the dark fall night.

About ten minutes later the Helmsman, who had been watching his depth finder, took the engines out of gear and the pontoon started gliding on a virtually glasslike surface. He walked to the inboard end of the crate and started pushing it up the ramp with the aid of the Driver and the Spotter until about a third of it stuck over the bow. Waiting until the pontoon had virtually stopped the Helmsman grunted and the three pushed the crate up the ramp with relative ease until gravity took over and the crate tilted, wavered, and then with a final shove slid over the side into Hibbard Pond. That final push changed the manner in which the crate went down. It was hard enough that the crate tilted forward and when it hit the bottom, it kept moving and settled on what had been the top before it was pushed off the pontoon boat. That was the second and most consequential mistake the Helmsman had made. The Helmsman went back to the con, slid the throttle from neutral to forward and turned the pontoon back the way it had come, not moving fast so as to minimize noise but this late in the season the lake was empty.

The Driver and the Spotter sat on the bench seat where the body had been and after a few minutes the Spotter broke the silence that had ensued from the time the truck entered the parking lot, "What did he do to deserve this?"

The Driver shrugged and said, "It doesn't pay to take the Boss's money or product."

Chapter 1

Just after two o'clock in the morning, the Witch of the North and the Witch of the East came onto the ice just south of the Loon Creek Inn. It was closed for the winter, so their cars could be parked there with no problem and not be seen. At approximately the same time, the Witch of the West and the Witch of the South came onto the ice from Timber Point. Basically closed for the season, there was a caretaking couple who lived there year round, but they were away on a well-deserved two-week cruise. If they had been in residence, the two witches would have parked their cars off the entry road and walked through the property to the lake. Instead they had parked very close to the lake. Like the witches of the North and East, they were tied together with a thirty-foot nylon rope, an end knotted around the waist of each one. The Michigan DNR (Department of Natural Resources) had issued its "Ice Unsafe" warning two weeks ago and all the fishing shanties had been pulled. The four witches knew the ice was unsafe, but it was the proper time and they had no choice. The day and hour was decreed by the Legend of the Ice Bear.

Despite the fact that the sky was partly cloudy and the moon was in its wane, the two groups showed no lights other than the dim blue screens of their smart phones used in GPS mode to be guided to their goal. The coordinates of their target had been set in the middle of the summer on a boat ride by the Witch of the East. It was over the hole that was the deepest part of Hibbard Pond: 110 feet. They moved slowly with the lead witch of each group poking the ice in front of her with the handle of a broom. And it was no ordinary broom because, of course, these were not ordinary witches. These were Besoms with handles of oak limbs cut live and bark removed. The bristles were thin branches of Birch trees that abound on the shores of Hibbard Pond and tied to the oak handle with ropes made from natural materials. Each group's path was not straight because weak ice was constantly encountered. Accordingly the journeys took close to an hour, giving them an hour to prepare and the preparations were numerous. While the lead witch carried a broom in one hand and smart phone in the other, the trailing witches carried the burden of necessary accessories. Following The Witch of the North, The Witch of the East carried metal buckets. In her left hand, she had two buckets nested together with the top one containing a two-gallon zipper freezer bag with four cloths soaked in kerosene. In her right hand, she carried two nested buckets with the top one containing six spray paint cans: two large red and four small gold. The Witch of the South, who followed the Witch of the West, carried a gas-powered ice auger and that required her to use both hands. To see them crossing the lake you would have believed they were witches because they wore black robes with bell sleeves and hoods that they had pulled up over their heads for warmth. Yet except for the color of the robes they could easily have been monks because of the similarity of the robes. They were two strange looking pairs: in both cases the lead witch was tall, the Witch of the North being five foot ten inches and the Witch of the West five foot eight. However, the Witch of the East was five foot two and weighed only a hundred pounds, yet she bore her load like a trooper. The Witch of the South was taller by four inches but weighed a good one hundred fifty pounds more.

Finally reaching their goal, they put down their burdens and three of them unfastened the safety ropes that had connected them. Then the Witch of the North stood on the ice above the deep hole of Hibbard Pond holding in her hand one end of a thirty-foot rope. The Witch of the East had kept the other end tied around her waist and she swept the ice clear of snow and debris as she walked counterclockwise in the circle dictated by the rope. When the first circuit had been completed, the broom was replaced by a spray can of red paint and a second circuit completed, moving clockwise this time, marking the circle. Once this was done, the other two witches used the brooms to clear the ice and snow from the inside of the circle just marked.

The area cleared, guided by her GPS, the Witch of the North moved to the exact northeast point of the circle and moving southwest marked her path with red spray paint while the Witch of the East did the same southeast to northwest. Then a small circle with a five-foot radius was made at the center, and two diameters made in the small circle, one north to south and the other west to east. Then the northeast point on the big circle was connected to the east on the small circle and the east on the small circle to southeast on the large and continuing until a four point star had been made.

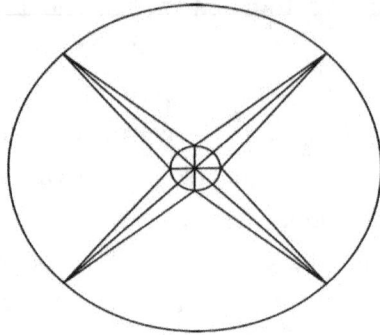

Then each of the witches used a spray can of gold paint to make strange rune-like words in the four open areas of the large circle outside the star. This work was all completed in a half hour. Then the Witch of the South used an ice auger to drill holes in the center of the circle and at the northeast, southeast, southwest and northwest points of the large circle. Each of the witches put a metal bucket containing a kerosene soaked rag into an outer circle hole. In this entire process, no areas of thin ice had been encountered but this was expected. After all, this rite had been preordained.

With ten minutes to go before the anointed time, the four witches gathered outside the circle to drink from bottles of water they had carried with them in pockets under the cloaks and to share tokes of a spliff (a marijuana cigarette rolled with some tobacco in it for better burning). Then feeling sufficiently fortified (although the South Witch would have traded the spliff for a pint of vodka), each witch took her place just outside the circle and watched her smart-phone. The North Witch was at the northeast point, East Witch at the southeast, and so on. Precisely at 3:20 an alarm sounded on each phone and the witches each used a butane charcoal lighter to ignite the kerosene rags in her bucket. At 3:23 they began to chant the words that appeared on the screens of the smart phones:

Je•jii•baan O•jib•we a•kiing nda nji•baa•mi,
bgo•se•ndi•mi•go•yin wii wii•doo•koo•yaang.
Mko•mii-ma•kwa, kiin ge•chi-pii•te•ndaa•go•zi•yin,
bi-di•shi•shnaang, mii•nzhi•naang nbwaa•kaa•win.

While these were words most people could not understand, they were not the kind of words that people would expect witches to say – rather they were Ojibwe, an Algonquian language spoken by the Chippewa Indians of Upper Michigan. They were words of an ancient ritual derived from the Chippewa Legend of the Ice Bear.

Each of them was so intent on the recitation that the Witch of the North almost didn't hear the faint boom that emanated from the darkness above them. For her the ritualistic chant had been memorized and she was able to move her eyes from the smart-phone to the skies above her without ever missing a beat. What she saw there brought terror to her heart. She had expected an emanation coming as a result of the ritual, but through the hole in the center of the circle, the one not filled with a metal bucket containing a burning kerosene soaked rag. But she had not expected to see a fiery ball plummeting earthward from the dark night sky and heading straight for them.

Douglas Ewan Cameron

~*~*~*

Available from
W & B Publishers
www.a-argusbooks.com

www.ingramcontent.com/pod-product-compliance
Lightning Source LLC
Chambersburg PA
CBHW051518260626
47170CB00003B/683